I0658704

THE IMMIGRANT'S GRANDSON

Vern Turner

Savant Books and Publications
A Division of K. Simmons Productions
Honolulu, HI, USA
2022

Published in the USA by Savant Books and Publications LLC
A Division of K. Simmons Productions
2630 Kapiolani Blvd #1601
Honolulu, HI 96826
http://www.savantbooksandpublications.com

Printed in the USA

Edited by Daniel S. Janik
Cover images courtesy of Pixabay.com
Cover by Daniel S. Janik

13 digit ISBN: 978-1-7376431-3-5

First Edition: March 2022
Library of Congress Control Number: 2022934535

Acknowledgement

Much of this story is my story, though, as with historical fiction, it imagines how things should have been and even as real events drive it. Howard Savage is a fictitious character I invented to represent the successes of generational accomplishment in the United States of the Twentieth century.

My grandfather did indeed emigrate from what today is known as Ukraine. Then, it was called Little Russia. Family legend has it he had a bearskin coat and worked with horses on a large farm. He reportedly walked to Trieste and took a ship to America. He worked in a brewery in Cleveland. I know; I've been there. My family didn't all pick up and move to San Diego, but I think we all would have loved to have done that. I did, however, end up living in San Diego for over 20 years, and, like the Savages, thoroughly enjoyed every year, earning an advanced degree from San Diego State University.

My mother was my grandfather's daughter, not Howard's father. The rest of the story comes from my own experience from the 60s to present.

Some characters in the aerospace industry and at NASA are actual. I used them as homage to their fantastic contributions to the accomplishments of those times during the middle years of my life.

This basic story idea came from my dearest and longest-known friend, Sally Baldwin Kling. My spouse, Elaine, single-handedly manages most of our household and encourages me to write. She endures my chattering about storylines and ideas, while offering insightful and sage suggestions based on her many years of reading all types of novels.

The passages concerning the horse-riding lesson came from the woman who tried to help me stay alive while I was on a horse. Nancy Melton Wubenhorst is a woman of great intelligence and talent. I wish only good things for her.

The Immigrant's Grandson is neither my first nor my last novel. It most certainly has been the most challenging literary effort for me so far.

I love to hear from readers. Please consider dropping me a note at www.vernturner.com after reading this book and any of the others you will find there.

Preface

Every human accomplishment has a back story, and THE IMMI-GRANT'S GRANDSON is one.

Following World War II, the United States and the Soviet Union engaged in a dangerous and rancorous Cold War. One of the major battles of that war was over the control of space. The essence of this particular battle was the fight for scientific and technological dominance. The United States created NASA to out-compete the Soviets, who had developed heavy-lift rockets to put various satellites into orbit around the Earth. Soon, all eyes turned toward that bright, shiny, omnipresent object in space called the moon, and becoming the first to explore and colonize the moon became the primary scientific and political mission for both countries.

History is filled with hundreds of backstories about the men and women who dedicated their lives in pursuit of landing the first humans on the moon and returning them safely to Earth. THE IMMIGRANT'S GRANDSON is, as I mentioned, one of those stories. From the humblest of beginnings on the frozen steppes of Eastern Europe in the early twentieth century to actually placing humans on the moon, THE IMMI-GRANT'S GRANDSON provides a ringside seat to witness the various sorts of characters who participated in perhaps the greatest human achievement in all history—so far. And this story may prove to be yet another backstory for an even greater human achievement: placing the first human colonists on MARS.

The Immigrant's Grandson

PART I
THE PATRIARCH

The Immigrant's Grandson

Chapter 1
Salt of the Earth

Known as Little Russia in 1908, Ukraine, as it is known today, was primarily agrarian with a feudal society and economy. Lords were typically addressed as "Master." Some masters were egalitarian, caring for and nurturing their "employees". Others were heartless, even cruel, maximally exploiting the "labor" that made them rich. The Didychi—*full, hereditary landowners—especially thought they could do anything they wished with their labor force, assuming, often correctly, that their illiterate, ignorant peasants had no where else to go.*

But intelligent people in any era have imagination: imagination that empowers their dreams to find ways to bring those dreams to reality.

The wind blowing down from the Siberian steppes was especially biting this night as it rattled the doors of the big barn. February in this part of Little Russia was always harsh when the Arctic winter weather gave its last burst of misery to all warm-blooded creatures huddled and trembling under their blankets, coats and furs. And so it was for Vasily Sovatislav, as he and his favorite source of winter warmth lay naked together wrapped in the giant Siberian brown bear coat that his patron had kindly provided. The companion in the bearskin was the assistant cook for the owner of the estate to whom they were both indentured.

"Mmmm, Vasily, that was *dyvovyzhnyy*—wonderful! But I need to do something about the wetness before the morning. Did you bring a cloth?" the woman asked in Ukrainian.

"*Tak*, Katia. You think I'm uncivilized at lovemaking? We are not barnyard animals."

"Well, here we are, in the barn, rutting like a couple of Master Gregori's goats, Vasily, so yes, I think we are just like barnyard animals. You are the billy. I am the nanny," Katia Ternenkova replied with a coy smile. "God forbid," she added, "I should turn up with child after all these long winter nights together. Master Gregori would cast us both out as food for the wolves."

"*Ne turbuytes*. Do not worry, Katia. You applied the goose grease before we, uh, made ourselves moist, yes?"

"Of course. My mother taught me well. After having two children in this very barn, she had to find a way to deal with the advances of her randy husband." she replied indignantly. "They eventually married…but that doesn't matter right now. Let's get some sleep before daybreak. Listen to the wind howl. It is singing us a lullaby, my dear Vasily."

Vasily brought Katia's ample body closer until her head nestled perfectly on his chest under his chin .

As sleep enveloped her, Katia began buzzing lightly and Vasily's thoughts wandered: *What a warm and willing lover you are, dear Katia. But I am just twenty years old—I think—and you are considerably older. And much more experienced than I. Oh, but you have taught me well, and I am proud to be such an able and willing student of your charms and skills. But this cannot go on forever. One or both of us must change our lives. You can read and write. I cannot. You can cook a feast from nothing, while all I can do is groom and feed horses and keep the troika repaired. More each day, I'm feeling the need to venture out, away from this farm, past the village. Fastin is just so small and all the young girls there are ugly. Well, to sleep. We both have work to do tomorrow.*

Vasily Sovatislav was indeed twenty years old in the year 1908. There were no formal records of his birth, so all he knew was what his mother told him before she died of a horrible chest affliction nobody understood. He was barely twelve when Master Georgi, for whom his mother had worked as a house maid, took young Vasily under his tutelage, teaching him how to train and tend the fine collection of draft horses, the pride of all the farms around Kiev. These days, Vasily stood just over 1.85 meters (six feet) in height and weighed a rock solid 100 kilos, about 220 pounds. His hair was coal black. His eyes, of the palest blue, were hidden beneath long, equally coal black lashes. His jawline was prominent and square.

He was as strong as he looked. His smooth muscles and sloping shoulders betrayed a power that few men ever attained. He always won the hay bale tossing competition between the other farm hands and could straighten a horseshoe with his bare hands. Nobody challenged Vasily to a wrestling match. He had no idea who his father was, but Master Georgi once told him that if his father was known, he would say that his son was a man amongst men.

Katia Ternenkova was naturally attracted to this strapping boy and seduced him with her special talent: cooking sweet treats that no healthy young man could resist. Then, of course, followed the moments of passion in the bearskin coat where the boy became a man.

The worst of the storm passed, leaving scattered clouds scudding across the sky, but leaving temperatures so cold that, while taking a piss in the snow, his stream crackled, freezing before hitting the ground. The bearskin coat was a treasure on days like this. Katia reluctantly exited it, quickly donning her own clothes, bundling up against the cold as she did every morning, and scurried back to the great house to begin her work before anyone awoke.

Later that morning, Master Georgi instructed Vasily and Oleg, the head cook, to drive the troika and team into Fastin to pick up the long list of supplies required for the coming feast presented by the richer famers to help relieve the burden of want among their families and vassals. Luckily, the last and harshest storm of the year had dropped little additional snow in its wake, so the road into the village was clear of drifts.

Peasants were still peasants in Little Russia during the period before the soon-to-become republic of Ukraine would come into being. People's lives were harsh, steeped in poverty; the struggle for bare subsistence being their constant companion. Peasants had to somehow curry favor with their master to obtain warm clothes and enough to eat. For a peasant to have a family of his or her own was out of the question, but pregnancies and births still occurred with regularity. Those children, if they survived their first two winters, simply became part of the peasant community for that farm. There were few "job promotions". Typically, there was only one overseer who kept all the laborers in line. Similar arrangements existed throughout the world wherever unskilled labor was relied upon to make the overseer and master rich. The Tsar and his family, for example, were said to live an opulent life, but after the first couple layers of ministers, the quality of life fell off a steep cliff, bottoming in the abject poverty that was "normal" to Vasily and other vassals.

Nonetheless, Vasily considered himself above the bottom, experiencing a gnawing ambition that he couldn't explain, and having few opportunities to develop enough critical or abstract thought to let his imagination become manifest. He looked forward to the ride into town with Oleg. Making friends with the cook was always a good idea for a strapping lad like Vasily Sovatislav.

The runners of the sleigh squealed loudly as they cut into the ultracold, packed snow on the narrow road to town. The trip was not long, only four kilometers (two and a half miles). Vasily pulled the team of three to a halt in front of the shop where most of the supplies would be purchased. Oleg plodded in with his list, telling Vasily to wait until called to help load everything into the sleigh.

"Vasily Ivanovich! What are you doing out there in the cold?" Nestor Busic, a shopkeeper and long time friend said loudly. "Come in for a few minutes for a taste of morning vodka. It will help warm your innards."

After ascertaining that Oleg was entirely engrossed in checking and selecting the various items on his extensive list, Vasily replied, "Why, *dyakuyu tobi*—thank you—Nestor Nikolaiovich. Nothing could be better to cut the grease from the breakfast sausage I just ate."

Inside the small shop, Nestor continued the conversation. "So, Vasily, I heard something from a traveling merchant. About America. He said the streets there were paved in gold. When I asked if he'd actually seen them, he said no, but he'd heard it from a reliable source. I, of course, told him that he was full of shit."

"Well, Nestor, did he say what the streets of America he'd *seen* were made of?"

"*Nemaye*, he didn't. But he said that everyone—well, almost everyone—had enough to eat and that the weather was a lot warmer than here."

"What else did he say about America?"

"His friend in the import business showed him some catalogs that offered EVERYTHING you could ever want. And the women in them were all slim and beautiful. Here, he left one. Take a look for yourself."

"What does the big writing say?"

"The salesman said 'Seers-Row-Buck', or something like that. He said they had big stores all over the country. What do you think?"

"My God, Nestor! Look at all this stuff! How do I get this beautiful shovel? Mine is falling apart!"

"I don't know. I think you must write a letter and send money."

"May I take this home and look at it a while? I'll bring it back next week."

"Sure. I'm not ordering anything. It takes hard currency to do that, and I have little."

"Where is this merchant from? How did he get all the way here to God's favorite country?"

"He says there are ships that come and go from a place called Trieste. That's in Italy. They take in and take out passengers from all parts of the world."

"How much, do you know, would it cost to go to this land of milk and honey, America?"

"I have no idea, but next time he is here, I will ask. Why? Are you planning a trip to America, Vasily?" Nestor asked with a smirk. "How is your English?" he added with a serious but mocking expression, then burst into loud laughter showing his bad teeth and his single gold crown in front.

Vasily didn't laugh. He was already contemplating about how to get to Trieste. *Maybe I could find a ship that would sail across the water to America. It would be a long way to Trieste, I'm guessing. How would I get there?*

The ride back to the farm seemed far shorter and faster. Vasily was unconsciously urging his beautiful, strong draft horses to move quickly. They relished the challenge, probably anticipating the bag of oats and the bale of hay waiting for them in the barn. The wind the speeding sled created stung the faces of the two humans who pulled up the collars of their coats and pulled down their hats so that only their watering eyes were left uncovered. After helping Oleg unload the sleigh, Vasily hurried back to the barn to tend the horses and look over the store catalog he had secreted away.

With his chores finished, Vasily went through each page, marveling at the variety of products pictured therein. He could not, of course, read a word of English—or Cyrillic, either—but he could read numbers and he guessed that the "$" meant money. Realizing this, he began pondering how to acquire enough money to make the journey to a land known to him only through the pages of a store catalog.

Each week, Master Georgi paid a few kopeks to his workforce so they could buy personal items, or blow it all drinking cheap vodka. Vasily had done that himself, but now began making excuses not to go drinking with the others.

With the coming of spring, the single road into the village turned to soupy mud. While pulling the supply wagon to town and back, Vasily had to often cut across the densely-packed grassland to keep from plunging axel-deep into the mire. Either way, the horses strained mightily to pull their load. By May, the roads had dried out enough that Vasily could drag a heavy timber along the road to town to flatten out the remaining ruts.

Wildflowers soon rioted, and the skies became a cloudless, cornflower blue...most of the time. Vasily managed to save his allotments, patching his worn, but barely useable garments. Katia surreptitiously smuggled him a newer shirt and an extra pair of wool trousers left by an overnight guest. These items, plus a couple of her needles and some thread she gifted him, he packed into a well-hidden rucksack.

During this time of hoarding, Vasily Sovatislav carefully planned his emigration. He confided only in Katia, and she proved more than a treasure to him. He still didn't know how to get to Trieste, but he was going, and Katia would help him prepare. During the course of the winter and into the spring, she taught him the rudiments of reading and writing their native language, including common words between Russian, Ukrainian, Hungarian and Polish. By the end of May, he was able to speak useful Russian and read the shop signs in town and even some of the notices pasted on walls and nailed to posts. Each evening they were together, she read to him by candlelight from the Bible. Soon, he was haltingly reading the Ukrainian words in it himself. He brought home a few Russian language newspapers and Katia helped him learn to read them and speak the words.

Chapter 2

The Migration

From conversations with friends in town—conversations that expanded his vocabulary too, Vasily learned the basic lay of the land between the village and the distant port of Trieste. He would have to cross the Carpathian Mountains and a few smaller ranges before he got to Budapest in Hungary. He estimated the total distance between one and two thousand kilometers, roughly 600 to 1,200 miles. Vasily calculated that if he walked twenty kilometers a day, it would take somewhere near 100 days to get to Trieste. That meant if he left in early June, he should just make it over the mountains before it started snowing. Knowing this helped him set the date of his departure, and he started hoarding money from everyone from whom he could borrow. He carefully asked Master Georgi if he had a used overcoat he could wear on the cold evenings when he stayed overnight in town.

"*Zvychayno*," Georgi Levchenko replied. "Of course, lad. Just last week a neighbor swapped a good coat for one of my bulls, so you may have my old one. I am not in need of two." Georgi pounded Vasily on the back and several minutes later handed over a heavily worn, but full-length wool overcoat that nearly touched the ground. Perfect!

The next day, a green monster of guilt started creeping into Vasily's thoughts. Having accepted the coat, he couldn't possibly tell Master Georgi he would soon be leaving forever. As equally embarrassed as fearful, he decided he would have to slip out during the night without further words. And so, on a mid-June morning, after all the lights were out, and under a full moon, Vasily hefted his rucksack filled with bread, sausage and two old vodka bottles filled with water. He tucked his new coat between the straps of the pack, and crept silently away. He knew the first part of his journey by heart. Looking a final time over his shoulder, he impressed on his mind the silhouette of his only known home. He then turned west, never to see Katia, his Master or the farm again.

He crossed Bessarabia, knowing nothing about that small sliver of a country, to face the daunting Carpathians, still showing vestiges of snow near their tops. Vasily's boots were fairly new and the soles solid. Even so, it took longer than he had imagined to cross the mountains, by trial and error searching out trails and passes that would get him through to the other side. Following goat trails and sheep scat signs, he was able to stay away from impassable cliffs and cross the numerous streams and rivulets at their narrowest. Still, the higher elevations quickly sapped his strength and he found himself having to stop and rest increasingly often. His food soon ran out. Weariness and the constant cold caused him to begin worrying if he might die in the mountains. He staggered in a daze the final few kilometers out of the mountains where he came upon a small farm.

Vasily's urgent knock on the door was answered by a plump woman in an apron and colorful head scarf or babushka. One look told her that the large young man was in distress, and she guided him to a chair at a rough-hewn wooden table and offered him water. While he gulped down the water, she filled a plate with sausage and bread and placed it in front of him. Neither of them had yet spoken a word. In his best Russian, Vasily introduced himself and explained he was on his way to Trieste.

The woman, Sophia, understanding enough of what Vasily said, nodded approvingly. When she pointed at the empty rucksack, he explained, in Russian, that he would happily work for food and a place to sleep at night in the barn,

Sophia abruptly held up a hand signaling him to stop talking, waddled out the back door and yelled for someone. A few moments later, a lanky, raw-boned man with straw still clinging to his sparse beard lumbered inside and stood beside her. Vasily repeated his introduction and offered to help around the farm for enough supplies to continue his trek.

Sophia and the farmer, whom Sophia called Yuri, conversed together until Yuri agreed. Yuri's grasp of Russian was far better than his wife's, so he and Vasily communicated in more detail. He showed Vasily out the door and walked him toward the barn. Pointing at the small herd of cows as they went, Yuri told Vasily to milk the cows twice a day and make sure they had plenty of fodder. Stopping in front of the barn, he asked Vasily if he knew anything about horses. Vasily's face immediately lit up like an oil lamp and he asked to see the stock. Yuri even took some time to correct Vasily's Russian.

Yuri's horses were in sad shape. They looked terribly underfed and badly needed their hooves trimmed. Vasily told Yuri that he would do what he could to bring the horses back to strength, enough to pull a plow or wagon. The man, smiling broadly, clapped him on the back, handed him a pitchfork and walked back toward the farmhouse.

Vasily worked on the farm for a week, asking only for his daily food, some supplies and water for continuing his journey. Yuri and Sophia became more friendly with their new employee as the horses rounded into shape—even after just a week. The night before Vasily's departure, Yuri suggested he take the farm road to a larger one, then turn west toward Budapest. He might be able to catch a ride on a supply wagon along the way, which would speed his journey.

The next morning, Vasily enjoyed a hearty breakfast of eggs, sliced ham and hot black bread covered with butter. Bidding his hosts farewell, he headed down the road with renewed strength and purpose. There was no sign to indicate when he crossed into Hungary, but large ones repeatedly pointed the way to Budapest. He did indeed catch a ride in a hay wagon, saving him days of walking. As the wagon crested yet another hill, he saw the city of Budapest laid out before him. In the distance was a large, winding river that he would later learn was called the Danube. Coming to some rail tracks, he jumped off, thanked the wagon driver, and followed the tracks to a train station. By now, it was late July and he was barely half-way to Trieste. A quick read of the station's passenger information sign told him that even a third class seat on a train to Trieste exceeded his remaining Russian currency by half again as much.

"How far get me?" he asked in badly broken Hungarian as he stepped ruefully up to the ticket agent's cage, showing the agent his palm and his money.

"That will get you to Ljubljana. In Slovenia. From there you can walk across the Transylvania Alps. Once you get off, follow the train tracks and they will lead you to Trieste. Good luck."

"Ticket Ljubljana," Vasily replied.

Three hours later, Vasily was watching Hungary creep by from his third class compartment's window seat. He was down to his last two kopeks, and had no idea how he would find enough food to get him to Trieste or, for that matter, passage on a ship.

The train pulled into Ljubljana late at night. The terminal was mostly deserted, and the few people there were happily greeting disembarking friends or relatives. Vasily found a bench in a quiet corner of the terminal, and slept deeply.

The shrill sound of a train whistle woke him with a start. He ate his last sausage and piece of bread from his rucksack, washing it down with the last of his water. Seeing a spigot, he tested the water, then filled his bottles from it. As instructed, he jumped off the platform and began walking the train track ties westward.

By noon, tired, hungry and desperate, he came upon a roadside stand where an elderly couple were selling vegetables. Vasily showed them his last two kopeks and asked for something to eat. The couple, who knew some Russian, cut an overripe melon for him to eat. Using his basic Russian and gestures he conveyed that he was headed to Trieste, but didn't know how far he had yet to go. He showed he had no money, no identification papers and explained he knew no one in Trieste.

"Didn't you have a good life back in Little Russia?" they asked looking bewildered.

"*Tak*. Suppose, yes, but urge to have adventure."

"So, how is that adventure going for you?"

This caused all three to laugh, as his plight was obvious. "Not as expected. Beggar, I am not. Work for food and place sleep. *Mozhesh meni dopomohty*—can you help me?"

"Why…Trieste?" the woman asked.

"Take ship to America…"

"Oh, America! Last year, one of our villagers had that same dream. He left and nobody ever heard from him again. Maybe he died or was killed by an American gangster?" the woman replied.

"Well, what you do is not our concern. Still, we have some vegetables that need picking and soil that needs turning for the winter. Walk up that path. There is a small tool shed. You can sleep there," the old man added. "I'll come up and show you around soon."

Vasily thanked the couple profusely and headed up the path that wound around, then over a hill. Below him, he saw a neat little farm with a large vegetable garden. The shed was located at the far end of the garden away from the main house. As he walked, he noticed cabbages and beets that looked ready to pick. The other vegetables looked ready to bolt, so he knew that any work would have to be done quickly. For once, he felt his timing was perfect.

Vasily worked days and slept in the shed seven nights. One of his socks had worn such big holes it was beyond repair, and he asked the old lady if she had a replacement. Digging around in one of her chests, she emerged with a pair of new, heavy woolen socks and handed them to Vasily. "These were supposed to be for my son, but he fell off a horse and broke his neck. You may have seen his grave behind the shed. I'm sure you will put these to good use in America." She smiled, showing several missing teeth.

The next day, Vasily set off on what he hoped was the last leg of his European journey with high hopes that he would somehow locate a ship willing to take him to America. He had no idea, of course, where such a ship would actually take him, as he knew only the one American city by name, Chee-cah-go, the purported home of the Seers-Row-Buck compa-ny. In Trieste, he would need to find more information about America and where exactly the port of Chee-cah-go was. Maybe in Trieste he could go to—what had the old man called it?—a library. Yes. A library. But he still had over a hundred more kilometers to walk—A week if he hurried and the ground was flat.

But the ground wasn't flat. It took two full weeks during which Au-gust inched ever closer to September with its accompanying cold winter rains and snow not far behind. Again, he had to stop and work for food, this time at a farm and farrier's shop in Dobrova, Slovenia. It helped that he knew how to make horseshoes and tend horse's hoofs. The farrier,

Mikhail Karlovic, in gratitude, paid him hard cash for his skilled work, and asked Vasily to stay. "*Príliš zlé,*" the man replied in Slovenian when Vasily hastily reaffirmed his intent to continue on his journey in his most rudimentary attempts at the same language. "Too bad. I could certainly have used a skilled horseman such as yourself. Do you have identification papers? It will be impossible for you to board a ship without them."

"*Nemaye.* No. Born in countryside, Little Russia. No papers. Work on same farm until die."

"I see. Well, I have a customer in a small town named Planina. It's on your way to Trieste. I saved a couple of his prized horses from their injuries, and he owes me a favor. I will write him a letter which you will deliver. He knows important people, people who have access to ways to get identification papers for travelers like yourself. It may take a few days, but you can work his horses for him while you wait for your papers. How does that sound?"

"Um…*khahrohshiy*! Good!" Vasily replied with a grin, understanding little other than his host's caring smile. "*Dyakuyu*! Thank you, Mikhail! Learn write letter when get to America. Send to you."

"I hope you get there, Vasily Sovatislav, and live your dream. You have come a long way, so your determination and courage can never be questioned. If somebody does, knock them flat on their ass and ask them if they could make such a journey." That produced a good laugh from both.

"The man's name is Josef Donorovic," Mikhail continued. "He will do what I ask. Now, here is a spare shirt and plenty of food. Hurry along. You must cross the Julian Alps before it snows."

With Master Georgi's greatcoat still draped across the rucksack, Vasily resumed his journey over hills and across fields, always heading west toward Planina. Once there, he asked haltingly where the Donorovic farm was. He was directed over yet another hill to a large, sprawling farm with numerous horses grazing in fenced fields and others in paddocks. He presented the letter of introduction to Josef Donorovic who eyed Vasily with suspicion. Donorovic knew Russian fairly well as he often did business with Russian customers. A few pointed questions removed any doubts and Donorovic immediately put Vasily to work grooming his horses, cleaning stalls and re-shoeing them as needed.

It was over a week before Donorovic called Vasily onto the porch surrounding the great house. "You have done very good work here, Vasily. That work confirms your validity. I sent a courier to see Mr. Karlovic and here are your identification papers. They are written in Slovenian. Can you read them? No? Right. Follow after me."

Josef read the identification papers for one Vasily Andreovich Sovatislav, having Vasily repeat the words until he could say them without coaching. "We didn't know your middle name, so I had them make one up. I hope you don't mind."

"No 'middle name' good. This one fine. Thank you for help."

"You earned it, young man. Oh, and it says here that you are twenty-one years old. That is the legal age almost everywhere." Josef stepped back to eye and remember the young man, then continued. "So! You should leave tomorrow. Tonight I will have the cook make enough food packages to get you to Trieste. It should take only five days, but the weather is unpredictable this time of year so I've provided a bit more. You'd better get going. Leave first thing in the morning, before it gets hot and by afternoon you'll be in the foothills of the Julian Alps. Here's my mail address. Write me from America after you get settled. Who knows, maybe some day I will visit YOU." The two smiled and embraced after which Vasily went to the kitchen where the cook was already preparing the food packages. He was going to make it to Trieste!

After that? Well, somehow he'd find a way to get on a ship for America. Somehow, someway, Vasily Andreovich Sovatislav would get to America.

Chapter 3

The Voyage

The descent out of the Julian Alps was a relief after two days of hard walking along roads that twisted, turned and frequently doubled-backed. There remained one more set of hills to cross before he entered the city, and what Vasily saw from the last hilltop was a sprawling, convoluted mass of stone buildings, narrow streets and a long, winding road that splintered into its heart in a maze of alleys and dead ends.

So this is what I walked for three months to find? Oh, there's the water! That must be the ocean. But what ocean? And is America really on the other side?

With these and a myriad of other thoughts spinning inside his tired mind, he lumbered into town, arriving in a small plaza surrounded by neatly kept shops and a restaurant. Mr. Donorovic had gifted Vasily enough money to survive until he found ship passage, But his growling stomach directed him toward the enticing smells wafting from a sidewalk cafe. Plopping down at a table, he placed his rucksack on the ground next to his chair. A harried-looking waiter arrived, threw a menu at Vasily and stalked off without a word.

The print on the menu was not Cyrillic, and was, therefore, unreadable to him. When the waiter returned, Vasily asked for the "*yeda spetsial'naya*"—the "special"—in his best Russian. The waiter rolled his eyes, grabbed the menu and left. A Few minutes later, a pretty young woman with blonde, double-braided hair came up to his table and spoke to him in perfect Russian. Vasily, ever so thankful, ordered two meat pies, coffee and a tart for dessert. It would cost him a good portion of his money, but he definitely deserved a celebratory treat for having made it to Trieste.

When the food arrived, he asked the young woman, again in Russian, where the ships were and if there were rooms for rent near the docks.

"*Da*," she replied with a smile. "Follow this street; it's one of the few that doesn't change its name three times before it ends. It will take you to *Riva del Mandracchio*. That street runs along the wharves. On the opposite side of the street are several inexpensive rooming places where sailors often stay. You should be able to find something within your budget. From where do you come?"

Vasily explained as best he could how he'd walked his way from a small farm near Kiev in Little Russia.

Anna switched languages to Ukrainian. "My name is Anna Petrokova. I came here from a farm outside Kiev, too. What are you doing here?"

It was a relief to once again speak his native language. "I want to take a ship to America," he answered shyly. "You? Will you wait tables for weary foreign travelers forever?"

Anna laughed. "I have met people from many European countries, some from Asia, too. I even met some *Amerikanskiy* sailors. That is why I can read and speak several languages. We are in Italy, so I had to learn some Italian, too. *Buongiorno!* That's 'good morning' in Italian. That menu you're holding is written in Italian. Can you read it? No? I think your adventure has yet to teach you more languages!" After a pause, she continued. "I want to have an adventure or two, also. Let's talk about our adventures tonight when I'm off work. Meet me here at six o'clock. If you have any money left, you can buy me a glass of wine."

"I have time to find a room and get here by six?"

"You should. It's only a short walk from here. Now, eat your dinner, find a room and come back at six."

After eating, Vasily found his way to the street paralleling the wharves and approached what looked like a reasonably priced hostel along the way. It was one block past the road that brought him to *Riva del Mandracchio,* so he could easily find his way back to the cafe to meet Anna. There was one bathroom on each floor and Vasily had to wait in line for his turn. He washed as best he could. After bathing in icy streams all summer long, the lukewarm sponge bath was greatly appreciated. He even shaved the stubble on his cheeks and throat leaving the coal black, curling mustache framing his mouth. He put on his clean shirt and brushed his hair, and shook as much trail dust off his pants and boots as he could.

Arriving at the cafe a little before six, he sat and waited at a table. Just after six, Anna Petrokova came bouncing out of the cafe door, saw Vasily and smiled widely. She had the same, earthy peasant beauty that he'd known in Katia, though his time with her seemed centuries ago. Anna had bright blue eyes to go with the straight blonde hair and fair, but not pale skin. She was much shorter than Vasily, and, to his appreciation, sturdily built. Her smile revealed straight, even teeth, making her broad face seem even brighter. She captured Vasily's heart immediately. They walked across the plaza to a bistro that served wine. Not knowing anything about the local beverages, Anna ordered for them both.

'*Oh, this is tasty. She knows what tastes good,* he thought.

"So, Vasily, you are by yourself, *da?*"

"*Da.* One day, I felt the need to get away from the mud and horses. A friend in our village showed me Seers-Row-Buck catalog from Chee-cah-go, and I think America is for me. So I saved up a little money, packed food and left. I think it was in June. What is the date now?"

"That is quite a brave thing to do. It's September tenth. You've been traveling for over three months. Aren't you tired?"

"*Da*. I will sleep all day tomorrow. I will then find a ship to America."

"I've been thinking about America, too. American merchant sailors often stop at our cafe and I listen to them talk. I've even learned a little English from them. Do you have papers?"

"*Da*. It is a long story, but I am now a real person!" That brought a laugh from Anna.

"I, too, have papers. What is a person without papers these days?" They both chuckled at that.

The conversation meandered along as they recounted their lives. They drank a second glass of wine.

"I like you, Vasily. Are you as strong as you look?"

"I suppose so. But I don't have any way to show you," he replied, grinning.

"Pick me up with one arm."

Shocked by her boldness, he nonetheless stood up and before she could rise from her chair, picked both Anna and the chair she was sitting in up with one arm. The effort brought their faces even, and she put an arm around his neck and kissed him fully and deeply.

"Your mustache tickles, and somebody taught you how to kiss very well."

He set the chair and its passenger gently back down. "Yes. She was our assistant cook and liked me, so one thing led to another," he said, repeating the phrase he'd heard from Anna during their conversation.

"Well, walk me home. It's just a couple blocks. I've enjoyed your company."

The two walked slowly up a street and over another to Anna's rooming house.

"Will you come see me tomorrow, Vasily Andreovich? We can talk more about America."

"Yes. That is a good idea!" he answered, wobbling slightly. "Mmm. I never drank wine before. Same time tomorrow?"

"Yes. You're so tall. Bend down and let me give you a goodnight kiss."

She encircled his neck with her strong arms and, while enjoying the sweetness of her kiss, he wrapped his arms around her and stood, lifting her off her feet, pressing her ample breasts against his chest.

"Mmm. You are strong, and you do kiss very sweetly, just as a woman likes. I'll see you tomorrow. Good luck with finding a ship."

Vasily awoke with a start and a low backache next morning, not being used to a soft bed. He dressed, washed and ventured out to the docks where he saw rough-looking men talking and working along the wharves where a few large ships were docked. To his eyes, the steam-powered ships looked like floating mountains. Marveling at their size, he walked past one while staring up at the masts and pulleys lifting crates up to the ship until someone yelled at him in a language he didn't know. In his best Russian, he explained that he spoke Ukrainian and basic Russian, upon which the speaker switched into a caricature of Russian that Vasily could somewhat understand.

After sizing Vasily up, he said something that sounded like, "You look big, strong. Can shovel coal into furnace all day?"

"*Da*," Vasily replied, bewildered. "But why do that?"

"Want fireman. Keep boilers pumping steam to engines. You want job?"

"On this ship?"

"On this ship. Ship named 'S. S. City of Trenton'. You want job or not?"

"Where going?" Vasily replied, cocking his head to one side.

"New York City. Leave two days. You want sign on or not?"

New York! Vasily stood, dumbfounded, looking from the huge ship to the man and back to the ship.

"Go to Chee-cah-go?"

"Not on ship. Must take train from New York."

"*Da*, I be your fireman?"

Continuing in his broken Russian the man replied, "First, need see papers. Then you sign contract. You get free passage, meals and two dollars a day. Need see papers."

Following Mr. Doborovic's instructions, Vasily carried his papers everywhere with him. Showing them to the man, he asked, "What your name, please?"

"Peter Molovich. First mate. You call me Mr. Pete," the man replied in English with a smile.

"Where you learn Russian?" Vasily ventured, curious about Mr. Pete's odd way of speaking.

"Little here. Little there. Go around world, learn enough languages to be boss, keep fed and out of jail," Mr. Pete replied heartily, laughing at his own Russian and humor. "Okay, Mr. Vasily Sovatislav, sign here."

After signing, Mr. Pete said in broken Russian, "Get things. Report back soon as possible."

Vasily walked swiftly to his room, packed everything and hurried back to the ship lest it sail without him. "Mr. Pete. Any passengers?"

"Maybe. Why?"

"Know woman wants go New York, too."

"Oh? Can she cook? We need cook."

"Yes. Can cook. I will bring her tonight."

"You'll sleep here tonight. Get her tomorrow."

After a quick tour of the ship, Mr. Pete showed Vasily a hammock strung between two bulkheads, barely large enough to accommodate him, and assigned him a small locker to store his belongings.

The engine room, where he would be working, was two compartments away from the crew quarters and kitchen/mess area. The boiler extended from the engine room to the top deck. Off to either side of the hissing boiler were two huge coal bunkers and two glowing furnace doors. "Keep steam up, enough run electrical generator. Makes hot water while in port. At sea, fresh water strictly rationed. Kitchen stoves also coal-fired. You tend stoves, too, when cook asks. Must keep steam up all night." At Vasily's nod, Mr. Pete, seeing disappointment in his new hand's face, continued, "Go see girlfriend. We try talk her into cooking for us, *da*?" Mr. Pete gave Vasily a knowing wink.

Vasily walked quickly up to the cafe, not knowing what an "electrical generator" was or even electricity. Inside, he found Anna working the counter.

"I have found a ship going to New York," he stated in hurried Ukrainian. "I will be the fireman. They need a cook. I told them you could cook. Can you cook?"

"Wait. What? Of course, I can cook. What are you saying, Vasily?"

"*Mozhet byt'* you go to New York…with me…er…us."

"And who exactly is this 'us'?"

"Er. Uh. Ship's crew, I guess. I signed up. What do you think? The ship leaves day after tomorrow."

"This is all so…sudden. Go. Sit at a table outside and I'll bring you a coffee. Let me think a little," she said, adding slyly, "You do look adorable when you're excited like this. Now, go! Sit!"

Anna brought him the coffee, smiled her broad, signature smile and left him sitting, wondering, '*What is the Russian word for making a 'quick decision'? Pospeshnyy? Bezrassudnyy? Yes, bezrassudnyy! Foolhardy. I am being foolhardy? But I like this woman and she, I think, likes me. She is also strong. Is she adventurous? I guess we'll see.*

Ten minutes later, Anna came out without her apron, carrying a tote bag. "*Moi nebesa*—My heavens! Let's go to the ship and see what we shall see."

When they got to the S.S. City of Trenton, Mr. Pete was pouring over papers while more boxes were being checked and carried aboard. He noticed Vasily and the short blonde woman with him. He walked over to them.

"So, you be cook," he stated once again in his strange version of Russian. "What can cook? Cook for forty men and women? We need good cook."

In her broken but understandable Russian she answered, "I can cook for one or a hundred. What kind of food do you have on ship? What meats? What vegetables? Flour? Eggs? Do you have plenty oven space? How many loaves of bread do men eat a day? These are details I need to know if I'm going to cook for this, uh, ship."

"Good questions," replied Mr. Pete, impressed. "We load plenty meat; in big cooler. Eat usual things. Lots Italian food. Many crew *Ital'yanskiy*. Need pasta. You make and cook pasta?"

"*Konechno*—of course!" replied Anna indignantly. "Let me talk with my friend for a few minutes," she stated, turning to Vasily.

"Vasily. I will sign up to go to New York with you, but I want to know what will become of us: you and me. What are your thoughts?"

"I like you very much, Anna. I have had only one girlfriend before you, so you would only be the second. Let's see how our 'adventure' goes on the ship; it will test us as a couple, I think? If we still like each other after a few weeks, I ask the captain to marry us. Okay with you?"

"Well, that is a marriage proposal I never expected to get. I accept, Vasily. If you turn out to be a shit, I will either throw you overboard or poison you. Okay with you?" she asked, breaking into a wide grin.

"I will take the challenge. Good. Now, we must get better...acquainted. I was just paid two dollars for my work today, so I'll buy us a little dinner."

"Save the money, Vasily, dear. I have a better idea."

Anna returned her attention to Mr. Pete, showed him her papers and signed on as the ship's cook. During a break in the loading, Mr. Pete took Anna on the required ship's tour with Vasily following along for a second tour and language "lesson." Listening to Anna querying the first mate during the tour proved she was smart, exceptionally clever and showed leadership. She looked carefully around the kitchen, cooler and pantry and made a couple of suggestions on the spot, Mr. Pete nodding his assent, thinking them excellent suggestions.

Instead of going back to the cafe, however, Anna took Vasily back to her room and proceeded to seduce him. Not that it took much effort. Both quickly discovered they were quite compatible, sexually, despite their height differences. Anna's body was not slender, but she wasn't fat. Her breasts were so firm they didn't even jiggle like Katia's at the height of their sexual encounters.

As they lay panting after their second episode of lovemaking, Anna said, "Well, Vasily Andreovich, do you think we have the necessities to be a couple? I don't know if I love you yet, but I do love doing this with you. I wonder if we'll ever have the time or the privacy to keep on exploring *polovoy akt* during the voyage to New York."

"I feel the same. You are beautiful. And the...*polovoy akt*— sex—is wonderful. We shall find ways to do more, uh, exploring on the trip. I look forward to your 'cooking'," he said, dead-panning his joke. The joke was met with a punch to his gut and a leap upon his body for yet another "exploration."

The next morning, Anna packed her belongings into two carpet bags, collected her back pay from the cafe, and walked to the ship. Vasily, having risen earlier, was already working on board.

They sailed on September twelfth, heading south into the Adriatic Sea for lands of mystery, unknown fortune and the "adventure" for which each had hoped.

The voyage out into the Mediterranean Sea, and through the Straits of Gibraltar into the Atlantic Ocean took two full weeks. The S.S. City of Trenton could barely make twelve knots, so once in the open ocean, the ship wallowed and groaned with each wave attempting to impede its progress.

In the Atlantic, everyone's daily routines were quickly established and perfected. The captain, a Jamaican, married Vasily and Anna to the delight of the crew, who cheered lustily knowing that they'd soon be downing the extra case of "secret" champagne put into the cooler on the day they sailed from Trieste. Vasily had befriended one of the engineers, who stood witness at their wedding. Anna loved being the center of attention, but after her second glass of champagne and a piece of the wedding cake which she'd made herself, went back to the kitchen to prepare the evening meal for the captain and crew.

Vasily, meanwhile, drank a little more champagne with his engineer friend, Abner Wentz. Wentz was German-born, but had learned Russian from his father's housekeeper, and English from his British mother. "Vasily, what you do when we dock in New York? Will you stay at sea?"

"*Nyet*. I try find Chee-cah-go. Get work with Seers-Row-Buck. Start family. Anna and I having great adventure, but soon must find way to feed ourselves in new country. Why ask?"

"I have a cousin in Cleveland, Ohio, who works at a brewery," Abner replied. "He is German, too. I am going to end my days at sea after this trip, and take a train to Cleveland where he has a job waiting for me. Why don't you and Anna come with me? I'm sure you'll find work there. Anna is a good cook. Maybe she can cook at a hotel or something. What do you say?"

"Must talk to Anna," Vasily replied. Still have time before New York. Wonder if I can walk without— *khytayuchys?*—sorry. Means "*osh-elomlyayushchiy*" in Russian—staggering—when go ashore, again?" The two men laughed over both Vasily's stumbling Russian and his all too appropriate question.

The Atlantic is rarely calm and their voyage from Gibraltar to New York did not upset that axiom. After a week of bobbing and wallowing with every swell, everyone came to anticipate the ship's next move well enough to keep from falling or smashing into bulkheads.

On October twentieth, the lookout called out that land was in sight. All those not on duty rushed to the top deck to catch their first sight of land. What they saw, to their collective amazement, weren't forests and tall trees, but human-made spikes of concrete and steel, thrusting into the clouds, welcoming them to the largest city in the western hemi-sphere, New York. Vasily took a break from the furnace and grabbed Anna from the kitchen for a quick look at their destination. That night Anna and Vasily agreed to travel with Abner to Cleveland. Abner looked pleased, then reminded them that first, the three would have to register on Ellis Island in New York harbor.

After docking, as the ship began unloading, Vasily and Anna were given their pay. Carrying their belongings down the gangplank they stopped, then together set foot on the soil of their new country, the United States of America. Abner directed them to the barge that ferried them to Ellis Island where they watched many long lines of immigrants slowly moving forward to be processed by dozens of harried-looking immigration clerks.

When it was their turn, they proudly stepped up as husband and wife, Mr. and Mrs. Vasily Sovatislav. Their clerk took one look at the name on their cards, turned it sideways and shook his head. Checking their immigration tags, even though the printing was in the same European script as on their identification papers, it proved just too much for the clerk. Nearing the end of his shift and, being very tired of trying to interpret foreign names in foreign-looking languages, he filled in the forms in his best English interpretation of what Vasily and Anna said were their names, names they would carry with them for as long as they resided in the United States. They would be known, henceforth, as Virgil and Anna Savage.

"Sorry, folks," the tired immigration officer said, "That's the best I can do. Besides, you're in a new land, so what's wrong with having new names? Welcome to the United States of America,"

"NEXT!"

PART II
GENERATIONS

Chapter 4

Depression

The Great War, later known as World War I, had drained numerous countries of their sons and their treasuries. The US. military "only" lost 50,000 soldiers in the eighteen months it was engaged. The European participants, however, were left barren of the workforce necessary to rebuild their economies. In the midst of all this, the Russian people rebelled against their ruling family and installed a new form of government.

The Communist Revolution seemed to push capitalists to distraction. In the United States average people began buying stocks "on the margin," borrowing money on what the market said one's existing stock was worth, or, if owning no stock, on the over-inflated "value" of any assets whatsoever. Between 1919 and 1928, the stock market boomed—on "margin"—and the "Roaring Twenties" roared like a bull with the appearance of jazz, open relationships, the prohibition of alcohol for human consumption, and a massive crime spree gripping urban America.

Then, something only a banker could understand happened. The banks needed capital to make legitimate loans, but most of their assets were tied up in "margin" accounts. When the banks began calling in the margin accounts, many stockholders were forced to sell their stocks below margin in order to protect their other assets. It took almost a year, but in 1929, the overall value of stocks tanked and those still trying to sell were left with nothing but debt. Banks, businesses and individuals went bankrupt and many faux fortunes were wiped out overnight. Failing businesses cut their work forces, leaving one in four workers with no source of income. The middle class stood in soup lines and begged for handouts from passers-by.

The squalling newborn boy could be heard the length of the hall in the maternity ward at Huron Road Hospital in East Cleveland, Ohio. Both parents grinned delightedly as Lois Savage stuffed a nipple into the gaping mouth that was emitting the loud "greetings" to the world. Frank Savage could barely hold still as his nervous fingers took yet another lap around the brim of his hat. "Let's name him...Howard," Lois Savage offered as the new being abruptly stopped screaming and began doing what all newborn mammals have done since the beginning of their time on earth.

"Uh, okay. But why...Howard? Why not Jack or Louis? Ya know, like the great boxers?" asked Frank, standing next to her bed, gaping at their hungry new addition.

"Well, he sounds like he's ready to fight the world, doesn't he? Howard? Well, he was my father's favorite brother."

"Wasn't he killed in The Great War?" Frank asked warily.

"Yes, but he was awarded the Distinguished Service Cross for heroism. The story goes that he dragged several wounded soldiers back to their trenches. He was wounded by a machine gun bullet, but he went back and kept rescuing more soldiers."

"So, you want to name our son after your war hero uncle, right?"

"Yes. But only if you agree," Lois offered.

"Well, why not? Maybe our son will grow up to be some sort of hero himself."

"He might. Now what would be a good middle name?" Lois asked, obviously relieved.

"You know that my father's name is Virgil. How about Howard Virgil Savage? That has a nice ring to it, dontcha think?"

"I like it, darling. Good choice! Gosh, this little guy is hungry. It feels like he's trying to turn my breast inside out."

Howard Virgil Savage entered the world on March 27, 1932, on one of the many similar days during the greatest economic depression in the history of the western democracies.

It was into this maelstrom of worldwide hopelessness, poverty and upheaval that Howard Virgil Savage arrived appropriately screaming his lungs out. Was he announcing his presence with authority, or declaring that he was a precursor of great things to come? He was the grandson of intrepid immigrants who had traveled from Eastern Europe, and the son of parents who were part of what would be later known as *The Greatest Generation.* Time and circumstances would dictate if he lived up to the expectations for his given name, and how he would honor the legacy given him by his ancestors.

Chapter 5
Working to Live

"Honey, I'm home! Got some good news, Lois...I think."

"I'm in the bedroom changing a diaper. Be out in a minute," Lois called, speaking around the safety pins still in her teeth.

Frank and Lois Savage lived on the top floor of a four-story walk-up near Shaw High School in East Cleveland, Ohio. Their East One Hundred and Forty-First Street apartment was barely six-hundred square feet, consisting of a single bedroom, a small living area, a dining area barely big enough for a table and four chairs, and a tiny adjacent kitchen. The bedroom was so small that their double bed only had one side free to enter and exit. The single closet overflowed with what clothes they both had, and the four-drawer dresser looked like it was ready to explode its contents too. There were tiny windows on the far wall of the living area, one in the dining area and one in the bedroom. The walls were covered with faded wallpaper that looked like fever dream images of a dying florist.

Lois emerged from the bedroom with young Howard perched on one hip while she carefully deposited the used diaper in the diaper pail. "So, what's the news?"

"WPA hired me! I start on a road crew Monday. Buck an hour. Not bad considerin' that the minimum is forty cents. Since I'm married with a kid, I got the better rate."

"Oh, sweetheart! That's great! Does that mean we can start eating steak again?" They both laughed ruefully at Lois' attempt at humor.

Frank had been doing pick-up and handy-man jobs since Howard was born, and was barely able to provide enough for the sixty dollars per month rent plus fifty more for food. Fortunately, Lois had kept nursing Howard as bottle milk and baby food were impossible to afford. "Good thing I've got big tits," she often added sarcastically.

"Well, they're sayin' I'll get at least forty hours a week and maybe some overtime if the weather holds. That would mean almost two-fifty a month! We might actually be able to afford a steak dinner once in a while. I'll even be able to walk to the job site. How's our boy doin' today?"

"Oh, he slept most of the day, so I actually got some mending done. I'm tired a seeing your toes stick through your socks. Maybe we could get a phone, if work stays steady."

"Why do we need a phone? Isn't Mrs. Matson across the hall good enough company?" Frank retorted with a frown and a twinkle in his eye.

"Very funny. I'd really like to talk to my mother sometimes. And what if something happened to Howard? I could call a doctor…"

"True. I'll ask around and see how much it costs for a phone to be installed. That payphone downstairs always seem to have a teenager hangin' on it."

"Here. Take Howard," Lois said. "I need to do laundry. We're outta clean diapers."

Lois loaded the diaper pail on top of the other clothes in the wicker laundry basket squeezed into the back of the closet. She grabbed the detergent and wiggled her way out the door, walking down five flights of stairs to the communal washing machine in the basement. Frank sat on the small, dark blue couch avoiding the spring that kept prodding everyone's backside. He bounced Howard on his knees while catching the pacifier that Howard insisted on throwing.

"Are you gonna be a pitcher or an outfielder, big boy? It looks like you're already warmin' up for the big leagues." It was clear to anyone watching, that Frank Savage saw the sun rising and setting in his beautiful son.

"How did I get so lucky to have such a perfect kid? You even drool like a champ."

Lois eventually returned with an empty basket after hanging the clothes on the outdoor line strung between the two wings of the apartment building. In winter the laundry hung on the lines strung around the basement. Her flowered print dress was sweat-stained from the effort. It was mid-July in Cleveland and apart from an unexpected thunderstorm, the summer air was almost always cloying. "The clothes should be dry after dinner," she announced, falling exhaustedly onto the sofa next to Frank.

"It's gonna be mac and cheese again tonight, darling. That'll fill us up. Just add some hot sauce or ketchup to give it more flavor."

Today, she would chop their last onion to give the dish added flavor. With effort, she rose from the too soft couch and walked into the kitchen, hand on her aching back. She smiled as she watched Frank play with Howard, who was giggling and gurgling in equal amounts. Grating cheese was a nasty chore with the old grater her mother gave her. The teeth were dull and she kept scraping her knuckles while bearing down. *I really need one of the new ones made out of stainless steel. They never rust or get dull.*

Lois turned on the small fan and set it on the sill of the open window in the dining area. The evening air was hot, sticky and humid. Looking into the living area, she thought, *Is it my imagination, or does Howard look like he's trying to dictate the terms of play with Frank? It's only been four months and Howard is sitting up by himself and focusing on objects. Maybe Frank is right. Maybe he will be a big leaguer. But I hope for Howard's sake that it's more than just baseball he's good at. I hope we can send him to college. I should start a savings account now with Frank's new job. It will add up over the years.*

At the same time, Frank thought: *Boy would I like to find a bigger place. When he starts walking I'd like it to be more than five steps in one direction.*

As for Howard, he finally ran out of energy, fussed and rubbed his eyes. Frank reluctantly returned him to the tiny crib that barely fit between bed and dresser. The boy almost immediately fell sleep. Frank set the table for dinner, sharing more of his excitement about finding steady work. He grabbed a cold cola out of the tiny refrigerator (they couldn't afford beer even after Roosevelt and the Democrats got the Twenty-first Amendment passed that overturned the Eighteenth Amendment banning the sale of alcohol), and turned on the radio to hear the news.

The familiar voice of Frank's favorite radio newsman, Walter Winchell, announced that unemployment was finally dropping as more people were employed on government-sponsored projects. A new idea from the Roosevelt administration, the Civilian Conservation Corps, or CCC, was taking unemployed youths who stubbornly remained illiterate and put them to work AND enrolled them in school. They would be sent off to camps to improve roads, rebuild infrastructure in national and state parks, and build housing for themselves as well as for the destitute, living rough all across the country. These young men were paid twenty-five dollars per week and half of it was sent home to their families or placed in a personal savings account. Meanwhile, they were taught the three Rs and a vocation: carpentry, electrician and plumbing—among other trades. Unemployed journeymen were paid to teach the classes and supervise the apprentices. Unemployed and retired school teachers taught the academic classes. Observers predicted huge success for the young men AND the infrastructure of the nation.

In an editorial aside, Winchell summarized the last few years: The country was still experiencing wide-spread starvation, and those who could find steady work were endlessly grateful for the steady income. Walking down any street in any town revealed people with a hollowed out look of fear and desperation. "How could this happen here...to us?" was the newsman's repeated question.

In less inviting news, a guy in Germany named "Hitler" was creating mayhem with his thugs harassing and injuring Jews, their businesses and all political opponents of his National Socialist Party. Chancellor Hitler, it was reported, continued to ignore the Versailles treaty and was re-building the economy and Germany's military might by enlarging the supporting industries that fed it equipment and weapons of all types and sizes. The good news was that the staggering inflation there seemed now under control, with people going back to work in droves. To those pay-ing attention in 1934, it seemed an odd juxtaposition that both a totalitar-ian/fascist regime and a democratic government were clawing their way out of the world-wide economic disaster at the same time, using similar methods to "prime the pump," but for vastly different reasons.

After listening to the weather forecast, Frank turned off the radio and sat at the dinner table. Lois placed his meal in front of him while he slid his hand up her skirt a little past decency and pulled her closer to him to bury his face in her tummy while murmuring tenderly.

"That's very sweet, Frank, but let's eat before the dinner gets cold," Lois chided. She pulled away smiling. She sat across from her beloved husband so she could look into his large, sad-looking blue eyes. Frank

Savage was not a sad person, it was just that the shape of his eyes produced a downcast look on his face.

Frank graduated near the top of his Collinwood High School class of 1930. He was the starting shortstop on the baseball team and was a member of the debate club. Even the thespians wanted his talents, but studies and baseball were more important to him. His father, Virgil and his mother, Anna, had always emphasized formal education since neither of them had any. They knew the struggles of not being fluent in the languages necessary to accomplish what they needed and wanted. Virgil Savage settled for taking his small family with him to evening classes in Cleveland to learn to read and write English. They never made it to the fabled *Seers-Row-Buck Company* in *Chee-cah-go.* They did, however, find a branch store in Cleveland and marveled at all the merchandise.

Anna, in the meantime, shopped by looking at labels with pictures of their contents. She discovered a bakery and butcher shop run by Ukrainian Jews who helped her learn more practical English words and even how to read an English language cookbook. Before long she was reading the newspapers that Virgil brought home for his own English language learning.

Virgil worked hard as a stationary fireman at the Cleveland-Toledo brewing company until prohibition shut them down. After that, he joined the un-employed masses taking up daily labor jobs whenever he could find one. For Virgil and Anna, America *was* a land of opportunity, and they intended to make opportunities work for their family's benefit. They insisted, therefore, that their son, Frank, finish high school and learn a trade.

While Frank attended elementary school, Virgil and Anna studied Frank's lessons that he brought home every day after he went to bed. They focused especially hard on English and math. Their hunger for learning earned them a respectable proficiency in both subjects. When Frank entered high school, they studied and learned more advanced material in more subjects including history. They were the epitome of self-taught adults.

Frank Savage excelled in all the high school vocational classes, but was especially brilliant as a machine tool operator. He could make precise pieces of metal from milling machines, drill presses and lathes better than anyone in the school. He'd hoped to land a good job as a machinist when he graduated, but The Great Depression put a screeching halt to industrial expansion, and people like Frank found themselves just trying to eke out enough of a living for the most basic shelter and food. Fortunately, he kept living with his parents and shared their household expenses.

Tent cities and shantytowns were the norm. Great dust storms in the drought-ridden midwest were driving people from their farms and into caravans migrating to the west coast states.

Lois Savage, nee Billings, was a dark-haired beauty at Collinwood who sang in the girls choir and finished second in the same class as Frank. She grew her hair long, instead of the more fashionable short cut styles of the late 1920s, and experimented with various ways to pile her hair up on her head. Her favorite style was a long, swishing ponytail.

Lois was on the tall side at just over five feet nine inches, and possessed a stunning figure that she concealed with loose clothing worn in layers. She and Frank Savage knew each other in passing at school and connected for keeps while Lois was working at Woolworth's soda bar on East One Hundred Thirty-First Street. Frank spent a good portion of his lawn mowing money on sodas and burgers just to sit at Lois' counter. From her tips and salary, Lois took correspondence courses in accounting and shorthand.

When The Great Depression hit, Virgil, having had extensive experience repairing wagons and sleighs in the "old country," discovered that he was very good at diagnosing automobile chassis problems. One of his neighbors, an auto mechanic, asked Virgil to come with him when he went on calls to get somebody's car started. Together they became a good team and developed many repeat customers.

When money dried up, people simply couldn't afford to buy new tires, get a tune-up, or replace a broken suspension, and their garage business simply died. The neighbor was forced to sell all his tools and equipment to pay debts. Virgil somehow managed to salvage his own personal tool kit, and ended up going door-to-door, soliciting car repair jobs for pennies on the dollar. He had a family to feed and it was, quite literally, a hand-to-mouth existence for the Savage family. With the election of Franklin Delano Roosevelt and the repeal of prohibition, breweries and distilleries began reopening and Virgil's old job again became available. This part of the recovery allowed Virgil to retain his home and later pay for a machine shop apprenticeship for Frank at a major tool and die shop.

Lois' father, Andy Billings, was a journeyman electrician. When the banks started calling in loans and mortgages, the home building business rolled over and died. And Andy Billings was one of the casualties. Andy had learned his trade from his father's best friend, Orville West. Orville, a self-taught electrician, had made lots of money wiring houses as electricity replaced gas lighting. Andy ended up working for Orville's business, and when Orville died, he discovered that Orville had left him the business. Andy soon discovered that the business was mired in debt. It broke his heart to sell off the equipment and supplies and close the business. Lois, her mother and her two sisters struggled with food supplies and household goods when Andy ended up working as a handyman often for bartered goods. It wasn't unusual for him to come home with a hat full of eggs or a baked pie.

Lois and her siblings were old and strong enough to do odd jobs, run errands and otherwise try to raise whatever money they could to help pay for food. Dorothy Billings, Lois' mother, had an electric sewing machine and eventually took in sewing and mending to help raise money. Anna Savage had a pedal-powered sewing machine and did the same after Frank brought Lois home to meet his parents. Their discussions regularly turned to ways in which they could help their husbands keep food on the table.

When Frank and Lois fell in love and married on September 21, 1930, their honeymoon was one night at the swanky Statler Hotel in downtown Cleveland, for which their parents paid. Their wedding gift was two one-dollar tickets to a Cleveland Indians baseball game at League Park.

Initially, Frank Savage—one of the lucky ones—found work as a machinist in a twelve-man company that made automobile parts. The company, Euclid Tool and Die, came about as part of Henry Ford's revolutionary manufacturing methods for building cars that working people could actually afford. ET & D cashed in on the car part manufacturing and repair demand. Business boomed until it didn't and on April 1, 1931, Frank was laid off. He and Lois had put a little money away while she continued to work at Woolworth's, moving up to retail where commissions added to her meager salary. They just managed to pay the rent for their East 141st Street apartment, but had to cut way back on everything else to survive.

In July of that year, Lois announced she was pregnant, and a whole new sense of urgency fell upon the broad shoulders of Frank Savage. He HAD to find work, but there was no steady work to be found. Somehow, the refrains of the song, *Happy Days are Here Again* had overnight changed to *Buddy, Can You Spare a Dime?*

Chapter 6

Growing Howard

The WPA job that kept the lights on and simple food on the table was, literally, a job digging ditches. The winters were the toughest, because the ground was frozen and the strongest men were used to swing pick axes to get through the few inches of frozen dirt. Frank would come home from work with muddy boots ("Leave your boots in the hallway!!") and soiled overalls ("Strip those things off in the bathtub and roll them up for the laundry!!"). Since he only had two pairs of overalls, Lois had to wash the dirty ones every day. Same with the work shirts and sweaters. The routine was a grind, but Frank and Lois bowed their necks and did what they had to do to keep that third mouth in their house happy and nourished.

And Howard *was* growing. He was beginning to find his land legs by ten months and walking without assistance at a year. After a few crashing disasters, Lois learned the long-known skills of baby-proofing her house. Her mother often came over to help tend the child while Lois got out of the tiny flat and did some shopping. "Mom, I don't know what I'd do without you."

One day, Lois came back from a grocery shopping excursion with exasperation written all over her. "Mom! I saw a colored lady in rags today outside the grocery store begging for any food we could spare. She was skin and bones and sort of tottered on her legs. She didn't look all that old, but I was afraid she might just up and die right there."

"Did you give her anything, dear?" asked Dorothy.

"Yes. I gave her two carrots and two apples. She grabbed my hand with both of hers and thanked me over and over. My God, mom, do the coloreds really have it that much worse than us?"

"Andy tells me from his time working down around Hough Avenue that those people live in dumps with rats running around and children barefoot and in rags. He said he couldn't get away from there fast enough, because it was so depressing. He also said that the only men he saw were really old and sitting around on stairs and such. It must be awful."

The decade of the 30s staggered along with an uneven economic recovery despite the interjection of public works projects, bank bailouts and a continuing stream of Federal and State legislation to ease the pain and suffering. Howard Virgil Savage kept growing and OUT-growing his clothes. Fortunately, Frank's mother, Anna, had saved her son's clothes from his various ages and gave them to Lois and Frank as required. Lois worked with Anna to alter and modify many of the child outfits, so they didn't look like the 19-teens and early 20s styles.

Frank kept his job and was even promoted to team leader with a small raise. The Savage household now had its first telephone. A new refrigerator was necessary, when the old one died one night and allowed all the frozen items to melt. Lois and her mom made a deal where Dorothy would sit for Howard, and Lois went back to her old job at the soda counter, but only part-time during the hours surrounding the lunch crowd. She served mostly WPA workers who were working the various projects nearby. Being the paragon of learned frugality, Lois kept a little back to add to Howard's college fund. It was adding up. Even with her part-time job and household management, she still had time available to spend with her son as he learned to play with his growing collection of toys. Building blocks were his favorite.

One day, Frank brought home a toy airplane. Howard was ecstatic with joy once he learned what it was and how he could "fly" it around the apartment and in the courtyard when he "helped" Lois or Dorothy hang laundry. As Howard became better at walking and running, his airplane became a faster flyer, too. He even slept with it in his crib. Ah. The crib. Howard's head and feet were touching each end. Growing the boy was starting to look a lot like growing the Savage living arrangements.

Chapter 7

Moving on up…

Thanksgiving dinner of 1937 was held at Andy and Dorothy Billings' home, a two story duplex on Fourth avenue in East Cleveland that they had purchased just before the crash and were able to keep because they rented out the bottom residence. That house had a full dining room and even a living room with fireplace. Instead of one bedroom it had two. The house's largeness inevitably led to a discussion about Howard and his growth that was met with both joy and concern. "We need to find a bigger place," announced Frank. "Howard is outgrowin' his crib and startin' to run into things. We got no place for another bed, so we gotta start lookin' for somethin' bigger that we can afford."

Brows furrowed. The table was silent except for Howard's demands for more gravy for his stuffing. After some minutes, Andy offered, "Frank, my tenants from downstairs are movin' out in a couple weeks. If you don't mind livin' under your in-laws, I'd be happy to rent it to you three. I don't know how much rent money Howard can generate, but I'll know where to find you if you miss a payment," he joked waggling his eyebrows.

After a pause, everyone burst into laughter. Lois' eyes filled with tears and she looked at Frank with silent hopefulness. Frank turned to Andy and said, "That would be great, dad. 'Course, we'll take it."

Lois flew out of her chair and almost toppled Frank in his with her powerful embrace. She sobbed her thanks into Franks collar while Andy and Dorothy looked on smiling beatifically. With Lois still draped around his neck, Frank calmly asked, "So, when will they be out?"

"December first. We'll help you clean the place up, maybe put a new coat of paint on the bathroom walls. The wallpaper needs some cleanin' and I bought some of that stuff that looks like green bread dough to do that. How much notice will you need to give your landlord?"

"He knows we're lookin'. I think he'll let us stay until we're ready to move. We never missed a rent payment, and I know he has a waitin' list. We'll have to clean out the place after we move all our stuff here. Do you know where I can rent a truck?"

"I do. Sounds like we have a plan."

"I've been thinkin' about this for some time. When I got my last raise to a buck fifty an hour, I saw that a bigger place was in reach. How much you goin' to charge us, dad?"

"Since you put it that way, how about what you are payin' now plus maybe ten bucks more for sharing utilities?"

"That'd be great. We certainly appreciate all that you do for us."

"Well, we'll also be glad to have our daughter closer and to watch our grandson grow up. I think I can say for both of us that this move will make us very happy. It's tough to find somethin' joyful these days, and this is one of the best moments we've had in years. You'll be able to put up a full-sized Christmas tree in your new home too. Won't that be great?"

This development created such a stir among the four that conversations buzzed on through dessert, clean up and the making of leftover plates. Andy took Frank aside and put his arm around him. "Frank, you have made my daughter very happy, and rentin' you the downstairs just seems like the best thing to do. I wish I could let you have it for free, but it pays for almost half the mortgage nut every month. You two are raisin' one fine young boy, and I gotta say that I'm selfish about havin' him closer now."

"Dad, I always wanted my own family, and I wanted it to be a happy one. I try to provide like I should, but times are really tough. I can't tell you how much movin' in downstairs means to us. Look at Lois. Her feet are barely touchin' the ground. We'll have to start packin' tomorrow just to use up some of her energy."

"Take it easy. You still have a week before you can help clean down here."

"I know, but I have the whole long weekend with nothin' to do but think about movin'. I gotta do somethin'!!"

On the Friday morning after Thanksgiving, everyone woke to fourteen inches of fresh snow. Frank Savage called his landlord and told him they would move out on December third. Then, at the last minute he asked if he could shovel off all the walks around the building.

"Sure, Frank. Sorry to lose you. Hey. I'll even give ya ten bucks for the shovelin'."

While Frank was clearing the walks of snow, Mrs. Slade, watching him from across the street, asked him if he could shovel her walk, too. Mrs. Georgia Slade was close to ninety, so Frank cleared her walk for free. When Georgia's neighbor, Harriet Clemens, saw what he was doing, she said she would pay Frank five dollars to shovel her walk and driveway. This went on along their end of the street through lunchtime, until Frank staggered home with an extra forty dollars of moving money in his pocket.

Slipping out of his goulashes, he flashed the cash and a big smile at Lois. "All that ditch diggin' got me in shape to be a proper snow shoveler. Maybe we should have steak tonight to celebrate."

"I'd like that. Put your goulashes back on and go see if Irv down at the corner store has some nice ones." With this added incentive, Frank began re-booting, but not before Lois had snatched all but the ten spot from his hand, smiling wickedly as she waggled her fingers at him while he prepared to leave.

The Savages waited impatiently for December third like horses in a starting gate. They arrived at the Fourth Avenue house with their rented truck packed high only to find that the previous tenants hadn't finished moving out. Frank and Lois shared a brief look of pique, then hopped out, Lois carrying Howard on her hip. Dropping her son off at her mom's place, she and Frank pitched in to help the departing tenants finish loading their trailer. Lois, Frank, Andy and Dorothy all began blitz-cleaning the downstairs apartment. They then moved Frank and Lois' belongings in while Howard cheered them on from a high chair Dorothy had rescued from the attic.

Their old furnishings didn't come close to filling the new home, but they were thrilled with having a new bedroom large enough for them to get out of bed on either side for the first time in their married life. It was these seemingly insignificant things that made their new house feel like home.

At the end of a long day, Dorothy called Lois up to help her prepare a common dinner, while Andy brought down a few beers to add to the refrigerator they had wrestled into place earlier. Andy and Frank drank quietly at the tiny dining table. Pushing his cap back, wiping the sweat from his brow and smiling, Frank said, "Well, here we are, dad. I never thought I'd say it, but we're gonna have to find some more furniture to fill the place up. Howard's too big for the crib, so first we need to get him a proper bed. 'Course that'll mean new sheets, too."

"I think we've got a spare set for a single bed upstairs. We'll wash 'em tomorrow. I suggest you take that truck down to the local furniture store, buy the bed and mattress, bring 'em back here and then turn the truck back in. It'll be an hour yet before the girls finish cooking"

"Good thinkin'. My head's swirlin'. Let's go peek in upstairs before I go to see what they have in store for us."

Chapter 8

1938

1938 was a watershed year in many ways. By March 27—Howard Virgil Savage's sixth birthday—Germany had invaded and occupied Austria. No shots were fired, but Chancellor Hitler returned triumphant to his nation of birth as its new leader, a forewarning of events to come.

Scientists in the United States and Germany discovered how to split atoms, releasing heretofore unimaginable amounts of energy. This led to a new understanding of the strong and weak forces that held the tiny atomic particles together. These forces complemented gravity and the electromagnetic forces that affect all the large bodies in the universe. It also kicked off the the science of quantum physics.

The RMS Queen Mary set a transatlantic voyage speed record. Howard Hughes flew a Lockheed Super Electra around the world in just over fourteen days. Then the ball-point pen, nylon, teflon, and freeze-dried coffee appeared, changing everyday life.

Oil was discovered in Saudi Arabia. The Spanish Civil War raged where Germany tested its new Luftwaffe. European nations began capitulating to Hitler's demands to annex the Sudetenland in Czechoslovakia hoping that a second world war could be prevented, while in Asia, Japan's unremitting thirst for resources gobbled up Korea, then Manchuria, then China. The stage was being set for a New World Order.

Disney studios produced a full-color, full length animated film titled

Snow White and the Seven Dwarfs. *Howard and children everywhere loved the film so much that they often begged to see it more than once. The Fair Labor and Standards Act formalized the minimum wage at forty cents an hour and created a standard work week of forty hours. Overtime would be paid at time-and-a-half.*

One other major piece of legislation was the introduction, debate, passage and signing into law of the Naval Act of 1938, calling for the building of 105,000 tons of new warships, increasing the U. S. Navy's power by 20%. This law's importance included impacting thousands of previously unemployed workers, thus helping reduce the idle skilled and unskilled workforce.

On a balmy, late summer day in 1938, Frank Savage came home from supervising his ditch-digging crew to announce that he'd applied for a machinists job at a large automotive plant in Cleveland. "Ya know, sweetie, it only costs seven hundred fifty dollars for a brand new car. If I get that machinist job, maybe we could afford one."

"Oh my! I'd never even dreamed…We've always taken the streetcar everywhere. Wouldn't that be grand?! What will this new job pay?"

"Don't know, but it'll be more than the dollar fifty an hour I'm gettin' now. One o' my men has a brother who's an accountant, who told him that Roosevelt is gettin' ready to launch somethin' called the 'Arsenal of Democracy' policy, so we may soon be makin' stuff for Europe as well as ourselves. That's gotta mean steady work and lots of overtime."

"Good to hear, but let's not get our hopes up just yet. First, let's see if that job comes through."

Howard's language skills were increasing daily. Nothing pleased his parents more, even when he began talking non-stop. Frank and Lois had learned from experience that language and education were the two keys to making anything possible in the USA. Frank's parents had emphasized learning English from his earliest memories, and Howard's inquisi-tiveness was pushing his language ability through wanting to know more and more about the world around him.

One evening, Lois, Frank and the Billingses discussed the topic of Howard's learning. Dorothy had saved the McGuffey readers from her child-rearing years and helped Howard learn from them when they babysat him. Virgil and Anna Savage were already involved in watching young Howard, and were always helping him learn words and encourag-ing reading. It helped them improve their own language skills too. The adults noted that Howard's public school didn't start teaching reading until first grade. But with everyone's help and Howard's curiosity, he was already reading the McGuffy books and the comics section of the newspapers—with the help of his father.

Just before his seventh birthday, he delighted everyone by reading out loud an entire McGuffey book without any coaching. True, it was jerky and halting, but he read clearly, seeming to be entirely consumed by the adventures of Dick and Jane and Spot. Lois had to hide tears of joy. Frank beamed like a thousand-watt bulb.

Virgil was still working at the brewery and Anna continued mending clothes. They visited Lois and Frank often, riding the streetcar from their Aspinwall Street home. Family gatherings were held at the Billings house as it was large enough to accommodate the entire family, includ-ing Virgil and Anna. Most holidays were celebrated there. Since every-one in the family was gregarious and talkative, they all got along well with much of the talk centering around the next generation in the person of Howard Savage. Every time Howard made a significant leap in his learning, Virgil showed little restraint at expressing his pride, fussing over his grandson every chance he got.

On November first, Thompson Products called and asked Frank to come in for an interview as soon as possible. "Oh, but he'll be all dirty from work," Lois replied, barely able to contain her excitement.

"Not to worry. We'll be here 'til seven tonight. We have a lot of slots to fill. When do you think he can get here?"

"Well, he's usually home by four, so I guess around five. Would that be okay?"

"Sure. My name is Nancy Greeley. Tell him to come to the main gate and mention my name."

Frank no sooner came through the door when Lois thrust the news on him. "Put your shoes back on and take the streetcar over to Thompson Products. You have a job interview with, uh, Nancy Greeley. Off you go."

Two hours later, Frank came home holding something in a paper bag.

"Why are you grinning? Did you get the job?" Lois asked anxiously.

"They offered me a machinist's job in the valve division. I'll be grindin' and polishin' engine valves for two twenty five an hour! I'll soon be gettin' overtime, too! I start on Monday! That's ninety dollars a week plus, Lois! You might be able to quit your soda jerk job, if you want."

"So, what's in the bag, big boy?"

"Oh, uh, a bottle of champagne. I thought we should celebrate."

"Quick, put it in the fridge. I've made spaghetti and meatballs, so champagne seems right!" Lois ecstatically announced, throwing her arms around Frank's neck and kissing him, grinning, kissing him again, then slow-walking him out to the kitchen without letting go. Just then, Howard came bursting out of his room and, sensing something good was happening, wrapped his arms around Frank's leg.

"Oh, I got somethin' for you, too, son," Frank added, pulling out the biggest chocolate bar he could find, and showing it to Howard. "This, my boy, is for dessert! Yer mother would kill me if I gave it to ya now."

"Thanks, daddy! When's dinner?" the boy replied, eagerly eyeing the candy bar.

Lois reluctantly extricated herself from Frank's embrace, pushed him toward the bathroom and ran upstairs to tell her parents the good news. "Stir the sauce while I'm gone, Frank! I'll be right back! Do take a shower while I'm away."

Yet, as important as 1938 would be to the history of humankind, 1939 would prove even more so. That year, the world would topple from the myriad regional conflicts into a time of worldwide destruction never seen before.

Chapter 9
Over the Brink

On September 1, 1939, based on a manufactured crisis at the German-Poland border, Hitler advanced his vast armies into that country, and the history of the world began a new, horrific chapter.

Frank and Lois Savage's pride and joy, Howard, graduated to second grade—he turned seven in March, outgrowing his baby fat into what looked like a miniature of Virgil, the family patriarch. His black hair glowed like that of a finely groomed thoroughbred's mane. His intense blue eyes, under dark brows and thick dark lashes, exhibited an intensity that some found threatening or even sinister. But when Howard Savage opened his mouth to speak, his voice was almost adult-like. He always seemed to have something important to say. His countenance lightened whenever he smiled, and he smiled often and laughed even more.

His father, Frank, purchased a scarcely used 1938 Plymouth sedan and the three Savages started traveling throughout northeastern Ohio as often as they could. Frank paid $600 for the 4-door touring model with less than 15,000 miles. Everyone who saw it ended up saying that Frank had gotten a "cream puff" car.

Frank's job at the valve factory was steady as the new model year was underway. He was quickly promoted to lead man of the center-less grinding and mirror-polishing departments, receiving a small raise and extra overtime. His supervisor, who had been with the company for over thirty years and ready to retire, pulled Frank aside and informed him he was grooming him as his replacement.

On a mid-summer day of that year, the owner of Thompson Products held an all-employees meeting in the huge cafeteria for a special announcement. The company had just won a major contract with three major aircraft engine makers in the United States, as well as the Merlin company in England, to make all the valves for their engines. President Roosevelt, seeing the growing war clouds on the horizon, initiated legislation that expanded the air forces of both the Navy and the Army Air Corps. Merlin, soon-to-be a part of Rolls-Royce, made engines for the already famous Supermarine Spitfire, the Hawker Hurricane and some advanced bombers nobody had yet heard of. With great excitement, Fred Thompson announced that the company was beginning a massive expansion in the valve division, as well as others to make parts for the new tanks and airplanes flying off the drawing boards. Until the company could hire and train enough new staff, overtime would become normal for all employees. A spontaneous cheer erupted from everyone gathered at the prospect of plenty of work and more pay. The "Arsenal of Democracy" had arrived at the doorstep of the Savages, and Frank, now twenty-seven years old, would be able to buy things he and his family had never allowed themselves to imagine, and begin saving for Howard's education. In a joking but serious manner, the owner of Thompson Products told everyone to take the rest of the day off, and go home to tell their families that they wouldn't be seeing much of him or her in the coming months.

Frank hurried home to tell Lois the good news, only to find her sobbing into crossed arms on the dining room table. "Whatsa matter?!" he asked, worried.

"Mother had a stroke this morning and died on the way to the hospital."

Dorothy Billings had been a hugely supportive influence on the family.

"When I told Howard that Granny had died, he closed himself in his room sobbing."

Frank went upstairs to find what looked like a sleepwalking Andy Billings trying to make sense of everything and arrangements he'd never expected or wanted to make. Frank gathered Andy in his arms and let him cry, something Andy had been too shocked and hurt to do while he began mourning his loving wife. Virgil and Anna soon appeared to console Lois and Andy.

Andy Billings had been working as an electrical contractor with a builder east of Cleveland.

The call from Lois to his work site had taken hours to reach him. Lois had called the ambulance when her mother beside her had simply keeled over while putting dishes away in the cupboards. Howard was "flying" his airplane around the house when she fell. He came running into the kitchen at the noise.

'Why is Granny sleeping on the floor?"

Lois, trying to maintain self-control, mumbled something about her wanting to rest, while thumbing frantically through the phone book for the number for the Huron Road Hospital. They dispatched an ambulance immediately.

Having no private transportation, Lois rode in the ambulance to the hospital, cradling Howard in her lap. They waited anxiously for half an hour before a young doctor came out to the waiting area and gave them the bad news: "We did everything we could, but the stroke was so severe that it caused her heart to just stop. I'm terribly sorry for your loss. We will have the necessary paperwork for you shortly and will hold your mother's body until you can make arrangements. Again, I'm sorry for your loss of a loved one."

The emergency room desk-nurse called a taxi for Lois and Howard. Lois, numb with shock, answered Howard's endless questions with platitudes. Once home, she explained to Howard that Granny had had a terrible accident and had died. Howard's shock broke Lois' heart all over again, and they cried in each others' arms until Howard broke free and ran to his room.

Frank and Lois made the funeral arrangements, organized the wake and otherwise comforted Andy who was so distraught he could do little but sit on his side of the couch, staring morosely at the spot where his wife used to be. The question in all the Savages' minds was how would Andy make the adjustment to being a widower. To their relief, as the weeks passed, Andy slowly returned to his normal, jovial self, but there remained times at the dinner table when he suddenly stared vacantly into space, stood up and walked upstairs without saying anything. Clearly, the loss of Dorothy continued to haunt him.

Two days after the news that Hitler had invaded Poland, Andy came down for dinner, asked for a cold beer and everyone's attention. "I read in the paper that the shipyards in California are looking for electricians to wire ships. The pay is supposed to be a LOT more than I'm makin' here buildin' cracker-box houses, so, I've decided to take a train out to San Diego and look into a company called National Iron Works. They build ships for the Navy. Surprised?"

"Yes," Frank answered warily. "When are you thinkin' of goin'?"

"I leave next Wednesday. It'll take three days by train. If I like the town and they offer me a good job, I'll take it. I'm only fifty-two, so I still got some life in me."

"WOW!" Lois replied. "San Diego! Well, we'll miss you terribly, of course, but I understand. Call us collect when you know something. Will you want us to run the house for you?"

"Hadn't thought that far, yet. But, good idea. You can rent out the up-stairs …if I don't come back."

He did call collect after having accepted a position as senior electri-cian, wiring big Navy support ships like tenders and oilers. The pay was astonishingly high, so he thought he would be able to buy a house in San Diego after a short while. He'd be home in three days to pack his things and sell off everything he couldn't take with him.

When he returned home, Andy Billings showed everyone a handful of postcards from San Diego featuring the beaches, the famous Hotel del Coronado and views from a beautiful peninsula called Point Loma. Everyone ooh'ed and a-ah'ed at the spectacular meeting of water and land. The harbor, of course, was filled with Navy ships of all sorts. "I already found a place to stay. It's in National City, just south of down-town San Diego along the bay. It's where the shipyard is located, too, so I can walk or ride a bike to work. I never smelled the sea before. It was pretty intoxicatin' for an old landlubber like me."

"Oh, daddy, We'll miss you so much. But it looks like a great place to live. Just look at those beaches! We could all get brown as coffee beans there."

Frank, initially silent and lost in thought, finally asked, "Do they have machine shops there?"

"As a matter of fact, Frank, there's a huge machine shop right at Na-tional Iron Works, and there are two, maybe three aircraft factories there, too. I saw a bunch of big seaplanes floatin' in the harbor just before I left. I'll check it out for you if you want— after I get settled. I'll write it all in a letter. Would you consider movin' to San Diego, Frank?"

"Well, Andy, right now it's just a thought."

"If we could somehow recreate what we have here and share the mortgage on a nice house…Sorry, daddy. My mind is running away with me," Lois added.

"Don't apologize. But let's not put the cart before the horse. Let's see first what happens with my job and what that lunatic in Germany is doin'."

Chapter 10

Sea Change

What "that lunatic" did was invade Poland, triggering the mutual de-
fense pact with Britain and France to defend Poland against Germany.
As 1939 staggered through its fourth quarter, the European War grew in
ferocity and intensity. Unknown to the rest of the world, the brink had
been crossed, and the doors leading to Hell were kicked open by a psy-
chopath's jackboot.

National Iron Works gave Andy Billings $300 to drive himself and
essentials to San Diego. Fortunately, Andy had enough in savings to pay
for a moving company. Lois excitedly offered to co-drive her father to
San Diego, and take the train back to Cleveland. When Andy quickly
agreed, Lois was ecstatic, having not had five days alone with her father
since she was a little girl. Anna and Virgil would watch young Howard
while Frank was at work.

Lois and Andy left Cleveland on 12 September, 1939, in Andy
Billings' 1937 Buick, driving south to Cincinnati on U.S. 42. When they
got to the Ohio River, they turned west onto U.S. 50. After awhile, Andy
started talking about Dorothy and their years together. "You and your
sisters are, of course, the lights of my life now. Your mother and I
couldn't have been happier when you married Frank. After your mother
passed, I couldn't live in a house so full of the memories I have of her. I
kept lookin' for her every mornin'. It was startin' to make me crazy. I

caught myself callin' her name and talkin' to her. That wasn't good. With you, Frank and little Howard now settled in the house, I felt free to do something else.

"I figgered I had the skills that were needed for Roosevelt's big buildup, so I went down to the library and started readin' out-of-town newspapers. The Los Angeles Times had a want ad for electricians in San Diego at National Iron Works. I thought, 'What the hell does an iron shop need with electricians?' As I kept readin', I discovered that they were a major support ship builder for the U.S. Navy. Then, I went to the Yellow Pages section of the San Diego phone book and looked up everything I could find about that town's realtors and such. That's how I found out about apartments.

"All this gave me a sense of purpose and stopped me mopin' around the house. Then, after callin' the personnel office at National Iron Works, I was invited for an interview and, well, you know the rest. They even reimbursed me for my train ticket."

"After your mother passed, the evenin's were hard, and those days when I made my own dinner were the worst. I found myself sobbin' as I was stirrin' the spaghetti sauce. I missed her so much. Dinners were when we used to discuss that day and the next day's activities. Now, there was just an empty chair and silence. Lois, I started drinkin'…and began goin' to bed pretty potted. Sometimes I even fell asleep in my chair and woke up in the wee hours wonderin' where I was. I'd heard about other men who had lost a spouse, and started goin' downhill, dyin' soon after. I think what saved me were my memories of your mother always encouragin' me. She always pumped me up when I'd had a bad day. When I closed my eyes I could see her smile and hear her sayin' those things to me. This time, though, it was somethin' like 'Get off your ass and do somethin' to make me proud'. I thought of you, your sisters,

Frank and Howard, and how much I love you all. I just couldn't disgrace the family by becomin' a drunk wallowin' in self-pity.

"There was this guy on one of the job sites who felt really sorry for himself when his wife died of cancer. She was only thirty-eight and he was barely a year older. He started showin' up at work with a load on at seven in the mornin'. He started makin' dangerous mistakes, and even fell off a second story scaffold. Thinkin' about him, I knew it was time for me to do somethin' different and special with my life. And I want to live and see Howard grow up. I have high hopes for him."

His heart-rending soliloquy took them to the Illinois state line at Vincennes, Indiana. Lois had remained mostly silent but attentive to her father's continued outpouring. Andy pulled into a truck stop and the two had a late lunch/early dinner. As they walked into the restaurant, Lois slipped an arm through her father's and smiled up at him with glistening eyes.

They stopped for the evening outside East St. Louis, Ilinois, and stayed in one of the new "motor hotels" now called "motels." Their rooms were not expensive and they both slept solidly after the long day on the road. Next morning after breakfast, they followed U.S. 50 across the Mississippi River into St. Louis, Missouri, until they reached U.S. Route 66. That highway led southwest all the way to Needles, California, where, with temperatures soaring well over 100 degrees Fahrenheit, they stopped for gas before turning south on U.S. Route 95. The service station owner advised Andy to buy a canvas water bag, fill it and drape it over the front bumper guard. "When yer drivin', the wind will keep the water cool. If yer goin' to San Diego on U.S. 80, there are some wicked hills and passes in the Laguna Mountains that will test your car's coolin' system. Don't be afraid to stop for an hour—if ya can find a shady spot —to let yer engine cool off some," the grizzled owner said, pushing back his straw hat and wiping the sweat off his dark-tanned, leathery brow.

U.S. Route 95 went back into Arizona, but kept them heading due south to U.S. 80. In Yuma, they turned west and crossed the Colorado River into California. The drive across the Imperial Valley was flat and hot. Andy had to pull over outside El Centro to cool off the car. There, he and Lois noticed a water tank with a black line painted halfway up that said, "SEA LEVEL". They looked at each other, the thought dawning on each that they were standing several feet below that line. They drove with all four windows rolled down on the Buick, but even at over 60 miles per hour, it was very uncomfortable. "You know, daddy, as hot as it is, I'm not sweating. Why is that?"

"Don't know, but it's so dry, must be no humidity. So our sweat evaporates instantly." Andy replied.

The passage up and out of the Imperial Valley began with a fifteen mile climb that, at times, seemed impossible to get any steeper. When they got to the summit, the temperature gauge needle on the Buick's dashboard was pegged solidly on HOT, so Andy pulled over behind a big boulder, opened the hood of the Buick and waited until the radiator was cool enough to check the water level. It was low, so he emptied the canvas bag into the radiator, silently thanking that station owner for the advice.

The drive through the coastal ranges of San Diego County proved a beautiful mix of high desert and oak woodlands. As they traveled further west, desert scrub gave way to chaparral, a mix of drought-resistant plants unique to southern California where it rained less than fifteen inches per year and not at all between May and October. Being September, everything looked crackling dry. The grasses were pale tan or yellow, though the oak trees remained green.

Rolling over a high pass near a town called Alpine, they began a steady descent toward the Pacific Ocean. They drove through another hot valley and a small town named El Cajon. Leaving that town, they passed out of a long valley of orchards and farms, called Mission Valley on the map. The air cooled significantly and the smell of salt water tickled their nostrils. In the distance, they saw a sea of ship masts as they turned south on the Pacific Coast Highway. As they did, a large transport plane buzzed directly over their car. "That airport," Andy reported, "is named after Charles Lindbergh. See that buildin' over there? That's where the *Spirit of St. Louis* was built by Ryan Aeronautics." It took another ten minutes to pass through town and into National City. Andy found his way to the small apartment Andy had rented on "C" Avenue and parked.

The movers arrived a little later that day. Lois and Andy both laughed at how, for once, the timing worked perfectly. "Ya know, Lois, we're really close to Mexico here. I tried some of the food over there. It's delicious. Let's have dinner at a little Mexican restaurant I know of located on Harbor Drive."

Lois' eyes grew large as she tasted the various items on the sampler menu. "This stuff is wonderful! I've gotta learn how to make this!"

The owner's wife waited on their table and Lois asked what she would need to take back to Ohio to make this wonderful food for her husband and son. In perfect English, Señora Maria Sandoval listed several ingredients Lois had seen on grocery spice shelves, but never had occasion to use them. "Mrs. Savage, you must buy *masa* flour and a good *tor-tee-ya* press. Every good Mexican wife must learn to make a very *theen tor-teeya*." she said smiling at her own affectation. "The press will get the shape and basic thickness right, but it is up to the cook to make it *theen*. You'll see when you try," she said, smiling.

"Where can I buy these items?" Lois asked.

"Go down Pacific Highway to Chula Vista. On the corner of Third and 'L' is a grocery store and next to it is a *tortilleria*. They will have everything. Thank you for asking. I don't meet many *gringas* asking how to make tortillas," she said grinning broadly.

Andy bought several bottles of *Cerveza* from Mrs. Sandoval to enjoy while they unpacked. It was dusty work, but with the windows open a cool sea breeze filled the apartment with that smell one never forgets once the sea air has tickled the senses and made a home in the memory banks.

After two hours, Andy Billings, feeling he was as settled as he could be for the day, father and daughter flopped down in chairs and drank the cold beer straight from the bottle. "'Mmm! This is really good, daddy! Did you try this when you were out here for the interview?"

"Yeah. The first one I tasted was so much better than the stuff from back home. Your father-in-law's brewery made good beer and ale, but this stuff doesn't leave your mouth feelin' lousy after."

"I want to smuggle a couple bottles home with me so Frank can taste it. What time does my train leave?"

"Just after nine in the mornin' from Union Station. We can have breakfast at Mrs. Sandoval's restaurant before we go.

"Will they be open that early?"

"I think so. They've four or five kids, so they'll likely be feedin' them and anyone else who shows up. Oh! Let's go find that *tor-ta-ree-ah* before they close."

Next morning, at the train station, Lois called Frank collect. It was Saturday, so he was home with Howard hovering over the phone waiting for it to ring. "So, how's San Diego?"

"It's *beautiful* here," Lois replied. "I've never seen such a blue sky.

The city surrounds a huge bay and the smell of the sea is wonderful. I wish you were here. So, I'm about to board the train for home and bringing some surprises. The schedule says I'll be there late Monday. I'll call when I get into Terminal Tower. See you soon. I love you."

Chapter 11

Decisions and Delayed Decisions

In 1940,the American war material buildup was in full swing, though in fits and starts. Shoddy equipment and overcharges were the norm. In the process of building the largest manufacturing facility in the world at Willow Run, Michigan, labor disputes broke out, much to the outrage of the United States State Department, which had promised our allies in Great Britain and the Soviet Union items that weren't yet being made.

Until well into 1946, blatant, unbridled savagery and tyranny from dictatorships were ascendent with new acts of inhumanity appearing daily. Newspapers described how entire populations were being destroyed. World War II was the first truly global war the world had ever seen.

"M-m-m! This Mexican beer IS good. We'd better not tell my dad about it," Frank said, wiping a line of foam from his lips. "He might not approve of us drinking a 'foreign' beer."

"I know. So, how'd you like the burritos?" asked Lois.

"Really good. Is this one of the recipes you got from the restaurant lady in San Diego?"

"Yummy, mommy! Can I have another one?"

"You sure can, honey. Here. I made plenty." Lois replied, placing another of the rolled burritos on Howards outstretched plate.

Frank eventually asked, "What's in this stuff?"

"Well, I used some spices that I've never used before—like cumin—to make the red *enchilada* sauce. Then, I added some hamburger, garlic and cilantro. While that was simmering, I took these pinto beans the Mexican lady said I *must* have for burritos. She called them *free-ho-lees* after being cooked in oil to make them soft. Right. Then I mixed the beans in with the hamburger, added some chopped onions and, well, here they are. I made *tortillas* yesterday while you were at work and Howard was at school. The process took quite a bit of time. Notice how thin they are," she said smiling over her shoulder.

"Is that supposed to mean somethin'?"

"Oh, sure. A good maker of Mexican food must be able to make a *theen* tortilla. That was my first lesson from the nice lady in San Diego."

"Well, it's all *delicious*. What's this red stuff in the Ball jar?"

"It's called *picante*. It's made with chopped tomatoes, small green peppers - she called *hall-o-pin-yos* - garlic, onion, cilantro and a little salt. The more peppers, the spicier it gets. Did you like it?"

"Yeah, sure! You can make this anytime. Your trip seems to have also piqued some interest in moving to San Diego."

"True," Lois added wistfully. " If we did that, what would we do with your folks? They'd miss us and Howard terribly."

"True. And my job is startin' to get really good. Got another raise last week. My supervisor's retirin' in a couple months and wants me to replace him. That would bring another nice raise. Dunno, sweetheart. It's tempting. San Diego looks exotic and everythin', but we've planted some serious roots here. Howard's makin' friends, too." Frank noticed Lois' scowl. "Now, don't get me wrong. I'm happy that your dad made the move. He needed a fresh start. All we had to do was rent out his place, and that's taking care of the house payment. Maybe we should buy out your father. With the rental upstairs and my raises, we could pay off the mortgage. Are you goin' to go back to Woolworth's part time when Howard's at school?"

"All good thoughts, my love. You're always the practical one. And, you are right, of course. With the sea still in my nostrils, I had visions of being tanned all year. I do see your points, though," Lois said with a pout. "Let's have your folks over for dinner. I can try out my new Mexican recipes on them. It'll be interesting to see their reactions to *tacos*."

"Good idea, dear," Frank replied. "Can't wait to see mom's reaction to this stuff. If she likes it, she'll probably want to start a restaurant that serves it." They both laughed at that, and then stopped in mid-chortle.

"You may be right, Frank. Wouldn't that be something?' Lois remarked dreamily. "Too bad they've never heard of jalapeno peppers. If your mother took one look at a *tortilla*, she'd say I didn't add enough yeast to make the bread rise." Lois said wryly. That brought a laugh from Frank.

With ideas bursting open in her head like newly blooming flowers, Lois wrote to her father and asked him to send her a package of *jalapeno* peppers, locally made enchilada sauce in quart jars and a starchy, but tasty fruit called avocado. She asked for a dozen of the hard ones to ripen at home. She added two dozen corn *tortillas*, and another big bag of masa flour to the list. To Lois' surprise, the local grocery store carried pinto beans, so she would only have to buy the lard in which to fry them into *frijoles*.

It took three weeks for the box of California groceries to arrive, and Lois unpacked it with delight and anticipation of meals to come. Her father also included a book of Mexican food recipes. While scanning it, she found a recipe for a warm salad. *Boy, this will be fun,* she thought with delight.

Lois asked Frank to invite his parents over for a "special" dinner. Lois simmered ground beef in enchilada sauce with plenty of chopped garlic added. While that simmered, she chopped a head of lettuce and six large corn *tortillas* into one-inch squares, reserving the other half of the lettuce. She then toasted the *tortilla* squares in the oven to crispness. Several handfuls of chopped tomatoes went half onto a plate and half into the large soup pot to which she'd already added a can of kidney beans. After simmering for a half-hour, she emptied half of the seasoned meat onto another plate and the rest into the soup pot. She then added the toasted corn chips. The final, "secret" pot ingredient was a bottle of French salad dressing. She stirred the mixture until everything was evenly distributed.

The doorbell rang, and Virgil and Anna walked right in. "Something smells good!" Anna announced. "If tastes good as smells...."

Lois greeted her in-laws, directing them into the living room to talk with Frank while she finished preparing the *tacos*. While Frank served up a cold beer to his dad, Anna walked into the kitchen to look over Lois' shoulder.

"What's green stuff on plate?"

"Chopped avocado, mom. It goes into the *tacos*."

"Humpf! Not American food, " Anna offered determinedly.

"Well, it actually, sort of is," stated Lois with equal determination. "It's originally from Mexico, but became part of California's and Texas' culture when they became part of our country. I sampled this when I took dad to San Diego, and it was love at first bite—ha, ha. So I decided then and there to learn how to cook it myself."

"What in pot?"

"It's a warm, Mexican salad," Lois offered hesitantly.

"What I smell? Very strong..."

"It's called cumin. You've seen it on the store shelves, but I've never used it…until now."

Anna peeked under the lid of the soup pot. As she reached for a spoon to dip into the mixture, Lois gently took the spoon from her and shook a scolding finger at her.

"No cheating. This is my 'cook's surprise' dinner. I should have shooed you out of the kitchen earlier. Here's a glass of iced tea. Go pester your son." All this was said with that special kind of familiarity found only in close-knit families.

When dinner was served, Lois had to instruct everyone on how to build a taco from the chopped and shredded ingredients served on separate plates. Lois had made her own *picante* sauce for the occasion using fresh cilantro, finely-chopped garlic and tomatoes along with more finely diced *jalapenos*. She simmered this mixture for two hours before letting it cool. It was a lot of work, but she smartly filled two quart jars of this good, red sauce for the refrigerator. She showed them how to build their tacos and add a little picante sauce on top of the layers. Lois went around the table heaping a large serving of the warm salad from the soup pot onto their plates. After she'd finally sat down, she looked around the table and waited.

Virgil was the first to comment: "Very, very good, Lois. Spicy very good. Warm salad also very tasty. I have more. Sorry, don't like—what you call 'em? - 'taco shells'? Break too easy. Need fork for spilled stuff. But taste very good, yes. What you call red sauce?"

"*Picante*, dad. It goes on everything, even scrambled eggs."

"This I like. Please give Anna recipe. We could use change of taste sometime." Virgil said the last sentence winking at his wife who returned the obligatory scowl.

Over the next weeks, Anna and Lois did indeed conspire to create a Mexican food menu for their hard-working husbands. Howard couldn't get enough of it, *burritos* being his favorite. Lois wrote to her dad in San Diego to send another large box of supplies and items that were totally unknown in northeastern Ohio.

On the cusp of this half-decade of all-out war for the United States, the family of Virgil, Anna, Frank, Lois, Howard and Andy carefully embarked on a decision pathway that followed the course of world events brought to their happy and cohesive family. Innumerable delayed decisions were uniformly put off until 1941, a year of significance that brought forced maturity to everyone and everything they did.

PART III
PEACE AND WAR

Chapter 12
Waves of Change

Anna and Lois Savage kept experimenting with recipes from the Mexican cookbook, producing variations on the traditional recipes that received raves from their families. One day she said to Lois, "Okay. Is time see if anybody but us likes these foods. I have idea, but need test."

Never short of ambition and imagination, Anna Savage went to her church and organized a "pot luck" luncheon where all participants would bring a dish based on the ethnicity of their choice. The event was planned for the second Sunday of January 1941. Announcements circulated among the parishioners and the church was full for the service. Afterwards, everyone hurried downstairs to either set up the buffet, or to be the first in line.

Each dish had a little card saying from what country or ethnicity the dish originated. Anna's, of course, said "Mexico." Howard had made a little Mexican flag and attached it to the card. As the pot luck progressed, people started coming back to Anna's table to either get second helpings or, following a friend's advice, sample Mexican food for the first time. By the end, Anna Savage's Mexican food dishes had been picked clean.

"Looks like Mexican food big favorite. You think maybe we open small diner or restaurant, you and me? Start small, see how goes," Anna offered while returning home with Lois,

"Interesting idea, but we'd have to import key ingredients from my dad. That could get expensive."

"*Da*. Let me talk to Irv at store. Maybe he interested in selling our Mexican food to customers. Make bigger, cheaper order maybe. You help me, *da*?"

"Of course. After all, I'm the one who got you started on this path." They both laughed and set about planning an in-house buffet at Irv Goodman's *The Corner Store,* that sat on the corner of Fourth and Hayden Avenues.

Irv Goodman, the son of Russian immigrants himself, offered his usual skepticism about anything new, but eventually relented before Anna's constant prodding. The buffet was a huge success and Anna, by agreement, shared the profits with Irv. For the next month, Anna's Mexican buffet continued its popularity—until the *jalapenos* ran out. Irv tried to import the green peppers from California distributors, but the shipping costs were so high Anna's profit share couldn't cover the expense.

Just before Howard's ninth birthday in March 1941, Frank came home with a look on his face that matched his slumping body.

"What happened, darling?"

"That supervisor's job I was gettin' ready for just got handed to the general manager's nephew. He's fresh out of Ohio State, and my department's supervisor openin' was the only one comin' up," Frank dejectedly explained.

"Does he know anything about machine shops, or making valves?" Lois asked, trying to cheer up her husband.

"I don't know. But I DO know that he is twenty-four years old and never worked in a shop before. Met him today. He looked like a deer caught in headlights. Everybody looked at me and just shook their heads. We all walked out of the office without sayin' a word to the kid. I feel like I'd been gut-punched."

"Oh, baby, I'm so sorry," Lois said, placing an arm around his sagging shoulders. "There'll be other openings, I'm sure. With the war growing, I'm sure they'll be plenty more opportunities. Already the draft is taking young men. Maybe he'll get drafted, and you'll get the job you deserve."

"Maybe," Frank replied, purposefully changing the subject. "How's Howard doin' in school?"

"He's doing great. His fourth grade teacher says he's a whiz at arithmetic and loves building things. The other kids seem to like him and he makes the girls giggle...I'm told. I think he takes after his father..." Lois said, wrapping her arms around her husband squeezing him tightly. "Now, guess what we're having for dinner."

"Mexican food?" Frank asked expectantly.

"Not tonight. We ran out of enchilada sauce and masa flour. I bought three nice steaks and sweet potatoes at Irv's. He started giving us wholesale discounts since our little buffet did so well," she replied, trying to cheer up. "Here's a cold beer. Take off your jacket and relax. The disappointment will pass. Take joy in your son and your wife," she said, giving him a broad wink.

Three days later, Frank came home once again down-trodden.

"Oh dear. What's happened now, sweetheart?" Lois asked, sweeping her husband into her arms.

"Well, the boy supervisor thought it best to move me to the dirtiest job in the department, mirror polish. Thing is, my valve seat grinding quality is the best in the department. I get fewer rejects than any other grinder. I think he wants me to quit so he won't feel the resentment from me and the others. Everybody knows I should have been made supervisor. I dunno, baby. Maybe San Diego isn't such a bad idea. I'm gonna call your dad and check into work there."

"Wouldn't be the worst thing to be close to my dad again, but what about your folks? They'd be a couple thousand miles away from us and Howard. But first, you need to talk with dad."

"You're right. It'd be a huge upheaval for everyone. Hell, I've never been outside Ohio…."

Frank's job didn't get better. Overtime was becoming required, and he was already working sixty hours per week mirror-polishing valve seats. The grit and grime was ground permanently into his hands and under his fingernails. Scrubbing simply did not remove the deepest particles. His mood soon reflected the grime embedded in his skin. The job's tedium greatly offset the money earned and reduced his energy while with this wife and son.

Frank and Lois spoke with Andy, Virgil and Anna about the situation. Andy was most encouraging regarding machinist jobs in San Diego. He sent want-ads from every San Diego Union-Tribune Sunday newspaper. Frank immediately saw several jobs perfectly suited for his skills and experience. Virgil and Anna wished Frank and Lois nothing but success in whatever decision they made.

"Of course, Anna and I want see Howard grow up, but understand you need think about family," Virgil explained to the young couple over a Sunday dinner. "We come halfway 'round world with nothing in pockets." Virgil paused to exchange knowing, loving smiles with Anna. "And we made good life here. Now you have own life think about. Frank, you our son. Will always be our son. Don't feel like you leaving us. We miss Howard, of course…Making big move is—how you say - complicated"

Lois looked up from her plate and said, "What if you two sold your house and moved out west with us? Mom, we could open a restaurant with dishes from different backgrounds. San Diego is a Navy town and those boys there are coming from all over the country. I'll bet they'd love some home-style cooking as well as the European dishes you make so well. And then there's the Mexican stuff we're perfecting..."

Anna looked searchingly at Virgil. Virgil returned the look. Then they both turned their heads in unison to look at Frank and Lois. "You want us come along? We good here. Cleveland home. I retire from brewery soon," Virgil argued without conviction.

"You wouldn't be taggin' along Dad. We'd want you to put the restaurant together. Lois and I have talked quite a bit about the move, but were afraid to bring it up. We wouldn't be runnin' *away* from Cleveland, but, like what you and mom did those many years ago, we'd be runnin' *toward* the next chapter in our lives. What do you really have holdin' you here? The brewery? You're gonna get your social security soon, so that will be some steady income. And Howard...You'd get to see your grandson grow.

"Mom. Dad. War's comin'. There'll be plenty of work in San Diego for everyone. San Diego is boomin' right now. We'd love to have you come with us, or at least join us soon after we move. As you can tell, we've pretty much decided to go. Three major manufacturin' companies, including Andy's shop, have advertised jobs for which I qualify, that pay twice what I'm makin' here, overtime not included. Andy's given us ownership of this house. We just assumed his mortgage—that wasn't that much. The equity from the sale would give us some cash for the next house as well as something to start the restaurant. I'm gonna take a train next week and accept one of the jobs I read about if they offer me one. We hope to time the move so Howard can start at his new school in September. That gives us three months to get everythin' settled. Won't you two think about joinin' us?"

Virgil stared across the table at his hard-working son and almost burst with pride. "You brave boy, Frank. I very proud of you." Exchanging knowing glances with his wife, he continued: "Anna and I know this day come when you 'fly from nest'. So, what we do to help?"

"You can help us most by coming with us," Frank said as tears appeared in his and Lois' eyes at the same time.

"Umm. We want be with you. Watch Howard grow into man, *da*," Virgil answered for the two of them.

"*Da*. We want see Howard grow up," said Anna, trying to keep calm, though her voice trembled with emotion. "We talk. Will tell you what we do tomorrow."

"*Da*, tomorrow," Virgil agreed, barely able to hide his own excitement.

Later that night, Virgil poured himself and Anna a shot of whiskey, toasting in Ukrainian, "Here's to our boy, his wife, our grandson…and us, Anna. May we all live a great new life in California."

They threw back their whiskeys, sat down across from each other and shared that special kind of intimacy that showed special familiarity. Anna continued in Ukranian: "My first thought is, 'I would love to have my own business.' The restaurant idea excites me. We should do this. Dear husband, look at all that we've accomplished. We were illiterate peasants. We traveled halfway around the world with nothing but a few kopeks. We are adventurers in our hearts, *neh*? With the money from our house and savings, we could move with Frank and Lois and Howard without burdening them. Your thoughts?"

"Ah, my beloved, we are indeed adventurers. But we were young back then and the world was ours to conquer. I'm a little bit nervous about selling this house, but we'll get another one. I agree. We must go. It will just be another challenge together. We're just in our late 50s and in good health. I want to watch Howard grow up too. I want to be near our family to help our grandson whenever he needs it."

"So!" exclaimed Anna, sitting straight upright. "It's settled. It's still early, so call your son and tell him of our decision." Adding, after lapsing back into English, "We go California!"

Chapter 13

An Offer You Can't Refuse

In 1941, relocating was a relatively simple process. Frank took his train ride to San Diego to seek new employment. As he rode the rails, he watched the scenery change from the rolling farm lands of Illinois and Indiana to the flat, grain-filled prairies of Kansas, Oklahoma and the Texas Panhandle. *My God!* he thought as the rhythm of the rails droned on. *My wife and parents hardly blinked about movin' to California. Must have felt my pain and disappointment at bein' stuck in a filthy, boring job. Or, maybe that's just me bein' self-centered. Lois' trip to San Diego with her father had set the ideas growin' in our heads. Cookin' and eatin' that wonderful Mexican food was the straw on the back of the camel, wasn't it? Lois and her father love San Diego. Wonder how it will treat me. Whoa! Listen to me! I'm lettin' my thoughts run wild.*

Gettin' anxious to get there. Andy said he'd set up my interview schedule, and that I could use his car while he's at work. He says National Iron Works *is boomin' with new ship contracts. Looks like we're going to get in that fuckin' war after all. Yesterday's paper said tensions with Japan have been growin' ever since FDR cut them off from our oil and scrap metal exports, because they refused to get out of Manchuria and Korea. Dad always told me to leave a cornered rat a way out. California's just an ocean away from Japan. Will they start a war with us? I never expected such tension or such excitin' times as these. Everyone's just tryin' to put food on the table, now this…*

The depression's been really tough on everybody, but our family is strong and doesn't give up. Am I givin' up at Thompson Products? Don't think so, but I'm not gettin' any younger and I've got a son to raise. I want him to have a better life than I've had, and that's sayin' a lot - at least as far as havin' a lovin' and supportive family. Haven't had any quarrels over the years. Lois and I simply work out our differences—which are few. Can't control what the management does at the shop, but here I am about to change my life…and that of my whole family.

My son's growin' like a weed. He's so damned smart, we have trouble keepin' up with his curiosity. About EVERYTHING! Going to be a handful for his teachers, I bet.

What station are we pullin' into now? The sign says El Paso. Where's my map?

Andy Billings was waiting for Frank at Union Station just off Broadway and Pacific Highway in San Diego. The train from El Paso arrived a little after 3 P.M. "How was the train ride, Frank? You look like you could use a cold beer."

"Good to see you, Andy. The scenery was better than watchin' western movies, that's for sure. Yeah. A cold beer would be great."

As Andy drove them south down Pacific Highway, he pointed out the bustle of naval activity in the bay. "That chunk of land over there is called Coronado. There's a naval air station there. They tell me we might soon see aircraft carriers docking there. Right now, they're all out in Hawaii. See the ferry terminal there? You can catch a ride across the bay every half hour. Saves driving all the way down to Imperial Beach and back up the strand on the other side of the bay to Coronado. That big, long hill to the west is Point Loma. That's where the big military cemetery at Fort Rosecrans is. Down at the bottom is a submarine base.

"Yeah. It's all Navy here. Here's my place."

Andy pulled into his parking slot at his apartment building and, while helping Frank with his luggage, invited his son-in-law into his modest flat. The living area had two easy chairs with an end table between them, a small coffee table, and a third, ladder-back chair opposite. The tiny kitchen had an eating area with a round, wooden table and two more ladder-back chairs.

"There's two bedrooms. I bought a roll-away for the spare room along with a cheap four-drawer cabinet. That's where you'll sleep. The bathroom is across the hall. Get your stuff squared away and I'll pour us a couple of *Cervesas*."

Frank unpacked and hung up his only suit and white shirt. The shirt, thankfully, hadn't wrinkled as Lois had packed it carefully with the folds just so. The roll-away already had a sheet, blanket and pillow in place. He extracted his toiletries kit bag and put it on top of the cabinet.

Andy handed him a beer as he exited the bedroom area, and Frank took a long, welcome swallow. "Was the train trip okay?" Andy asked.

"Never sat still for so long in my life. They had an observation car, so I stayed up there mostly. Man, this is one big country with a LOT of empty space. The cows looked like specks in the distance. I didn't see any mountains until near El Paso. Las Cruces was pretty spectacular, but New Mexico flattened out until Arizona. That was this mornin'. Like to see more of the country some time with Lois and Howard. Maybe take a scenic route—if I land a job."

"Oh, I think you'll get one. I'll bet you another beer that you'll be signin' papers tomorrow if somebody makes you an offer you can't refuse. That's how it was for me."

"Hope you're right. I'm on pins and needles. It's been too long since I worked on real machine tools other than that goddamned grinder. Hope I haven't lost my touch."

"I doubt it. Those are skills that stay with you...I think." They both laughed at that.

Andy collected the empty beer bottle from Frank. "Let's walk down the street. I know this cute little restaurant. I'll buy you dinner. When you get your job, you can buy dinner and champagne."

"Sounds fair. Let's go. I'm starved."

Andy ordered a steak and baked potato with all the trimmings, and Frank, the same. As they finished dinner and their second glass of wine, Frank's eyes began drooping. "The travelin' is catchin' up with me. What time is my first interview tomorrow?"

"It's at nine o'clock. You have time for a good sleep. I'll be out of the house by six, so I'll set the alarm for you and leave some warm coffee in a Thermos. Find your way around the kitchen for breakfast. I promised Lois I wouldnt 't spoil her husband," Andy said, wagging his eyebrows at Frank.

"Very funny. She has me make dinner sometimes, and I always make my own breakfast as I'm up so damned early. I even make and pack my own lunches. I'm sure I'll recognize what is and isn't real food in your kitchen."

"Okay, let's get your butt into bed so you're bright and alert tomorrow. Tomorrow you start at Ryan Aircraft just down Pacific Highway, then it's down the road a couple blocks to Consolidated. They're building B-24s there. I think Ryan is buildin' scout planes and trainers. Next day, you'll join me at National Iron and speak with George Granger, our personnel manager. I've met him once. Seems like a good guy. Here. I've drawn little maps for you to find your way. A guy I work with will pick me up so you can have the car."

The first interview with Ryan Aviation went well, but the offer seemed low-ball, barely more than he was making at Thompson Products. Frank demurred, saying he'd get back to them.

The next interview was with Consolidated Aircraft Company. The personnel director, Al Green, conducted the interview along with the machine shop foreman, Arnie Steppe and the area manager, Craig Benson. The three men grilled him for an hour about all aspects of precision machining. It was a jovial interview, but Frank was leery as many of the questions seemed like traps, trying to catch Frank in any fabrications of his stated knowledge and skills. Finished, the three men asked Frank to wait outside the office.

Fifteen minutes later, all three men emerged from Al Green's office, and shook Frank's hand. With the two floor managers bidding him farewell, Green took Frank by the arm and said, "Let's have lunch downstairs. Our cafeteria makes a pretty good lunch. My treat."

Al Green directed Frank to a smaller, quieter dining area adjacent to the main cafeteria. "Okay, Frank, it's like this: Arnie and Craig would like you to start work tomorrow. We have a pressing need for a skilled machinist like yourself who can set up and run all the machine tools. How soon do you think you can get back here?"

"So, I'm guessin' you're offerin' me the machinist job, right?"

"Yes. But it is a *master* machinist position we're offering. We don't see your kind of experience and knowledge that often. I'd already talked with your shop teachers at your high school and they not only gave you their highest marks, and also told me how exacting their programs were. Actually, they said you were the best student they'd ever had.

"It used to be that the aircraft industry was mostly like a giant model shop. Now, though, we've become a production line factory and that means more of everything including machined parts that can be taken directly to points of assembly on schedule. Your high-volume experience at Thompson Products will be very useful here. Having an expert ma-chinist who is flexible enough to operate several different machine tools with precision is going to be a key piece of the puzzle for us."

"Maybe I shouldn't ask right away, but how much is the pay?"

"Oh. Right. Well, we can start you at four seventy-five an hour. There'll be overtime at time and half. The Army wants us to start turning out a bomber every couple days. How much you making back in Ohio?"

"Well, to be honest, about half that, so, your offer sounds pretty good. My family's already decided to move here and have started the house sellin' process, so getting everybody out here will take a few weeks, I guess."

"Look, Frank. We really need you at work right away. I'll authorize a plane trip back to Ohio so you can get back here as soon as you can. How long will it take you to drive from Cleveland back to San Diego?"

"If I push it, maybe three days. My father-in-law works at *National Iron Works*, so he could probably find us some temporary livin' quarters."

"Good. Housing is getting scarce. I suggest starting that process right away. How about if we fly you home day after tomorrow? Meanwhile, here's a phone number to call to locate a temporary apartment until your family gets things sorted out."

His lunch untouched, Frank Savage pushed his chair back and stared at Al Green. "WOW! My head's spinnin'. Why do I get the feelin' life here is lived in high gear?"

"That's because it is. Everybody here knows a war is coming, and San Diego, being a Navy town...well, it's going to get very, very busy here very, very soon. Are you in for this job?"

"I need to talk to my wife, Lois..."

"Not a problem. Let's go back to my office after you eat your lunch.

You can call her from there."

In the office, Al provided Frank an outside line and left to allow Frank and Lois to talk in private.

"Oh, my God, Frank! That's almost $10,000 a year before overtime! I won't tell you what to do, but that sounds like the offer you wanted that you can't refuse. What will you do?"

"Well, your approval just made up my mind. I'll accept. Mr. Green will fly me home. Your dad will help me find a temporary place here until the houses sell. I had plenty of time to plan the move on that long train ride. I think my folks would be willin' to live in the same residence as us…if we can find the right place. So, that means we sell our duplex first and you put our stuff in storage. You bring Howard and the car with essentials and we find a place to live for all of us. How does that sound?"

"Your plan will need some fine-tuning, but I'll start pushing the realtor here a little harder. When will you be home?"

"In a couple days. Call you before I leave. Never been in a airplane before. Yikes! Lots to digest. Talk to you soon."

Frank hung up and opened Al Green's office door. "Mr. Green. I'm finished talkin' with Lois."

"Great. Have you decided?"

"I'll accept the offer as a master machinist. The move will be a little complicated, but my wife is very capable. We'll have to buy another car so she can drive our son and some short-term stuff out here after the house sells. My parents will be comin' along sometime later, I guess, so…you see, it's complicated."

"Not to worry. Frank. We're very happy to have you on board. Today is Wednesday, June eleventh. How about we peg your starting date as Monday, June twenty-third. That should be enough time for you to disengage from Thompson Products and drive back here. Let me introduce you to Molly, our senior secretary. She will guide you through the necessary paperwork."

The two shook hands warmly. Al introduced Frank to Molly Atkinson, a middle-aged woman with bright red hair. After filling out and signing innumerable forms—including, to Frank's happy surprise, family health care supplements—something Thompson Products had never provided its employees. Finished, she reminded, "We start new employee orientation at seven o'clock on Monday mornings. I'll have a cup of coffee ready for you on the twenty-third. Welcome aboard. See you in a couple weeks."

Chapter 14

It's Complicated

Frank Savage's "direct" flight back to Cleveland took more than twelve hours since it involved three stops. Upon finally landing in Cleveland, Frank was greeted by Lois and Howard. As he descended from the silvery new American Airlines DC-3, he saw them. They were easy to spot as they were jumping up and down and waving. He waved back. Stepping away from the line of disembarking passengers, he trotted over to his wife and son.

"Welcome home, darling! How's my travelin' man? New job and everything...Wow! There's champagne on ice waiting at home!"

On the way home, Howard asked questions about where they'd be living, how long would it take to get there, and would he be able to play and make friends.

When they got home, he asked, "Daddy, will you be going to war?"

The champagne glass stopped halfway to his mouth. Frank answered hesitantly. "Honestly don't know, son. Technically, we're still at peace. But bad things are happenin' in other parts of the world. So far we've been spared. Why do you ask?"

"Well, Billy's dad said he'd join the Army if we got attacked, and that if other dad's didn't do that they were traitors and cowards. What's a traitor?"

"A traitor is a person who gives aid and comfort to an enemy of our country, Howard. Where did Billy get this?"

"I asked him that, and he said his father and his father's friends were talking about it one night."

"Okay. Look. Goin' around accusin' people of being traitors is not good. Treason is a terrible crime and requires plenty of proof. But don't you be gettin' in arguments or fights with other kids about things like this, okay?"

"Sure, daddy. But if somebody says you're a traitor or a coward, I'm still gonna punch him in the nose!"

This last comment was the most astounding thing Frank had ever heard Howard say. Howard was only nine years old, but he sounded more aware of things than many adults he'd known. Frank's pride swelled, but he felt obligated to say, "There's gonna be a lot to do in the comin' weeks, Howard. We can't be worried about you gettin' in trouble. Promise me you'll just walk away from that sort of nonsense."

"Okay, daddy," Howard replied. "I'll just find somebody else to play catch or stick ball with. Billy is a kind of bully, anyway," adding after a pause, "But somebody needs to push back against the things he does and says to the other kids."

"Really? What does Billy do?"

"Oh, he pushes girls around , hits them and laughs. Any boys who try to defend the girls get punched. Billy doesn't play ball at all, so he takes his—I don't know the word—out on everybody else."

"The word is 'jealousy'. You could also say 'envy'. Those words mean that somebody is really weak inside and has a poor spirit." After a brief pause, Frank asked, "Does Billy ever punch you?" Frank had put down his glass and, with Lois, were closely attending the conversation.

"Nope. I never give him the chance. I can run faster than him, so I get away. He just stands there shaking his fists at me and calling me names."

"Really? What names?" Frank continued.

"His favorite is 'chicken shit'. Is that bad?"

"Yes, it's very bad. But what he's really sayin' to everybody is that HE's the one who's a coward. I'll bet he never picks on anybody his own size or larger."

"Nope. So, am I being a coward by running away?"

"Not at all, Son. In fact, you are bein' brave and smart to avoid people like that. There are grown-ups like that too. You'll have to learn to deal with them in life. You're on the right track.

Look, Howard, I gotta leave in a few days and drive to San Diego to start my new job. Your mother is going to need every bit of help you can give her to get everything packed, stored and ready to move when we find our new house. You think you can do that? Can you be the man of the house while I'm away?"

"I think so," Howard replied, thinking. "I'm strong enough. Mom is already teaching me how to pack stuff. How will mom and I get there?"

"Good question. You and I and mom are gonna buy a second car big enough to haul enough belongin's so we can get by until we find a house. It'll be like camping out. Won't that be fun?"

"Yes! Do I get to pick the car's color?"

"Don't see why not. Just don't pick somethin' that everyone will groan about."

Frank Savage's heart swelled. His own father exhibited that same attitude when he decided to move to San Diego. *Maybe it won't be as complicated as I thought.*

But is *was* complicated. Lois had already informed their upstairs tenants that they were selling and that they'd have to negotiate with the new owners when the time came. Virgil and Anna had listed their house for sale, and it sold in a week. The buyers were anxious to have Virgil and

Anna out quickly.

Virgil and Anna ended up staying with Frank and Lois until their house sold. They stored their household goods and furniture in the younger Savages' garage. Howard moved into his parents' bedroom and slept on a cot allowing his grandparents to sleep in his room. Planning around the single bathroom was the greatest challenge.

Buying the second car was the easiest part of the process. They found a clean-looking 1939 Ford station wagon with good tires, no rust and low mileage. It cost $550, and when Howard gave his stamp of approval to the salesman over the dark maroon color, everyone had a good chuckle. "When will you be old enough to drive?" asked the smiling salesman.

"Hmmm. Maybe in a couple years. I'm growing fast, and I plan to start taking driving lessons as soon as I can reach the pedals. Right, daddy?"

That produced an eye roll from Frank. He gave his son a big hug to seal the deal.

Frank gave notice at Thompson Products, much to the chagrin of the personnel manager, Gary Childs. "You're not giving us the usual two-week notice, Frank. Have we treated you that badly?"

"Not really. But Consolidated made me an offer I couldn't refuse and, with things in the world the way they are, they want me to start right away. Thompson Products was good, steady work, but being stuck in mirror polish wasn't my idea of a good career position. Once the supervisor's job went to the kid, I started lookin'. Do you understand?" Both men looked down at their feet. "I think I was a valuable employee..." Frank trailed off.

"You *were* a valuable employee. It's too bad about the supervisor position. That decision was not in my control. Well, you've accumulated some retirement. I'll cash it out for you and, despite the short notice, I'll make sure you get two week's severance pay. Is next Friday your last day?"

"Yes, Thanks, Gary. I appreciate what you're doing."

"Okay, I'll have the papers and your checks ready first thing in the morning. I'm sure you'll want to say good-bye to your co-workers."

"I will. Might even have some advice for that kid supervisor. He might end up gettin' drafted, you know."

"Many young men will find their lives changing dramatically in the near future. Heck, here you are, only twenty-seven, heading all the way across the country. Thanks for stopping in today and giving me the bad...or, in your case, good news. See you tomorrow."

Frank dealt with the upsetting thoughts about parting from his wife and son for the long trip to San Diego by packing, re-packing, checking maps and otherwise acting like a caged lion. The anticipation of the next phase in his family's lives kept him on edge.

There was solace for him in knowing that the cash from the two Savage houses would be more than adequate for a serious down payment, or maybe even completely pay for a new dwelling in San Diego. His parents' house had sold quickly and for the full asking price. Since it was clear of debt, the cash went straight into the bank. Virgil, nearing retirement age, had accumulated a nice benefit package too. His twenty years of service accrued a nice lump sum and ended up providing the senior Savages with $20,000 over and above the $35,000 from the house sale. This money, added to the savings they'd managed to squirrel away over the years, provided sufficient capital for their next life adventure.

"No more shoveling coal for me, Anna. I now gentleman and restaurant manager. How that sound?" he asked in his best English.

"Yes, my dear. You already work enough for two lives. Now you work for yourself and family."

The relocation plan centered on finding a duplex where Virgil and Anna could live near to Frank, Lois and Howard. After considerable discussion, it was decided that the cash from the sale of Frank and Lois's duplex would go to the new place in San Diego, while Virgil and Anna's capital would be used to start a family business. If everything worked out as planned, Frank, Lois, Virgil and Anna would be able to make a cash offer on the new house without the need for a mortgage.

Andy, in the meantime, was scouring real estate ads both for Frank's temporary residence and for the new Savage living arrangement. Prices were rising quickly due to the rapidly expanding job market and population influx. This was primarily due to the gathering clouds of war.

Before departing for San Diego, Frank announced, "Lois, you're just gonna have to trust Andy and me to find a place. We need to get goin'. Real estate prices are startin' to go up fast. What I need from you and the folks is a check list of features that we *must* have and another with those that would be *nice* to have in the new place. When I find something, before I commit, of course, I'll call and tell you about it. Sound like a plan?"

"I couldn't agree more," Lois said. "Let's all discuss this over dinner, tonight. We can begin making the lists and, at the same time, set financial limits. We need to include Howard in the plans, too. He needs a safe place to play outside. Which reminds me, you'll have to check for a nearby school. Oh, and another thing: What about all our furniture? Do we want to pay to move all our old stuff, or should we buy whatever we need when we get there? Maybe when you find the place, you'll have an idea about what we need to keep and buy…"

"Good idea," Frank agreed. "Means I'll need to look at San Diego furniture prices, too. But we'll definitely get a better couch. I'm tired of feeling the springs poking me. How does Howard like his bedroom furniture?"

"Let's ask him! Howard! Come sit with us a bit," Lois called. When he joined them she asked: "Do you like your bed and chest? Would you want us to move them to California?"

"Ummm. Sure. I could really use a bigger box though for more toys."

That brought some much-need laughter, Frank replied, "Of course. We'll get you a bigger toy box when we settle in."

"I would also like an Erector set," Howard excitedly interjected. "I like building things. Can I get one of those sets after we move?"

"We'll look into that, I promise," Lois replied. After Howard returned to his room, Lois turned to Frank and said: "We can probably fit a change of bedding and towels in the station wagon along with a few of our favorite dishes, glasses, pots and pans. And we should be able to squeeze in almost all our clothes. We can probably wait for the movers to pack our winter stuff, though..."

That brought a stunned look to Frank's face. "Maybe we don't need winter clothes. It doesn't get colder than forty degrees there even on the coldest of nights. That's sweater weather for us."

Lois got up to call Virgil and Anna while Frank started listing their general home requirements. They'd need a minimum of 1,500 square feet to give everyone enough space to not feel crowded. Their current house floor space was about 1,200 square feet, but the kitchen was tiny. *We're gonna need a good, big kitchen for starters...*

Lois interrupted Frank's thoughts. "What do you have there?"

"Space requirements. We'll need maybe fifteen hundred square feet with a much larger kitchen. That tiny kitchen we have is just not enough. Wadda ya think of a bigger kitchen with around two-hundred square feet?"

"Oh YES! Perfect! Right! Let's start going room-by-room..."

The complications became fewer as everyone contributed ideas. Frank was due to leave for San Diego in three days, so he had the tires checked and the Plymouth serviced. When the day to leave finally came, Frank packed the car to the gills with his personal stuff, shop tools and anything else he thought he'd need getting settled. He would stay with Andy until he found his own studio, or some such place to stay. Hugs, kisses and tears were exchanged between the three Savages. Frank had bid farewell to his parents the previous evening.

It was just six o'clock in the morning, but the excitement and anticipation were shared by Frank, his wife and son. He climbed into the heavily-loaded Plymouth, backed slowly down the driveway, cringing when the back bumper scraped the pavement. Turning, he waved goodbye to his wife and son standing in the driveway and waving back. Never had he felt so much love, respect and determination as he did just now. He watched his family slowly grow smaller in the rear view mirror until he turned the corner and they were gone.

Chapter 15

First Step

An hour south out of Cleveland, Frank turned on the radio and found some Tommy Dorsey band music. He hummed along as the miles slipped by. Traffic was light and Frank made good time on U.S. 40, getting to the Indiana border outside Richmond by 10:30 A.M. After winding through Indianapolis traffic, he stopped for lunch at a roadside table. Lois had lovingly made him some sandwiches and an apple to go along with the Thermos of coffee.

Another hour and a half on U.S. 40 brought him into Illinois. There, he looked at his map and calculated that he could get through St. Louis and maybe as far as Rolla, Missouri, before it got dark. Crossing the Mississippi River, Frank marveled at its width. He imagined seeing Tom Sawyer and Huck Finn on a riverboat, but what he did see were flat barges filled with coal or crates. He picked up U.S. 66 just past downtown St. Louis.

There was one hotel, The Fairweather, in downtown Rolla, and it had a room available. The room was small with wallpaper peeling along the ceiling and in the corners. After unpacking the essentials, he located a restaurant across the street from the hotel where he enjoyed a hearty meal of barbecued ribs, fried potato slices and a decent salad. Two cold beers gave Frank the good sense to go back to the hotel and bed.

As it grew darker, he noticed a flashing neon sign from across the street with JESUS SAVES sending its hopeful message to the unrepentant and onto the walls of his room. Frank got up, pulled the curtains shut and thought, *Jesus will have to save my immortal soul some other time. Right now, I need sleep.*

Frank's alarm clock jarred him out of deep, dreamless sleep at 5:30 A.M. Jesus was still flashing his somewhat less visible message through the threadbare curtains. Frank rolled out as if getting up to go to work realizing that, in a sense, it was exactly what he was doing.

Showering himself awake, he brushed his teeth, dressed, packed up his used clothing and shaving kit, and headed down to the Plymouth. He tossed the key to the night clerk and asked, "Where can a guy get a good breakfast at this hour?"

The clerk raised his balding head from the paper he was reading and looked over his wire-rimmed glasses as if Frank had just landed from Mars. "Depends on which way you're headed, friend."

"West. I wanna get to Texas tonight."

"Then ya better git movin'. There's Mildred's Cafe near the end of town. She makes great blueberry pancakes. She's good folks."

"Thanks." Frank drove to Mildred's and, after a hearty, ham and eggs breakfast with a side of Mildred's famous pancakes, filled his Thermos with good, dark, fresh coffee.

The rolling hills of central Missouri's contribution to Ozark country soon gave way to flatter, browner land with fewer and fewer trees as he headed west. Route 66 took him through Tulsa, Oklahoma, an oil and cattle town. Soon the land flattened even more until the hills vanished altogether. By mid-afternoon, he passed through Oklahoma City, deciding to stop at the first town in Texas for the night. As Lois suggested, he bought two canvas water bags in Oklahoma City to hang on his front bumper.

While stopping for gas and a rest room, he noticed that the air was getting hotter and drier while the attendant's accents became more twangy—like the country songs he'd been listening to. West of Oklahoma city, the flat land became increasingly parched, covered only by dry grass. He saw some cattle and many, lazily rocking jack pumps. When he stopped for gas and asked the attendant what they were, the man snorted and said something that sounded like *awl*. Then Frank smelled it. *Ah, the man meant oil.*

Radio stations became fewer and harder to find, so he spent the hours driving with an elbow out the window, resting on the car door. Then, BANG! Frank gripped the steering wheel reflexively as the car lurched toward a ditch at the side of the road. He barely managed to keep the Plymouth from sliding off the road and nursed the Plymouth to a stop. *SHIT!!*

The right front tire had a hole big enough to fit an orange through. Cursing his bad luck in the ninety-seven degree heat, Frank unloaded the packed trunk, pulled out the jack and wrestled the spare tire onto the sizzling pavement. His buddy Ernie at the *Sohio* gas station back in Cleveland had made sure all his tires, including the spare, were up to par. '*Thank you Ernie. Boy, thought I was gonna lose it there for a minute. That ditch is pretty deep. God, it's hot!*'

The sun began casting long shadows before Frank found his way into the small town of Shamrock, Texas. What greeted him was a tall building called a grain elevator, a general store, a Fleet-Wing gas station named *Magnolia* and a small, neatly kept hotel with two of the sign's letters burned out. The main street was lined with shops and a few late model cars parked at oblique angles along the sides. Next to the general store was a cafe called the *U-Drop In Cafe.*

Frank wisely chose to first register at the hotel. They had one room left. "We're fixin' to get the rodeo crowd in tamarra, so yer purty dern lucky to get a room, boy. Where yew from?" asked the sunburned desk clerk, fingering a double-bend briar pipe. His sandy hair was combed over to the side and he had the brightest blue eyes Frank had ever seen.

"Cleveland. On my way to San Diego."

"Hmph. Yankee. Shoulda knowd. Okay, Yankee, Mr. Frank Savage, yer in room eight down the hall. When ya leave, ya kin leave the key in the room. Nobody at the desk until nine o'clock or thereabouts."

"Thanks. Does that cafe over there serve dinner and breakfast?"

"Boy, that road there is root sixty-six. We get traffic all hours. Mo and Alice run that place twenty-four hours a day. Been doin' it since the awl boom in nineteen and thirty. Yer gonna hear trucks come through here all night."

"Okay. Say, I blew a tire up the road a ways," Frank continued. "Can I get a new one at the garage over there?"

"I reckon yew kin. Abner Moss and his son Ronnie've run the *Magnolia* station fer years. They got rich from the awl boom and jes keep gettin' richer. Then, the Fleet Wing gas company sold them what they call a franchise and they jes kept on pumpin' gas. They sleep in the back, so's if you wake 'em gently, they'll set yew up."

"Thanks again. And what's your name?"

"Me? I'm Lew Bannon. Been here in Shamrock all mah lahf. Used to own a ranch until the dust hit. Lotta people got run off and starved. It was bad. If it weren't for the awl, the town would prob'ly been vacated. How'd y'all do in Ohio during the depression?"

"My wife and I banged on a lot of doors getting odd jobs whenever and wherever we could. Had a kid in thirty two, and had to hustle more to keep him fed. He's nine now and growing like a weed. That's why we're moving to San Diego. Better job. MUCH better pay. A lotta people starved in Cleveland, too. Many of our so-called best citizens showed no civil decency toward those who were suddenly poor. 'Colored' people suffered the most..."

"Yeah, well, our black folks didn't do too good here, either. Lot of 'em ended up grubbin' the fields and sleepin' wherever they could. There was work here 'cause of the awl bidnesses, but they didn't hire them people much. Weren't surprisin' to find some o' them poor folk lyin' dead by the road or under a bridge any day."

"Lew, I'm pretty hot, sweaty and tired. Is there a bath in the room?"

"Nope, but there's a shared bath down the end of the hall. Yew might have to stand in line," Lew said chuckling, showing tobacco-stained teeth, the few of them he had left.

"Don't mind. But first I'm gonna try some of Mo and Alice's cooking at the *U-Drop In*. Thanks for your help."

"Yew bet. Welcome to Shamrock."

Frank ordered a T-bone steak, fried potatoes, and iced-tea instead of beer this night. He was very thirsty, needed to drink a lot of fluids and didn't want to get drunk. He'd ordered his steak rare, and when it arrived, it's sides draped over the huge platter's edges. He was surprised to find the inside bloody and cool to the taste.

"Ma'am," he said, calling Alice to the table. "The steak is still cold in the middle."

"Yew ordered it rare, didn'cha? Yer a Yankee, ain't ya?" Alice replied, grinning. "Well, here 'n Texas, 'rare' means still mooin'. Here, let me take it back and make it *medium* rare fer ya."

Frank responded meekly. "I didn't know..."

"Not to worry, Yankee. Y'all been coming' through here a lot since the awl boom. I jes have fun teasin' y'all. More tea?"

The tea was extra sweet, but Frank decided not to complain. He didn't want to be seen as any more a Yankee here than he already was. The steak came back perfectly done. It needed only some salt and pepper. It was delicious, and with the assistance of a little ketchup on the potatoes, his hunger was satisfied. He paid his bill at the counter cash register, but left a $5 tip on the table. He didn't want Texans to think that Yankees were cheap skates.

From the restaurant, Frank walked to the *Magnolia* gas station. A young man was washing a car's windows. When he finished, Frank asked him about tires.

"Sure. We got tires. What you drivin'?"

"A thirty-eight Plymouth. Tire blew outside of town this afternoon. It looks unrepairable to me, so I think I need a new one. Six by sixteen size. Can you help?"

"Yep. Jes got a new shipment of tires in from Amarillo. Roll th' blown tire down here so's I kin make certain th' size."

"Thanks. Name's Frank Savage."

"Howdy, Frank. Ah'm Ronnie Moss. Nice ta meetcha."

Frank extracted the blown tire and walked it to the garage in back of the station. Ronnie had already pulled a tire down from the rack and was unwrapping the spiral of shipping paper. "Let's make sure th' size," he said, examining the damaged tire. "Yep. Ah, guessed right. Lemme git you a new tube too. This un is blown all to hell."

Twenty minutes later, Ronnie bounced the newly installed tire on the floor. "Here she is, Mr. Savage. That'll be twenty bucks. The rim ain't damaged, so I 'spect it won't be rubbin' a hole in the new tube. Hope ya have a safe trip to Californee…"

Frank shook Ronnie's hand, rolled the new tire back to the car, and once again had to re-pack the entire trunk. Frank's hands and fingers still carried the embedded grit from mirror polishing valves, so Ronnie's garage dirt didn't add much to the color of his own hands. The horizon, now full dark, signaled it was time for a bath and bed. Frank wanted to get up early for the drive across the New Mexico desert.

His alarm clock woke him at 5:30 as planned. He washed his face, brushed his teeth and consulted his map to plan the day's travel. It was then that he noticed that Shamrock, Texas was 2,800 feet above sea level. Once entering New Mexico, he'd steadily gain altitude all the way to the continental divide west of Deming. He quickly charted his route from Shamrock, through Amarillo and into New Mexico on U.S. 66. In Tucumcari, New Mexico, U.S. 66 would continue west from Santa Rosa, but Frank would instead stay on U.S. 54 heading southwest to Alamogordo. There, he would take U.S. 70 south to Las Cruces, then turn due west crossing the Rio Grande River. Quick calculations showed that getting all the way to Tucson, Arizona, by tonight would be unlikely. Deming, New Mexico, looked a better stopping place.

It wasn't until he passed Alamogordo and through the small town of Corrizozo that the desert landscape turned picturesque, with cone-shaped extinct volcanoes dotting the landscape. The highest was the well-named Blanca Peak. When he stopped for gas, he noted there were still faint patches of snow on the highest slopes of the 12,000 foot mountain. *WOW! This is the most beautiful place I've ever seen! The people are all speaking Spanish. Well, dummy, you're in New Mexico.*

What a treat for the eyes after driving so far for so long across flat landscape. Lois told me about some of this from her drive out here with Andy, but to see it myself! What will tomorrow bring?

Near Las Cruces, New Mexico, the jagged peaks of the surrounding mountains were older than those he'd just seen in Corrizozo. The wide, sloping peaks had eroded, leaving ancient lava plugs resembling gnarled fingers, reaching upward from the bowels of the Earth.

The road on the other side of Las Cruces rose steeply until it leveled off onto a flat plain. As Frank looked ahead, the road narrowed as it approached the horizon. At dusk, 150 miles out of Las Cruces, he pulled into Deming, to find a meal and a room. After dinner, he called Lois and Howard to report his progress and assure them he was safe. He then called Andy to tell him of his progress and that he would arrive in San Diego hopefully late tomorrow afternoon or early evening.

"Take it easy comin' across the desert, Frank," Andy advised. "When you get into California, you'll be below sea level and it will be HOT. Past El Centro, you'll have to climb up some mountains through *Devil's Canyon*. Make sure you cool the engine and fill the radiator before attempting it. It'll be well over a hundred degrees, and I'd hate for you to boil over or blow a hose. If I was you, I'd get up REAL early and skedaddle across Arizona before it gets too hot."

"Okay, I'll get up before three, then. Should get me to Yuma by maybe nine or ten, and from there, only two to three more hours to San Diego."

"Sounds right, Frank. But be careful and watch your temperature gauge."

After the call, Frank was asleep before his pillow got warm.

Frank's alarm woke him at 2:30 A.M. He rolled grudgingly out of bed, washed up and placed his packed suitcase in the car. He ate breakfast at the truck stop diner across the road and was back rolling along U.S. 70 by 3:15. As he approached Lordsburg, New Mexico, he passed a sign announcing he had crossed the continental divide. Looking back in his rearview mirror, he watched the dim image of the highway disappear over the still dark horizon. In front of him the road was straight and flat as far as he could see and he wondered exactly what the divide was for.

Just at the crack of dawn, Frank entered the small, eastern Arizona town of Safford. There, he turned south on U.S. 191. The 34-mile drive to U.S. 80 was gloriously beautiful with the deep violet Pinaleno Mountains silhouetted against the brightening sky.

With his first glimpse of the magnificent Sonoran Desert, Frank reminded himself how glad he was there was no traffic. His head was constantly swiveling left and right at each new visual wonder. He opened his driver-side window and relished the smell of sage, creosote and clean, cool, desert air as he drove. *I gotta pull over and get full measure of this lovely place.*

Frank watched in wonder as sunlight crept across the desert floor. He spotted a lizard scurrying somewhere, and several birds flitting about between the plants. The haunting song of the black *phainopepla,* a bird unique to the American southwest, held his ear until he spotted one perched on a gangly stalk of an *ocatillo* cactus. *Wow! The silence. The smell. The incredible beauty of the desert. It sure isn't like I imagined from the western movies. Okay, sightseein's over. I'm definitely comin' back to this desert some day.*

Going west on U.S. 80, he chased his car's shadow into Tucson, Arizona, past Casa Grande, Gila Bend and on to Yuma. The highway descended for several miles through forests of saguaro cacti as he approached that small dusty town on the border with California. He stopped for gas in Yuma, and could feel the heat building. It was 9:30 in the morning, but the temperature was already over 90 degrees according to the gas station's thermometer. Crossing the Colorado River, he saw the "Welcome to California" sign and began the several mile drive through huge sand dunes bordering the highway. For a moment Frank imagined himself as cowboy Gary Cooper in the 1940 movie *The Westerner.* Every so often, small sand fingers drifted across the highway that made the Plymouth bounce. Once clear of the sand dunes, the road proceeded arrow-straight until it approached the small, agricultural town of

El Centro, in the lower Imperial Valley. From here, Frank could see the wall of mountains that awaited him.

At the little crossroads village of Ocatillo, situated at the base of the Laguna Mountains, he pulled over, as suggested, to let the engine cool all the way down. At the small gas station, the attendant, a small, sun-baked man wearing a beat-up straw hat turned up at the edges, blue jeans and cowboy boots came out and bade him *buenos dias*. After filling the gas tank he made sure all the dusty Plymouth's fluids were full while Frank checked the two outside water bags and topped them off. The drive up the eastern slope of the Laguna Mountains was steep, barren and rugged beyond anything Frank had ever imagined. After several miles of steady climbing, the road flattened and began winding through piles of boulders seemingly strewn at random by some gigantic child who threw them about in a fit of temper. *Devil's Canyon indeed!*

The road continued its meander through the mountains, passing through small towns with unusual sounding names like *Jacumba* and *Campo*.

Devil's Canyon finally gave way to scrubby brush, some cacti and valleys filled with spreading oak trees. The tree lines followed the drainages from what little water this area received. As Frank concentrated on managing the twists, turns, climbs and descents of the highway, more and thicker vegetation appeared. At one high point, a quick look ahead revealed a grayish blue horizon. The town he had just entered was Alpine.

The road from Alpine serpentined down, down, down into a weird, three-sided valley to a scruffy looking town called El Cajon, "The Box". There he pulled over to consult Andy's map. Ahead, U.S. 80 kept going west through what Andy had labeled Mission Valley. *Why Mission Valley? What secret mission was this valley privy to?* he wondered.

Then he noticed Andy's marginal comment: "San Diego Mission De Alcala". Andy had told him that San Diego was the first Spanish Catholic settlement in California. It was established by a priest named Junipero Serra. Almost at the same time that Frank remembered that fact, a white structure on top of the hill to the North revealed itself. The distant, red tile roof was suddenly clearly visible against the gray, cloudy, mid-June sky. He saw a small sign with an arrow pointing to the mission up the hill.

So, here I am in San Diego. Looks a lot like farm country in this valley. That's what Lois told me she saw when she and Andy drove by here. I'm only a half-hour from his place.

Suddenly, the smell of the sea filled his car and nostrils, and the cloud cover became thicker the closer he got to Pacific Highway. There, he turned left and headed south to National City where Andy lived. He knew the way from here on, having driven it less than three weeks ago.

I guess this is where the the next chapter in our adventure begins. Every journey begins with a single step. Wait. Some guy named Confucius said that, didn't he? This is definitely the end of yet another first step for our family.

Chapter 16

Collecting the Family

The next day, Andy Billings took Frank on a half-day tour of the San Diego area. Up from downtown, he stopped on Fifth Avenue in front of an apartment building. "I took the liberty of rentin' you a furnished studio until we can do some serious house huntin'. I bought you some sheets and towels for the place. I hope you like it."

"Gosh, Andy! Thanks. Is it my snorin' that made you find me a place?"

"Not at all," Andy deadpanned. "Just thought you'd appreciate some privacy and be able to better conduct the business of getting the family out here as soon as possible without any interference from me. The phone company will install your phone on Monday. Then you can call Lois and your folks directly."

"Andy, I can't thank you enough. Let me buy you dinner. Is there a place near here?"

"I was hoping you'd ask. Sally's Steakhouse is just down the avenue near Laurel. Let's go. I'm starved."

Their early dinner finished, Andy drove them back to his National City apartment, where he handed Frank the keys to his car and studio, and bade him good night. "See you in the morning. Pick me up at eight and we'll do some house huntin'."

Andy then hugged Frank, patted him affectionately on the cheek and watched from his doorway as Frank drove off.

At the studio, Frank pulled a double-sized bed out of the couch, and sat, testing it. It creaked and groaned, but as Andy had promised, there were clean sheets on the bed. In the kitchen, he found cupboards containing basic dishware, glasses, pots and pans. There was even a stove-top percolator coffee pot. When Frank opened the small refrigerator he saw that Andy had added the basics, including a few bottles of Mexican beer. The small pantry had been stocked with the necessary makings for a couple of breakfasts, lunches and dinners. A cold *cerveza* in hand, Frank sat on the couch, thinking.

This is great! Andy is doing his best to make the move here smooth. I don't know how I can repay him. I am truly one lucky guy. No wonder his daughter is such a terrific woman. I think we're goin' to like it here.

Next morning, Frank banged on Andy's door.

"Mornin', Frank. How'd you sleep?"

"Like a log. Thanks for everythin'. Don't know how I'll ever be able to return the favors."

"Forget it. Just be good to my daughter and raise me a great grandson. Think you can do that?"

"Absolutely."

"Want some coffee before we get goin'?" Andy asked.

"Nope, already had two cups and am ready to look at some places."

"Met this guy, Archie Ballard, from Pacific Coast Realty. I gave him your checklist. He's waiting for us at a place on Villa Terrace. Let's go have a look."

The building on Villa Terrace was a duplex with six bedrooms and six bathrooms, large enough to be a rooming house. The open, Spanish-style interior was trimmed everywhere with dark wood. The backyard was small, but beautifully landscaped with several palms, a banana tree and some brightly flowered, spiny, vine-like plants Archie called *bougainvillea*.

"This is beautiful, Archie, but don't know how my folks would like the living arrangements. They're gonna want a private entrance. I think that's on the checklist."

"It is," Archie answered, "but I wanted you to see what homes up here are like,

"Up here" meant *Banker's Hill*.

"What's a place like this sell for, Archie?"

"The owner is asking eighty-five thousand, but I'd guess they'd take eighty."

"It's a great home, but it's not for us. What else is on your list?"

"Sure. Okay, there's one on Front Street that I think will meet your expectations."

They drove a few blocks and stopped in front of a large home with a facade that looked like that of a Spanish mission church. It was situated up the Laurel Street hill from Consolidated Aircraft, Frank's new employer.

When he stepped through the arching front door, the building sang to him. It had two separate floors of 2,000 square feet each. Each floor had three bedrooms with the upstairs unit having a private entrance out the back. An interior staircase lead up to the second floor living area, kitchen and bedrooms. There was a lockable door at the top of the stairs. As they toured the first floor, the high ceilings, wooden floors and adobe walls captivated Frank Savage.

Never in my dreams did I imagine living is such a place as this.

The large kitchen featured skylights, a six-burner gas stove and a walk-in pantry. Frank stepped out through the back door to a patio surrounded by Bird-of-Paradise plants, an orange tree laden with ripening fruit and…a detached apartment/guest house. There was no car garage, but the weather in San Diego, he reminded himself, was never any more dramatic than a brief, heavy rain. Archie then showed them the basement housing the common gas-fired hot water and heating unit. There was also space for laundry machines. Along another basement wall were three large storage lockers.

"Andy! This place is perfect! What do you think?"

Archie said, "You haven't seen the inside of the guest house, yet."

The guest house was actually a one-bedroom apartment with full bath and kitchen. The living room and dining area adjacent to the kitchen was large enough for a table and four chairs.

"This is really nice. Maybe I could live here too."

That comment brought all conversation to a standstill.

Frank looked at Andy's face and, seeing his wistful expression, replied, "Andy, this is how I can return all your favors! We'll talk details back at my place."

"Archie, if my wife approves we'll take it. She gave me decision makin' power, but I still want to discuss the details with her before we decide. Do you need a deposit to hold it until, say next week? Oh, what's the sale price?"

"The owner is asking seventy-eight five. Depending on how you want to pay for it, he might take seventy-five. A hundred bucks would be sufficient for me to present an offer, which would give you two weeks to make a final decision."

Frank turned to Andy, who nodded eagerly. "Okay. Then that's our offer…if we decide to buy it.

"Thanks for your help, Archie. Let's go, Andy. We have phone calls to make. Oh. May I keep the information sheet so I can read it to my wife?"

"Sure, Mr. Savage. Here's my card. Before we go, let's fill out the offer sheet along with the deposit."

That afternoon as they drove back to Andy's apartment, Andy said, "Frank, I like your decisiveness. That Front Street place seems ideal for your folks and you guys…"

Frank cut in before Andy could finish. "…but what tipped it for me, Andy, was that we could have you there with us. The guest house is just as big as your apartment without the second bedroom."

"Yeah. And I can store my extra stuff in one of the lockers in the basement. It should work."

Lois' reaction to Frank's message was a burst of gleeful cheering followed by, "Let me tell your folks and call you back."

A half-hour later, Frank was describing the place to his father who asked questions about the structure, heating, plumbing and if all the light switches worked. "Good questions, Pop. I'll go back tomorrow, check and get back to you,"

"What price asking?" he added.

"Seventy-eight five, but we offered seventy-five, cash."

"Hmm. Yes. Good. And Andy comes, too. I like this. We pay cash and have money for starting business. You my son. If you think this good deal and right place for us, then I say, buy house."

"'I'm gonna get a camera and take pictures. I'll air-mail 'em as soon as I can get 'em developed. The realtor says we've got about a month before the owners move out."

"A month. Okay, we move into your house. Here is Lois."

"Well, I liked the sound of that conversation from this end," she said.

"It's a beautiful place. Any offers on our place?"

"As a matter of fact, the realtor called last night and said someone offered fifty-five five for our place. That's top dollar in our neighborhood.

Should we accept?"

"Yes. As soon as they formally accept the offer, I'll call you and tell you how to wire the cash. It's time to start linin' up the moving vans. With your dad joining us, he'll be chippin' in, too. He's workin' a lot of overtime and says he has more money than he knows what to do with. I'll probably see some overtime as soon as I start work too. This town is buzzin'.'"

"Okay, darling. I'll start the wheels rolling here. Howard is bouncing around the room. I told him he'd be able to play baseball all year 'round. He keeps yelling, 'palm trees, palm trees'!"

"Well, here we go, sweetie. I miss you very much. I'm glad you enjoyed the drive out west. We'll be living' in a beautiful house that will seem huge and mostly empty until we can fill it."

"Not a problem, dearest. The six of us will fill it with plenty of love.

"The Ford will fit the four of us. Oh. Does your dad know how to drive? I might need some driving relief."

"I doubt it. Maybe you should teach him and get him licensed."

"Good idea. I'll see to it right away.

"I know you start work on Monday, so enjoy the rest of your weekend. Gawd, I'm excited! I wish I were there so I could attack you."

"Don't worry. You'll get your chance soon enough, and I promise we'll schedule some extra time to make up for this separation." They both laughed, then rang off after heartfelt I love you's.

With city map in hand, Frank drove up Fifth Avenue to an area called Hillcrest. He found a camera store on Fifth and bought a small Kodak camera along with several rolls of the new "color" film. Driving to the Front Street property, he shot both rolls and rushed them back to the camera shop.

After the day's excitement, he drank *two* beers and made himself his first bachelor dinner in ten years. He fell into bed as exhilarated and fatigued as he'd ever been.

Frank woke on the morning of 22 June 1941 to brilliant sunlight playing across his eyelids. He'd forgotten to close the drapes last night. *Okay. I'm up. Make coffee. Eat breakfast. Tour the town, again. Find the parkin' lot at Consolidated for Monday. All the things I need do the Sunday before I start work.*

Over breakfast, he turned on the radio to listen to the morning news. What he heard sent a dark chill down his spine: Germany had just invaded the Soviet Union. The news commentators kept frantically blaring out details, such as they were, about two million German troops storming eastward across the Polish frontier in what they were calling a *blitzkrieg*—a "lightning war."

I'll bet we'll be in this thing before long. FDR must be going nuts. He listened for an hour, but the details remained sketchy. He turned off the radio. Though the news was upsetting, there wasn't anything else he could do. Right now, he needed to take care of himself, get ready for his new job, and do everything he could to prepare to receive his family next month.

Consolidated Aircraft clearly knew what they were doing with in-processing new employees. The Human Resources Department conducted a plant-wide tour for Frank Savage and the other twenty people being hired that day, 23 June 1941. The tour lasted two hours and covered the entire, sprawling facility. At one end of the vast property were buildings committed to making tools from the smallest used for making sub-assemblies to the very large ones used to bring sections of wing and fuselage into position and fasten them together. This would be Frank's area. Frank was especially impressed by the size and efficiency of the main assembly areas at the far end of the property where the giant bombers were being pieced together.

After the tour, Frank's foreman escorted him to his home department. There were fourteen other machinists and clerks in Frank's department, the tool-making/production machine shop. Arnie Steppe, the foreman, spoke to the gathered machinists: "This is Mr. Frank Savage. He's our new master machinist. He'll be working on all the machines, and I expect all of you to help him be part of our group. Frank is from Cleveland where he worked in high-volume production of engine valves, some of which are probably in our B-24 engines down in main assembly. Today's his 'in-class' day. I want each of you to give him a rundown on what you do. Any questions?"

Several hands popped up. "Clive Whitworth," he said in a pronounced British accent. "What brought you here away from those glorious midwest summer days?"

Everyone chuckled.

"I wish I had a snappy, one-sentence answer, but it's complicated," Frank replied to the group. "To begin with, summers in Cleveland are anythin' but glorious. It's hot, muggy and rains a lot. The bugs are fierce, and after several weeks of 'glory', it snows."

That brought knowing nods and more laughter.

"Truth be told, my father-in-law took a job down at National Iron Works and when my wife helped drive him here, she came back ravin' 'bout the town and the smell of the sea. Lake Erie, by comparison, smells like dead fish." More laughter.

Someone piped in with, "Wait until you smell the rotting kelp on the beaches here." Rueful laughter followed.

"So, to finish my story—which I don't mind sharin'—Andy, my father-in-law, mentioned the aircraft industry was lookin' for machinists, electricians, engineers and assemblers, so I started applyin'. Consolidated made me an offer I couldn't refuse, and here I am. Nice to meet you all. Lookin' forward to workin' with you every day. From the news, it sounds like we'll be gettin' a lot of work."

Questions completed, everyone dispersed and Arnie pulled Frank aside. "I'm gonna turn you loose so you can look at every machine and get to know better every operator. You okay with that?"

"Can't wait to get started," Frank replied eagerly. "Oh, do you mind if I take some time at lunch? Gotta set up a bank account so my wife can wire me the down payment on our new home."

"Sure. I know you have a lot on your plate, so, just keep me informed. You have to punch in and out on the time clock. Wear your badge at all times when on company property."

"Thanks, Arnie. Well, there's a half hour until lunch, so I'll start at the big turret lathe."

"Good choice. Have you ever run a shaper?"

"Yep. My high school shop had one. The trick is to keep the cutting tool sharp and properly 'relieved'. If the chips build up, the part is gonna get screwed up."

Arnie gave a smile of satisfaction, patted Frank on the back, and left the office leaving Frank to walk over to the Warner and Swayze turret lathe. It was un-manned, so Frank checked it out, rotated the tool holding turret and started the chuck spinning. The machine was new and hummed quietly. It still showed the factory polishing marks on the slides and ways.

Instead of lunch, Frank opened a savings and checking account. He had brought considerable cash with him to San Diego and was relieved to deposit it in a bank. Then he made the necessary arrangement to telegraph money from his bank in Ohio. The bank gave him an information sheet with contact and account numbers to aid Lois in making the transfers.

Back at work, Frank watched some of the machinists work on mostly aluminum parts. One milling machine was working on steel, and Frank asked the machinist how the parts would be used.

"They're for mounting the gun turret on top of the bomber," the machinist replied without stopping. "Those fifties they shoot would rip aluminum to shreds with all the vibration, so we gotta make sure the guns are stable and the airframe is protected against the hammering."

"I see I've got a lot to learn about building airplanes. Thanks for the lesson."

And so it went for the rest of the afternoon. The drive from his studio in the morning took only five minutes, but during the evening shift change, it took ten minutes just to get out onto Pacific Highway. A note was stuck in his door telling Frank he now had a telephone. Inside, on the small table next to the studio couch was a shiny black, telephone. The finger holes had numbers AND letters in them just big enough to read. The center hub of the dial displayed his new phone number: *LIberty* 0084.

He took a beer—*cerveza*—from the refrigerator and dialed the operator for long distance, giving her Lois' number. After a few minutes of clicks and buzzes, he heard a phone ring followed by a tinny, "Hello?"

"Hi. It's me. Gotta phone and you're my first call!" Frank said happily.

"Oh, hello, sweetheart. I'm so glad you called. What's your number?"

Frank read it to her, then asked about the progress selling the house.

"Nothing new to report. Your folks' stuff is in the garage, and they're settled, sort of, upstairs. They're anxious to get to our new home too. I can't wait to see the pictures."

"The pictures'll be in the mail tomorrow or Wednesday. I'll air-mail 'em, so you should get 'em pretty quick. Oh, and I opened a bank account. Here are the numbers for wiring money to our new bank. Did you find a mover?"

"Yes. The people who moved your folks do cross-country, too. They saved us a place on their schedule. When will our new place close?"

"Archie said we'll get the keys two weeks after I pay the money and sign the final paperwork. Let's hope the timing works well. I don't want to be rattling around in a big, empty house.

"The new job looks like it's goin' to be really good. The guys in the department all seem helpful and friendly. I miss you and Howard SO much! Can't wait to have you in my arms, again. I know. Just gotta be patient. Things will come together in due course. At least that's what I keep tellin' myself.

"I gotta call Andy and give him my phone number and the news from Cleveland. I love you."

"I miss you and love you, too," Lois replied sniffling. "I'll pester that realtor to push things along as fast as possible. I don't think we'll make it for the fourth of July, but definitely before August. God that desert is going to be hot! We should plan to drive across Arizona and the California desert at night so the car doesn't die. We'll be loaded to the gills. It may take an extra day to get there, but the point is getting there, and in one piece. So much to consider…"

"Say hi to Howard and my folks for me."

Chapter 17

"It Never Rains Here"

With storm clouds of war looming, the American attitude was, "Let's get rich selling stuff to Europe but otherwise stay out of the war." Few imagined Hitler was all that dangerous, or that our allies would not be able to pay for the tanks, planes and trucks that America was now producing en masse.

"Have you heard Benny Goodman's latest tune? Man, that guy can really play!" reflected the general attitude surrounding America's growing prosperity.

But Benny Goodman was also Jewish. That didn't matter to diverse Americans who simply wanted to accept the entertainment irrespective of their religion. George and Ira Gershwin, the great music writers, were Jewish and Ukrainian, having grown up not far from where Virgil Savage lived and escaped.

Frank Savage had been asleep for barely an hour when his phone rang. "Hello?"

"Will you accept a collect call from Lois Savage?"

"Yes. Of course."

"Go ahead, please.

"Hi, darling. We're in a hotel in Lordsburg, New Mexico. We just got in. We're gonna spend tonight and tomorrow here, and leave for San Diego about eight o'clock tomorrow night. That should get us there by four or five in the morning. Will you be awake enough to meet us?"

"Of course. The movers got everythin' moved into place, both upstairs and down. Andy moved in yesterday. We knew you'd be comin', so we filled the 'fridges and pantries—yes, we have a walk-in pantry! Andy and I may have to help my folks shift their heavy stuff, but everything else is set up.Arnie gave me a couple days off to receive the furniture and greet you. It'll be wonderful to have the family together again."

"That was nice of him. Okay. You go back to sleep, and we'll see you morning after next. Bye."

The night before the family's arrival, neither Andy nor Frank were able to sleep. Andy, seeing lights on in the main house's downstairs, kitchen, tapped on the door.

"C'mon in, Andy. Figured you'd be up early."

"Yeah. Is the coffee ready?"

"Almost finished. Let's take a couple of folding chairs out front and wait for the great arrival while we drink it."

The pre-dawn air was cool, still and fragrant, as the two men, sipping their coffee, were swept into the peacefulness of the moment. The flowers in bloom around the neighborhood added sweet smells to the morning. An upstairs lamp cast a warm glow over the multi-colored stones of the walkway and the pale yellow of the stucco coating of the building. "Does it get any better than this?" Frank asked rhetorically.

"Not much. But the best part is that it never rains here."

Both men laughed, but Frank stopped abruptly to ask, "It doesn't? But it must. Everything's so green...at least in most places."

"The natives told me we get around ten inches of rain per year between October and April. There are spells of hot, dry Santa Ana winds that sometimes occur in the fall and winter. The wind comes roaring in from the deserts to the East and sends temperatures soaring. But ninety-five degrees with ten percent humidity isn't really that uncomfortable."

"Gosh, Andy, are we in paradise?"

"Maybe. We definitely coulda done a hell of a lot worse." After a few moments of silence, Andy continued. "I'm really lookin' forward to seeing our girl. Whenever there is a challenge, she leaps in and solves it."

"You're tellin' me. The food, the restaurant idea, the decision to move here…her enthusiasm and lack of fear is really somethin'. Howard's takin' after her in that regard. He's turnin' into a good kid with great leadership instincts. He's not afraid to take charge of a task. I'll bet he was right there helpin' his mom organize the packin'."

That brought another chuckle.

"Well, Andy, it's coming' on four o'clock. Wouldn't be surprised if they come roaring up the hill any minute."

The conversation dwindled and the men retreated into their own personal thoughts, sipped their coffee and waited. Frank rose to turn on the front house lights, and had barely gotten reseated when a dark maroon Ford station wagon rumbled up to the curb and screeched to a halt. Frank checked his watch. It was exactly four-thirty. *My wonderful wife would have it timed perfectly, of course.*

The overstuffed Ford rocked from side to side, looking like a clown car at the circus as everyone piled out. Lois and Howard were the first up the walkway and leaped into Frank's arms. Lois made the sounds of a loving spouse too long absent, while Howard wrapped his arms around his father's legs. When Frank set her down, she ran to her dad and hugged him long and hard, wetting his collar with tears of joy. Howard stayed glued to his father until Frank grabbed him under the shoulders and lifted him up so he could wrap his small arms around his neck.

"I'm so happy to see you, daddy."

"Good to see you too, son. Telephones don't do justice. Let's go unpack the car."

As that drama unfolded, Virgil and Anna walked up and embraced Frank and Andy. Until now, Frank had never seen his father weep, but tears of joy flowed from both his parents.

"Well, we here. What we do now?" asked Virgil as he wiped away his tears.

Everyone started laughing.

"Shhh! The neighbors are still sleeping. Come on, let's grab what we can and sit down together for breakfast," Frank said around the hugs of his parents.

"Show us house, first," Virgil said. "Show us new home."

"Oh, sure, Dad. Let's go."

Frank walked everyone inside and upstairs pointing out where he'd directed the movers to put things. "I guessed at the furniture layout as they brought the stuff up the stairs, Mom, Pop. I'm sure you'll have your own ideas. Andy and I will help you move things around..."

Virgil and Anna stood and nodded silently as they looked around their new residence. Anna went into her kitchen and made approving sounds. "There is pantry I can walk into," she exclaimed. "Oh, Frank. Is wonderful!" to which Virgil added, "Okay. Now let's eat."

Seeing her kitchen, Lois chimed in, "Frank, this is so much better than the pictures you sent. It's BEAUTIFUL!"

"Glad you like it. Poke around everywhere you want. Andy, could you please begin unloading the car while I make breakfast. Full bellies will surely send everyone to their new beds."

Looking up from his breakfast, Virgil asked inquisitively, "Where garage?"

"Well, Dad, we don't need one. The locals say it doesn't rain here."

Chapter 18

Last Months of Peace

On September fourth, the U.S.S. Greer fired on a German submarine in the Atlantic that was attacking a convoy the destroyer was escorting, and the drums of war grew louder.

The Savage family quickly adjusted to their Front Street "mansion". That's what Anna dubbed it after seeing the entire house in daylight. Frank resumed his work at Consolidated while Lois located a school for Howard adjacent to Balboa Park, nearly a mile from their home. Together, she and Howard walked around the park and the San Diego Zoo to Roosevelt Elementary School. There, she enrolled him. School would start on the day after Labor Day, September 2nd, in a couple of days.

Consolidated Aircraft was among the many defense manufacturers that felt the vibrations from war drums. The U.S. government quietly increased its orders for all types of military aircraft, including for the B-24s that Consolidated was making. Frank began working ten hour days with frequent overtime. He enjoyed his job and was quickly learning the intricacies of the aircraft industry. He met often with the tool and aeronautical engineers to learn more about *why* his group was making the parts they did. He often shared these details with his ever-inquisitive son.

Howard just couldn't get enough of airplanes. He especially loved watching the constant line of military aircraft taking off and landing at nearby Lindbergh Field.

On the last Saturday in August, Consolidated Aircraft Company held a Family Day/Open House for its employees. Buffets were strategically placed throughout the sprawling campus. Supervisors and managers acted as tour guides. Frank brought his whole family, including his parents.

Howard was totally mesmerized by the huge airplane assemblies and delighted in crawling around in the display models as well as the finished bomber set aside for just such purposes. He peppered the guide with so many questions that he asked for relief to personally take Howard around and explain what every part on the plane did to help it fly.

"What's your name, boy?"

"Howard Savage, sir. My daddy's a master machinist here. What's yours?"

"It's Basil Rankin."

"You talk kinda funny? Where are you from?"

"I'm from Dorchester, England, Howard."

"Really? How did you get from there to here?"

"Oh, I took a holiday from home and never went back. I do love it here."

"We just moved here from Cleveland. Ever heard of it?"

"As a matter of fact, I have. One of my assemblers is from there."

"What's this airplane called? Don't all airplanes have a kinda pet name?"

"They do, and this one is the *Liberator*."

"It's really big."

"It's the biggest in the world. Let's have a look around inside, shall we?"

Basil walked Howard "upstream" from the completed bomber, explaining how each sub-assembly was built and how they were designed to fit perfectly together at final assembly. After an hour, Basil took Howard back to his parents, who were busy munching fried chicken. He congratulated them on raising such a curious and obviously bright son.

"Thank you. He does to us every day what he just did to you," Frank answered. "He wears me out with his endless questions. You should have heard him when we went to the shipyard for an open house. His grandpa, who works there, got the same treatment. Howard just seems to have a natural talent for complex machinery and machines. Maybe he'll be an engineer some day. Anyway, thanks for your patience. We appreciate it. It gave us a chance to grab lunch." Everyone laughed, while Basil returned to his station at final assembly.

"Daddy. That nice man let me sit in the pilot's chair! He showed me how to make the plane go up and down, and side-to-side. I could look out the window and see the, uh, a-ler-ons move. He called the control wheel the 'yoke'. Did you know that the B-24 *Liberator* has four of everything?"

"I did, son. It's a four-engine bomber, so the pilot needs to have control over each engine and even the fuel designated for each one. He can even send fuel from one gas tank to another."

"Wow. Do you think you can buy me a model kit so I can build one for my room?"

"As a matter of fact, Howard, there's a company in Cleveland that makes and sells all sorts of airplane model kits. I'll see what I can do. I built a few when I was a kid, mostly World War I biplanes."

Several days later, Frank located a Cleveland balsa wood and tissue model kit for a Hughes H-1 Racer. The advertised wing span was thirty-three inches, so the parts whould be big enough for Howard's hands to manage.

Howard was over the moon with joy when Frank brought the kit home, and together they patiently assembled the model, talking all the while about each and every part and its function.

One day as Howard returned home from school, his mother greeted him with a glass of cold lemonade. "Let's go to the patio and enjoy the cool shade while we drink our lemonade." As he stepped through the doorway, a bright, shiny object caught his eye. It was a brand new bicycle. "WOW! Is that for me?!"

"Of course it's for you," Lois exclaimed, as she grabbed Howard's lemonade glass. From behind Andy's residence walked Virgil and Anna. "Your grandfather bought it for you, Howard. Do you like it?"

"It's BEAUTIFUL! Thank you, Grandpa! Can I ride it to school?"

"That was idea," Virgil confirmed. "Get you to school and home faster. Make more time for homework. Happy you like it. You know how to ride bike?"

"Uh, I don't, but I'm gonna learn really fast." He paused. "Is it hard?"

Lois replied, "Not really. Once you find your balance and learn how to drive a straight line, it'll become second nature. Shall we give it a test spin before your daddy gets home."

It took Howard about ten minutes to get the feel and the balance while pedaling. Lois walked along side to spot for him as he gained confidence and balance and as he acquired basic maneuvering skills. Howard soon stopped wavering and started to maintain balance even when turning. "Don't turn too sharply," Lois yelled, watching him zoom around the driveway on his own. "If your pedals touch the ground, you could fall over."

Just then, Frank walked around the corner onto Front Street, and saw his son, riding his new bicycle. Howard came speeding toward him yelling that grandpa had bought him a bicycle. "Look, daddy! I can ride my new bike! Isn't it beautiful?"

"I see, Howard. I have a couple other things you're gonna need inside. Let's go in."

With the new bicycle parked in the back, Frank produced a chain and a lock, then a rucksack with shoulder straps. "What're they for?" asked the startled boy.

"The chain and lock are so you can lock your bike while in school so nobody will steal it. The rucksack is to carry your books and papers to and from school. Try it on. Let's fit it for you."

Frank took Howard outside and showed him how to lock his bike to a fence post or tree. He then produced another item, a key chain. "Here. Give me your house key and I'll add the lock key to it on this keychain. Never, ever lose your keys. Always check that you have your keys. If you lose them just once, you'll understand what I mean."

Howard kept going out before and after dinner to admire his new bike. Next morning, Howard was up, dressed and downing his breakfast in anticipation of his bicycle ride to school. With a wave to his mother, he began pedaling his way to up the street.

September oozed into October. To the Savage/Billings clan's surprise, no leaves turned color. No frosty mornings greeted them. There was no real chill in the air. In fact, the air temperature remained as warm as Cleveland's in July. People were still wearing short-sleeved shirts and shorts. Lois bought herself some sandals, as it seemed to be the footwear of choice in San Diego. People kept telling her that it would rain some-day soon. Sure.

Meanwhile, Virgil and Anna took Lois with them on restaurant hunt-ing tours. Having no idea how to begin their new business, they ate at all the restaurants along Broadway. They took notes from each place. While reading the classified ads one day, they came across a "For Sale" ad for a place along Pacific Highway south of the San Diego Bay Ferry wharf. Visiting it, they saw that it had twelve serviceable tables, as well as four booths along one wall. The kitchen, however, was a disaster. The stoves and ovens were black with burned-on grease. The pots and pans looked to be of Civil War vintage. The walk-in coolers and the large, walk-in freezer, however, were fairly new and clean. The wooden preparation tables were heavily sliced and dirty. A lingering smell of spoiled fish hovered in the air. Anna thought, *How on God's green Earth did this place not end up making people sick?*

Despite these observations, the three called the representing real estate company and asked the agent to meet them at *The Swordfish*. Mr. Aaron Darby appeared with the owners, Mr. and Mrs. Orville Muncy. Not surprisingly to Anna, there were no customers present.

Lois asked the first question: "So, why are you selling your restaurant?"

Mr. Muncy, a tired-looking, plump little man, gazed at Lois through rheumy eyes and replied, "We've been saving up and feel it's time to retire. We found a nice place up in the mountains near Julian, and we're gonna retire there. Amy and I are originally from the Cascades in Oregon near Sisters. We miss the mountain air."

"Meester Muncy," Anna asked, eager to get down to business. "How much you want for restaurant?"

"We'd like to get thirty thousand for it." As is. We don't owe anything so that plus our nest egg should get us through the rest of our lives. I'll be sixty-eight next year. Amy here's a little younger…" Amy just smiled. "We're just tired of the restaurant business. I want to read some books, drink beer and watch the deer run by."

"Please excuse, Meester Muncy," Anna asked the couple, who rose and began walking wistfully from the restaurant and out into the kitchen.

"Are you planning to make an offer, Mrs. Savage?" agent Darby asked.

"One minute, please," Anna replied. She was clearly taking charge of the situation.

She looked at Virgil. He replied to her silent question, "Mmm. Much work to get place ready for customers. Place stinks and is filthy. Take weeks just clean stoves and ovens. What you think, Lois?"

"We knew we were going to have to put in a lot of work from the beginning, but now that I see the reality, it's a pretty daunting task. We'd have to get all new cookware."

"*Da*. Cutting tables no good. Not usable now. Must clean and sand."

Lois summed up the situation. "We've got enough money in the bank to buy this place and fix it up. It will take us a month, maybe more, to start making money once we get it ready. In addition to all the cleaning, it'll cost at least a thousand dollars for new cookware, patch and re-paint the interior, change the name and get a new sign, as well as produce menus. Then we'll have to clean everything. We can do most of the work ourselves, but the materials will cost more money. And we haven't even looked at the dishware, flatware or examined the tables and chairs. We could easily find ourselves spending much more on new stuff."

Anna, satisfied that they discussed the necessary points, switched to full business mode. She'd seen how the restaurant business worked back in Trieste and when she ran her own kitchen aboard ship like her own fiefdom. "So, should we make offer, my darlings?" she said with sparkling eyes and a calculating voice.

Lois looked at the realtor with steely-eyes. "What if we offered twenty-five thousand. What do you think they'd say."

"*Da*. Yes. Meester Darby? What you say?" Virgil added.

Aaron Darby didn't hesitate. "Good restaurants are going to be needed in large numbers if the Navy keeps growing its fleet and especially if we go to war. This is a premium location, and, as you've pointed out, the owners haven't kept it up. If they accept your offer, you'll have to do some advertising, too. So, add that to your overhead costs. Don't forget, once you get the place suitable for customers, you're going to have to buy supplies and food. That will cost you more out-of-pocket cash. With that in mind, I'd offer them twenty thousand and see what they say."

Calling the Muncys back to the table, Anna resumed her leadership role. "We offer twenty thousand for everything. We pay cash. What you say?"

The Muncy's, non-plussed, looked at each other, shrugged and Mr. Muncy replied, "Make it twenty-two five and we have a deal."

Everyone shook hands. "See you all at my office at two o'clock tomorrow. That should be enough time for me to get all the papers in order. Virgil, Anna and Lois, be sure to bring the cash. Mr. Muncy, bring the deed, your account books and the restaurant keys."

Everyone shook hands again and left *The Swordfish*. Lois was the first to speak, "Well damn, Momma! Here we go on another adventure. I'm getting excited now, to get started. We gotta think of a new name and write up a menu too. I can think of a hundred things to do right away. Won't Frank and my dad be surprised when they get home tonight?!"

"*Da,*" Anna said with finality. "I born to do this. We turn grease pit into money-making business. Serve best menu in San Diego. Yes, my dear, is very exciting. But tonight we must still feed family."

That evening, Frank was shocked and pleased at the same time. "Wow! That was fast! Are you sure this will all work?"

"We *make* it work," Anna replied, "and you will help."

"Of course. Lois is fizzing around wanting to get started. Let's set up a work schedule too."

Thus *Momma's Home Cooking* came into being by consensus; the name an honorific to Anna. The cleaning went faster than expected, but the stoves and ovens required special attention with Howard assigned to cleaning the brass pulls and handles. New dishes were bought. "New" cookware was purchased from a second-hand store after a large estate sale donation. Two tables needed their legs repaired. Light bulbs were added to empty sockets and burned out ones replaced. The toilets, cracked and stained, were replaced by Frank and Virgil. Frank, Andy, Howard and Virgil all spent time on their hands and knees removing bad floor tiles and replacing them with new ones.

One of their Front Street neighbors, an artist, painted a sign for over the door and a somewhat cherubic "Momma" on the front window inviting people into the restaurant. *Momma's Home Cooking* was now ready to be called a business.

After three weeks of hard labor, the first food shipments showed up. It took a full week to get everything in place, so the grand opening of *Momma's Home Cooking* was set for Sunday, 23 November 1941, the Sunday beginning Thanksgiving week.

Lois placed an ad in the San Diego Union-Tribune announcing the grand opening. Opening week was a huge success as the word spread rapidly among both civilian residents and the Navy. They were open Thanksgiving, of course, and the line to get in stretched down the street as people waited for the turkey dinner, mashed potatoes, gravy and pumpkin pie special. Howard was tasked with taking trays of small perogies to the waiting customers along the street. The little "pigs in a blanket" proved a huge hit, making waiting in line a pleasure while having a nine year-old boy serve them. That one day, spanning almost twelve hours, produced enough revenue to nearly cover the cost of all the ancillary equipment the Savage/Billings enterprise had spent in preparation.

At ten o'clock that evening, the exhausted family washed the last dishes, pots and pans. Howard, ever the energy dynamo, happily wiped and put away the plates and flatware, while Frank, Andy and Virgil wrapped sets of tableware in napkins for the next day.

And the Thanksgiving success just kept going. *Momma's Home Cooking* suddenly became the go-to eatery along the eastern shore of San Diego Bay. People living on Coronado Island ferried over just to taste the multi-ethnic foods prepared fresh every day. The family rotated duties for lunch and dinner. and after that first, busy week, they realized they would have to take a day off each week to perform management tasks and just put their feet up. They chose Monday, 8 December 1941, as their first day of rest.

Chapter 19

The Day of Infamy

Three factors kept the attack on Pearl Harbor and Hawaii from being the success upon which the Japanese military was counting: First, the American aircraft carriers were not in the harbor. Second, the Japanese bombers neglected the huge fuel oil farm adjacent to the Pearl Harbor anchorage. Third, since it was Sunday, many of the service personnel were not on board their ships or on their bases. Had these targets been attacked, the outcome of the Pacific war might have been different.

The United States of America had been attacked and everything, from that moment on, changed. It ultimately presaged the discovery and weaponizing of the power of the universe. Humans had just created the means for their own extinction...and the fear that someone would do it on purpose.

Sunday morning 7 December 1941 began in San Diego with a blazing red rising sun casting a blood-red sheen on the windows of all the Front Street homes facing it.

At 6:35 A.M., Pacific Standard Time, Frank Savage rolled out of bed, slipped on his robe, visited the bathroom, retrieved the morning paper from the front porch and set about making the first pot of coffee for the day. Lois just groaned and rolled over.

At just after seven o'clock, Howard wandered sleepily into the kitchen and greeted his dad who had just started the percolator. "Good mornin',

Sport. Pour us some orange juice, will ya?"

"Good morning, daddy. Sure. Juice comin' up."

Three time zones to the west, the Japanese battle fleet of six aircraft carriers and their escorts plunged through rough seas, heading south. The air crews feverishly fueled and armed the bombers, torpedo planes and fighters even as wind and spray swept across the flight decks. The pilots had been roused from their bunks and made themselves ready for combat.

Lois Savage made her way to the kitchen at 7:45 A.M. and poured herself a cup of the rich, black coffee that Frank loved to make. He was on the back patio with Howard reading the paper. He finished the front section and sought out the sports page. Howard was giggling over the comics. Lois looked at the front section headlines. More war news from Europe. The Luftwaffe was still bombing the hell out of England. Wolf packs of submarines were sinking tens of thousands of tons of shipping. Fruitless discussions with the Japanese embassy yielded nothing. The military draft increased its numbers. More economic sanctions against Japan for their invasions of Manchuria and China. Good news seemed in short supply, and the world seemed to be careening toward a terrible abyss.

What started all this mayhem? Why are people so eager to kill each other? What did the Jews ever do to the German people that caused so much hate? Why did Germany invade Poland, then the Soviet Union? What was so goddamned important to the well-being of the German people that their military had to go and kill innocent Poles and Russians? Have we gone mad as a species, or is this how we've always been?

At 9:00 A.M. San Diego time, Frank turned on the radio to listen to the news. The item that caught everyone's ear announced that Hawaii and the Philippines had been put on full war alert footings *last* week. That news had only now leaked out.

In the waters 230 miles north of Pearl Harbor, the six aircraft carriers of the Japanese Navy turned east into the wind and a very heavy sea that caused the decks to pitch up to fifteen degrees, barely safe enough to launch their planes. But launch they did without a single mishap. The cheering deck crews watched the exhaust port flames from the fighters, the bombers and finally the torpedo planes as they rolled down the carrier decks and lifted into the air. After forming up, the airborne armada headed south. Their planning was impeccable and their luck at not being detected held. The aircraft set their radios to Honolulu radio stations and, with their direction finders, flew a straight line to their respective targets.

At 10:00 A.M. San Diego time, Anna came downstairs to collect the three Savages to accompany her to the restaurant to get ready for the Sunday lunch customers. Virgil was already there, letting the baker bring in the freshly-baked breads, rolls and donuts; the latter reserved for the Savage family. As everyone took to their duties, Frank turned on the restaurant's radio to fill the room with music. It made preparing for lunch much more pleasant for everyone. Anna happily hummed along.

Howard set the tables with freshly filled salt and pepper shakers, sugar bowls and mustard and ketchup bottles. Frank was busy slicing the leftover turkey into sandwich pieces; they were going to serve open-faced turkey sandwiches with Anna's delicious gravy. The burrito mix was bubbling happily and Anna was stacking the tortillas for the Mexican side of the menu. She'd become a master tortilla maker and took great pride in making them very thin.

At one minute before 8:00 A.M. Hawaii time, the first bombs fell on airfields, barracks and the ships anchored in Pearl Harbor. The attack caught everyone there by surprise and chaos ensued. The attacks lasted nearly two hours. Ships were sunk, planes destroyed and many military and civilian personnel killed or maimed. The Japanese military, deeming the attack a success, steamed back to Japan at flank speed.

Virgil opened the front door at 11:30 A.M. and flipped the CLOSED sign on the glass door to OPEN. Customers who'd been waiting, entered. Howard took pride in greeting and seating everyone. It was a nice touch for a family restaurant to have a nine year-old boy, big for his age, seat them with a smile and a menu.

The six tables and three booths were soon filled with diners, planning to enjoy their midday meals. The music was suddenly interrupted by a harried-voice announcing the attack on Pearl Harbor. The announcer, breathless, re-read scant details intercepted from Hawaii radio broadcasts and telephone calls to the mainland. The news struck the entire restaurant like a thunderbolt. Forks dropped on plates. Shocked expressions appeared on everyone's face.

Three of the diners threw money on their tables and dashed out the door. One customer, a Navy commander, asked to use the restaurant's phone. Returning to his table, he paid his bill and, with his officer companion, dashed out the door. The local radio announcer started warning every American citizen to be alert for unknown aircraft and that from this moment on, wartime blackout rules would apply.

All military leaves were cancelled and all personnel were ordered to report to their duty stations immediately. The National Guard was activated and ordered to deploy to the beaches, anticipating invasion. A San Diego policeman walked into *Momma's* and ordered the Savages to drape their windows as soon as possible. The entire Savage family was in shock. Virgil was the first to recover enough to see that their lives would quickly change and their business boom.

"Paint inside of windows. Is cheaper than curtains. Tomorrow, order more dry goods. Buy meat. Fill cooler and freezer. Must get ahead of hoarding and rationing. Shortages for everything coming."

"I have to report to work," Frank stated haltingly, still in a daze. "Lois, you and the family will have to prepare the restaurant and our house for what's to come."

Anna volunteered to take charge of buying foodstuffs for the business and home. Howard was instructed that he would go to school tomorrow, but would help when he finished his studies.

The Savages closed the restaurant early and went home for a good night's rest. Tomorrow would be a very different Monday than any they'd ever experienced.

This Day of Infamy brought the entire family closer together than ever before. *We are at war! We have to win! There is no other option!*

Chapter 20

"Whole Family Must Fight!"

The general mood in the Savage family was one of determined resignation. "It looks like everyone will have very few days off for the foreseeable future," Frank said, sitting at dinner that night. Everyone agreed.

Moments of silence acted as much-needed insulators, allowing everyone to deal with their own thoughts. The Savages, however, shared one overriding fact: This day represented the most direct threat to their security and way of life they'd ever known. As a group, they suddenly understood the gnawing beast of fear and terror gripping the hearts and guts of people throughout Europe and Asia. As the shadows lengthened, gloom seemed to grow with them.

Howard, aware of the gravity of the situation, reacted to the solemnity by asking simply, "What can I do to help?"

"You gotta keep goin' to school, Howard," Frank said. "Your education is gonna be even more important in the comin' years. We expect you to maintain high grades, and I know you want to pitch in around the restaurant. We're all gonna be very busy, but we'll still find a little time for a game of catch now and then."

Virgil Savage, looking like a storm cloud shooting lightning bolts, said with the kind of finality only he could generate: "Whole family must fight! Our people go to war to face enemy. Many be killed. We all Americans. Must give soldiers every support. Their pain, our pain. Their sacrifices, our sacrifices. No complaining. No wanting day off! We in war now, and we must FIGHT! Soldiers not have days off. I speak for everyone here, yes?

"Yes, Pop. Lois?"

"Of course. We have to save our country for Howard and everyone else."

Andy, still looking stunned, finally agreed. "Sure thing, Virgil. Stickin' together is what we do best, and we must all do everything we can. I'm gonna go eat and get to bed. Tomorrow is gonna be one hell-of-a-day at the shipyard!" Andy kissed his daughter, hugged his grandson, shook Virgil's and Frank's hands and gave Anna a deeply affectionate hug."

This scene was repeated everywhere across the country that evening. Roosevelt asked Congress to declare war on the Empire of Japan the next day calling December Seventh, 1941, the Day of Infamy.

Chapter 21

Putting in the Time

On 11 December 1941, Germany declared war on the United States of America as part of their agreement of mutual "defense" with Japan and Italy forming an Axis of tyranny. Thus the Second World War began as a global event. It would last until September, 1945. Before it was over, 75 million would perish. In 1945, the last year of the war, more deaths would occur than the three previous years combined.

The war's effects on the west coast of the United States included fears of a Japanese attack or invasion, and determination to work to do whatever it took to win the war. The port and naval base of San Diego exploded with ships of all sorts bringing supplies, food, munitions and other necessities to the Pacific Fleet, and to the support businesses serving the Navy. Overnight, the population nearly doubled.

Momma's Home Cooking extended its hours and was packed most of the time. Anna hired additional waitresses and cooks to run the night shifts, while she and Virgil took turns supervising operations in twelve-hour segments. Lois kept the home hearth going, pitching in with Frank, Howard and Andy at the restaurant whenever they could. Frank and Andy began working twelve hour shifts for six and a half days a week, depending on scheduling demands. Consolidated was tasked with turning out a fully operational B-24 every 24 hours. Consolidated couldn't hire assemblers and support personnel fast enough. Once Anna and Virgil had everything in order at the restaurant, Lois hired on at Consolidated and became one of the famous "Rosie the Riveter" assemblers.

Being photogenic, LIFE magazine photographers singled her out during morale tours of west coast factories. Howard and Virgil teased her mercilessly about her picture appearing in magazines. The San Diego Union-Tribune interviewed her in an article about how war workers were supporting the effort.

On his tenth birthday in March 1942, there was barely time to gulp down cake and ice cream with his family, before everyone went to bed. Virgil returned to the restaurant for his night shift. Howard recognized and accepted the situation where celebrations took second place to more important matters. It was a far more mature response than his years would suggest. At home after school, he washed and dried the breakfast dishes, and put them away. His experience at the restaurant taught him to start dinners to the point where all Lois had to do was turn on the stove or oven. After dinner, he pitched in with the dishes, drying and putting them away. He helped Lois prepare everyone's next day's lunches. The sandwich-making assembly line had all the sandwiches made, wrapped and in lunch boxes in twenty minutes.

Rationing of essentials like gasoline and meat were particularly onerous hardships for everyone. Frank received "A" ration stickers for gasoline, and he carefully hoarded them whenever possible. He and Lois could walk to their jobs, but Virgil and Anna had to drive to the restaurant. The two quickly learned the trick of taking the car out of gear driving downhill, coasting to save gas. Driving home, they took streets with the shallowest hills.

Anna was the genius at stretching the meat rations for the restaurant. Hamburger went a long way under the supervision of Anna Savage—having learned to stretch meager commodities as a peasant and ship's cook years ago. Powdered eggs eventually replaced the real thing, but with the right spices and skills, became more than just edible. Few restaurant customers complained about the short rations. Those who did complain were often shouted down with comments like: *"Don't you know there's a war on?"*

Frank fitted a wire basket onto Howard's bicycle handlebars as well as two across the back fender acting as saddle bags. The city of San Diego regularly conducted drives for excess cookware and scrap metal to build tanks, planes, rifles and ammunition. Howard peddled around the neighborhood asking for anything the residents could part with for the drive, always astonished at how much he collected. He often had to walk the overloaded bike for blocks until he came to the offload station in Balboa Park.

In April, 1942, an obscure Lt. Colonel devised a plan to launch B-25 Mitchell bombers from an aircraft carrier near enough to Japan to give them a taste of what being attacked felt like. The raid inflicted minor damage in Japan, but it raised morale in the United States significantly. *We're fighting back!*

It also precipitated the plan by the Japanese to take Midway Island, just 1,200 miles west of Hawaii. Using the principle of calculated risk, Admiral Raymond Spruance led a task force of the three operational air-craft carriers left in the Pacific fleet to win that battle, sinking four Ja-panese carriers in the process. In addition to the four, front-line carriers, dozens of Japan's most experienced pilots were killed. It was a devastat-ing defeat for Japan's navy, and they never ventured further east the rest of the war.

In August, 1942, American Marines invaded Japanese held islands in the Solomon chain near the Coral Sea. This was America's first major pushback against Japan's drive toward Australia. This operation was also the first real combat for U.S. forces against a determined and experienced foe since World War I. It took until February, 1943 for the battle to be won, but at the cost of many lives on both sides.

On one bright, sunny, but cool afternoon in February, Howard Savage, riding his bicycle home from school, noticed a dark blue sedan parked in front of the next door neighbor's house. Two smartly dressed Marines exited the car, the driver holding their rear door for them. The two U.S. Marine officers were dressed in formal dress blues, white hats and gold braid. They walked solemnly up to the front door and rang the doorbell. Howard stopped, captivated by the scene.

What he heard next chilled him to his bones. Mrs. Peabody opened the door, paused and let out a long sobbing wail. She then collapsed into the two men's arms. Howard, unsure about what just happened, started to cry in sympathy. He dashed inside, running into his mother's arms. Lois, having just come home from her shift at Consolidated, asked, "What's the matter, Howard? Are you hurt?"

"No. Mrs. Peabody screamed and cried when two Marines came to her door. It made me cry too. What happened? Why was she crying? She's always so nice and friendly."

"Oh dear. Howard, look at me." Lois bent low and held him by the shoulders.

"I think maybe she just learned that her son was killed in the war. The military sends uniformed officers to inform the family when that happens. I'm going to go over there and help console her. I'm afraid her blue star will turn to gold now. Okay. Let me go see Mrs. Peabody."

Lois returned a half hour later. Howard immediately joined her in the kitchen. His mother's eyes were red from crying. She stood still, shaking her head sadly.

"What's wrong, mommy?"

"I was right, honey. Her son Tommy was killed on some godforsaken place called Guadalcanal. He was a Marine lieutenant killed in combat. Poor Margaret is devastated. I held her while she cried. I didn't know it, but she's the daughter of a career Navy commander who is at sea on a cruiser somewhere. Her husband is an engineer at Ryan. She just got off the phone from calling him when I came over. But she's strong. She knew this could happen. We're at war and our fighting men are at risk. She'll recover, but her heart will always bear the weight of her loss."

Howard stared at his mother as she recounted the details.

"Sorry, baby. I just had to talk about it. Thanks for listening. Now, give me a hug and go back to your homework."

Frank had left for the night shift just before Howard came home. Lois wrote him a long note about the Peabody episode that he'd find when he got home after midnight.

The war years in San Diego, California, were tumultuous, exciting, busy and productive. After initial fears of a Japanese attack waned, people went about their business with firm resolve. The American government sadly, hypocritically rounded up the Japanese-Americans along the west coast, citizens included, and sent them to heavily guarded concentration camps similar to what the Germans were doing with European Jews. Their businesses and possessions were impounded and confiscated. War paranoia and inherent racism helped create this most egregious episode on American history.

The remarkable irony from this action was the creation of the 442nd Infantry Division primarily consisting of Japanese-American troops. The "Go For Broke" division became the most highly decorated unit in the United States Army during this war. One of its soldiers, Daniel Inoue, was awarded the Medal of Honor for valor. To conclude the irony, he eventually became a United States Senator from the great state of

Hawaii.

Frank Savage worked months between days off. B-24 *Liberator* bombers were rolling out of the factory on Pacific Highway. Lois Savage worked there almost as much as Frank, but was allowed a limited work week of forty hours because of their school-age child, the grandson of Virgil and Anna Savage.

Her "Rosie the Riveter" persona followed her everywhere as did her picture from LIFE with her sleeve rolled up, in abstract form, ending up on posters across the nation. The magazine purposefully omitted her name and where she worked, but people at Consolidated and at the restaurant recognized her. When she worked at *Momma's Home Cooking*, customers greeted her as if they'd known her all their lives and encouraged her to keep up the war effort. She was often asked for autographs, but she would just smile, politely decline, say, "Thank you," and keep working.

Andy Billings worked equally long hours at National Iron Works wiring Navy ships. Everyone around town, it seemed, worked overtime. Movie houses stayed open twenty-four hours so shift workers could snatch some entertainment to lighten their fatigue. The bars and restaurants stayed open long past their peacetime hours for the same reason. The price the war effort exacted from American families was huge. Excessive alcohol consumption injured many, destroyed many marriages and caused public displays of violence and mayhem. Many citizens suffered stress-related emotional breakdowns. Some would later say that America got off easy from the horrors of war, but that was not true. The non-combat war environment held its own unique horrors, leading some authors to later write of the citizens looking like "walking dead."

Yet, with all the difficulties, the broken homes and marriages, the fatigue and long hours, enough people stayed on the job doing excellent work. Early on, greedy corporations took outrageous profits from government contracts while producing poor quality goods. It took a Senate commission led by Harry S. Truman of Missouri to sort out the corruption and assure the fighting men and women that they received the best quality American industry could produce.

And yet...In spite of the war and the necessities it asked of the home front, racism in aircraft factories, shipbuilding facilities and elsewhere remained in full throat.

Frank and Lois Savage, with the help of Andy, Virgil and Anna, tried to make the lessons in bigotry and racial animus known to their son and grandson with the hopes that he would grow up to be a *whole* citizen who put kindness, cooperation and respect ahead of fear, ignorance and hate. Howard grasped their ideas and lectures and even commented about the people at school who were not of European ancestry. He said that some of his teachers and fellow students had Spanish names and noted that *their* ancestors came to America from Mexico. "Mommy, I don't see anything wrong with them. Why do people hate people of different colors?"

"They hate because that's what they were taught by their parents, family, friends and even some of their churches. You're being raised differently. Remember, your Grandpa and Grandma came here from a foreign country too, not able to speak English. They were shunned and abused for years. Why? Because some people saw these newcomers as threats to themselves. They feared the foreign languages, the foreign food and the foreign customs. It took many years for your grandparents to overcome these bad behaviors in others. Ask them about it sometime.

"I was lucky. My parents were very accepting and understanding of the newcomers. My dad worked with many of them from all different countries in Europe and Asia, as well as with our colored people in

Cleveland. They worked hard and performed very well. My dad, your Grandpa Andy, learned to respect those people and passed that along to me. They're Americans too. Everybody's blood is red. The color of their skin or the language they speak at home shouldn't make somebody afraid. Now we're ALL in this war and we ALL have to work together to defeat the really bad people causing it. Do you see?"

"Yes, mommy. I don't like to be afraid or angry. Is that what hate is; the kind you're talking about?"

"Exactly. It's a waste of energy! Now, don't you have homework to do?"

Chapter 22

1945: A History Lesson for Mankind

The world war raged on. Hitler avoided an assassination attempt and took charge of all military maneuvers and directives, creating chaos in Wehrmacht command. Many senior officers no longer obeyed his directives, instead tried to save their men from total slaughter.

Soviet prisoners joined the other "undesirables." They were used as slave labor to keep the German war machine functioning. "Arbeit Macht Frei,"—literally "work makes one free"—took on a new meaning, where the only way to be free was to die. In paradoxical manner, this became the new slogan of Nazi Germany, applying to everyone.

The fighting in Europe officially ended in May *1945.*

On the other side of the world, the Japanese military totally embraced the Bushido warrior code and literally fought to the death for every inch of every island. Casualties soared on both sides. Surrender was seen as a disgrace and was, therefore, not an option.

On a cold, rainy July morning near Alamogordo, New Mexico, an intensely bright flash of light was seen for miles around, signaling mankind's entry into the Atomic Age. In the pre-dawn hours of 6 August, 1945, three B-29 Superfortresses took off from Tinian atoll in the Marianas chain. Two were camera planes. They flew due north to the port city of Hiroshima, Japan, dropping the first atomic bomb, nicknamed "Little Boy". On 8 August, Nagasaki was the target for "Fat Man", the second atomic bomb. Together, these two weapons indiscriminately killed over a quarter million military and civilian personnel. These two attacks precipitated the surrender by the Japanese government to the allies and thus ended World War II.

In San Diego, the military mecca of the west coast, the VE celebrations were muted. *Momma's Home Cooking* gave free lunches to all military personnel in uniform. And there was dancing in the streets. At one point, Virgil Savage had to rescue his grandson from being trampled by hoards of revelers.

"Howard, war not over yet."

"But, Grandpa, everyone is having so much fun. Why can't I?"

"When war over, have fun. You big boy, but not ready for, uh, kind of fun these people having." Virgil glanced outside the restaurant window just in time to see a sailor run his hand up the dress of a pretty lady as they waited in line and danced to music blaring from a loudspeaker somewhere. Turning to Howard he concluded, "Not yet. Not yet."

The news of the atomic bomb stunned the Savage family. Frank and Andy had heard vague rumors about an American "super weapon," but had no idea of its destructive power. When photos and articles began appearing in the papers and magazines a sense of foreboding swept over the family, accompanied by a weird kind of joy that at last the United States had the biggest stick in the fight. There was no mention of the destruction or numbers of lives lost, just pictures showing the giant mushroom clouds.

On the other hand, in September, V-J day triggered unconstrained joy and parties throughout San Diego. Fireworks, tugboat sprays, horns honking, music blaring and dancing in the streets were the order of the day. *Momma's Home Cooking* closed and the Savage family joined in the revelry on Pacific Highway. Auto traffic stopped while military personnel stationed around town left their offices, desks and billets to join in the partying.

Howard walked up Broadway watching the parties unfold, and found himself outside a club where men and women dancing to big band music poured in and out. He stood there looking in wonder at everyone's expression of joy until a tall, very pretty dark-haired woman took him by the hand and started dancing with him. Howard was growing quickly, and had passed five feet nine inches. The woman, in heels, was about an inch taller than him, and he was just learning to dance, but this woman knew exactly what to do with her handsome young partner, whipping him around and crushing him into her ample bosom.

Howard stared into her brown eyes that joyously stared back. Her lips were on the full side and covered with red lipstick. "How ya doin', big boy? So ya like to dance! Well, I'm Rita. What's your name?"

"Howard. Howard Savage."

"Well, Howard Savage, you wanna be my boyfriend for today? I'm tired of sailors. All they want to do is get their hands up my skirt. Are you a good boy? You treat your women good?"

"Sure. I've never been somebody's boyfriend, but I like dancing with you. Where are you from, Rita?"

"Iowa. Came here for a job just before the war broke out. Small town girl…at least I was back then. C'mon, let's grab a free drink."

Rita Collins took Howard's hand and dragged him into the club, ordering a whiskey and soda for herself. "Wadd'll ya have, Howard? You look kinda young to for booze."

"Yeah. I'll have a ginger ale."

"Good choice," Rita said, smiling. "So wadda ya do here in San Diego, Howard?" She asked leading him to a booth.

"I'm in eighth grade, and I work in the family restaurant a couple blocks from here."

"Yeah? What's it called?"

"*Momma's Home Cooking.* You should come visit. Great food. If I'm on duty, I'll give you the best seat. Bring your boyfriend."

"Oh, honey, I don't have a boyfriend. I just have lots of friends. Hey, I think I may have eaten at your place once. There was this short, strong-lookin' woman working the kitchen and this tall, pretty lady came out to take my order."

"The cook was my grandma, and the waitress was my mom," Howard offered. "We take turns doing all the jobs. When I'm not sitting people, handing out menus or taking orders, I wash dishes and help in the kitchen. Since the war started, we've been working a lot of hours. We had to hire more help to spell us when we opened for twenty-four hour service. Boy, sailors sure are hungry and loud."

"Honey, you have no idea. You're sweet. Do you like girls, Howard?"

"Oh sure. My teachers and I get along great, and a couple girls at school keep asking me to walk them home. Stuff like that. I'm so busy with schoolwork and the restaurant that I haven't thought about having a girlfriend.

"Well, I wanna be your girlfriend today. Is that okay?"

"Okay. Sure. You seem nice, too. I like dancing with you. Where did you learn to dance like that?"

"Around here. I work at this club, and dancin' with lonely sailors pays the rent. They buy me drinks and things. They have to pay a little to the club for the dances, then the club pays me. I make enough to pay my bills. I try to make them like me so they'll leave a nice tip, know what I mean?"

"Uh, no, not really. How do you make them like you?"

Rita leaned over and kissed Howard full on the mouth. "Like that. Did you like that?"

"Oh. Uh. I've never been kissed like that. Is that how sailors kiss? I've seen kissing in the movies, but you're my first real grown-up kiss."

"Yes...sort of. Don't worry, Howard, I won't eat you. You're a sweet boy, and I'm enjoying being with you and away from all the grabby sailors, ya know?"

"I don't know, because I've never been grabbed by a sailor."

Rita laughed, and gave him a hug. He could smell her perfume and body.

"Finish your ginger ale and take me back outside for some more dancin'."

After another energetic jitterbug, Rita stopped to catch her breath and turned to Howard, "You're a very nice boy, Howard. I've enjoyed meetin' and dancin' with you. Now, you better go back to your restaurant before somebody misses you."

"Oh, we've closed for the day while all the celebrating is going on. Thanks for teaching me to dance. You're a nice lady. Come to the restaurant some time when I'm working and we can chat more. Now that the war's over, business should slow down and I'll have more time."

"Sure, Howard. Maybe I'll come and ask for a job. I've waited tables before. Piece o' cake." Rita left him with a big smile, tapped the tip of his nose lightly, and walked unsteadily back to the club.

Thus ended Howard Savage's unforgettable V-J day celebration. For him, Rita Collins was his "girlfriend" and his adulthood had just begun.

But 1945 still had three months to go, and America began welcoming home its returning heroes, its shattered survivors and those lost souls who had nowhere to go once they stepped off the ships. Many of them stayed in San Diego. It was a beautiful city. The weather was great, and it seemed that jobs awaited for a discharged sailor or Marine. Except that there *weren't* that many opportunities. A few found employment in the skills they were taught, but most had to take menial jobs. The gap between the jobs that the ex-enlisted and ex-officers could find was huge. Most officers, being college educated, stepped into white collar jobs. Smart enlisted personnel used the new GI Bill to go to college or trade school.

The last quarter of 1945 was tumultuous, but peaceful...for the most part. Dark-skinned men returning from war found their station in American society hadn't changed. Prejudice and bigotry often transcended their service to their country. Medals no longer mattered. Men of color who had fought bravely for a country that was based on the premise that all men are equal and was the land of the free, were faced once more with hypocrisy. In fact, many soldiers of color serving in Europe found girlfriends and wives in male-decimated Europe and stayed.

World War I, The War to End All Wars, simply never ended. World War II would be quickly replaced with other wars between nations and political entities. Howard Savage, in 1945, was about to enter into a new kind of war resulting in decades of tension, fear and, yes, accomplishments beyond imagination.

PART IV
HOWARD

Chapter 23

Growing up

His bicycle quickly became Howard Savage's closest ally. It liberated him to tour the city and its environs. One day during the summer of 1946 he rode all the way to Ocean Beach, a sleepy part of town on the western slope of the Point Loma peninsula. Locking his bike, he splashed in the surf that cloudy June morning. Since the war ended, traffic had greatly diminished, so he pedaled happily along Harbor Drive. Across the bay, the aircraft carrier U.S.S. Bunker Hill loomed from its berth on North Island, while the insular town of Coronado nestled quietly against the naval air base that still flew missions from its airfield.

It's neat to just be here all by myself without anyone knowing me. The waves just keep rolling in, and the time between them seems constant But sometimes there's a lull. Why? How do the pelicans manage to fly so close to the water without catching a wingtip? And look! A dolphin is riding a breaking wave. Do they do it for fun, or are there fish in the waves they're trying to catch? Why is it always cloudy along the beach in June? Someone said deserts heat up and the hot air rises, drawing in the cooler, wetter sea air. I wonder how that works. Why is hot air lighter than cold air? "Man, I gotta start learning all this stuff. *My folks are good at explaining things, but they're not teachers. There must be books that answer my questions.*

As he had in the past, he rode along the fence separating Lindbergh

Field runway from Pacific Highway and Harbor Drive. He remembered standing there for hours watching planes land and take off. The B-24s were massive and loud, but many other plane types used that airport including, of course, the commercial versions of DC-3s, DC-2s, the new DC-6s as well as a host of smaller aircraft.

How do pilots know when to cut their engines? How often does their landing gear break? What's it like to go on a real bombing mission? Or even take a ride in a DC-3? Dad said he really enjoyed flying. I really love airplanes. Why do some planes have two wings instead of just one? Man, I wanna learn this stuff!

Of his junior, then high school science classes, Howard liked chemistry and physics the most. These seemed to best help him understand how things worked. One day in his junior year, his science teacher showed his class a film about the V-2 rockets that Germany had built during the war. The narrator said they could achieve speeds of several thousand miles per hour and fly into space. *WOW!* This started him reading everything he could about rockets, engine design and aeronautics. Much of it was mysterious because he lacked the mathematical background to fully grasp all of it. That would soon change.

At sixteen, Howard Savage began filling out, morphing from a gangly kid with black hair, blue eyes and a crooked smile into a good looking, well-built, six-foot tall young man. He soon discovered and delighted in lifting his mother off her feet causing her to squeal. He still worked at the restaurant before and after school and during summers, but made time to play baseball with the Hoover High School team.

Since he was tall and interested in baseball, the coach positioned him at first base where he became known as a glove man, fielding countless errant throws from the infield. His hand-eye coordination wasn't limited to glove work. He could HIT.

On a winter's day, while Howard practiced infield drills, the coach yelled at him to come and meet someone. The coach was chatting with a handsome, tall, dark-haired man dressed in a casual suit. "Howard, I'd like you to meet Ted Williams."

For one of the rare times in his life, Howard was speechless. "Hi, Mr. Williams," he eventually said. "I'm Howard Savage. Nice to meetcha."

"Same here, kid. Coach tells me you can hit a little. I watched ya, and you gotta natural swing. My best advice is to develop bat speed, so you don't want a heavy bat. I like your power. You're not gonna see many sharp-breaking curve balls in high school, but if you go up the ladder, pitch selection will become more important. And always look for your pitch until you get two strikes. Then, protect the plate until you get one to drive. Maybe I'll see you around."

"Thanks for the tips, Mr. Williams. Hope you do good next season."

They shook hands and as Williams walked away, Howard couldn't erase the stars in his eyes, and felt giddy at having personally met one of the greatest hitters of all time. *Wait until my folks hear about this!*

Chapter 24

Rescuing Rita

By October 1945, the celebrations had ceased, and the tens of thousands of ex-sailors and Marines had finally dispersed to their homes. San Diego Bay was less populated with ships and businesses were noticing a downturn in customer traffic. One such business, The *Tin Can Dance Club*, started laying off waitresses and dance solicitors. On October tenth, Rita Collins found herself unemployed.

Feeling gut punched at being summarily removed from her main source of income, Rita wandered along Pacific Highway. Staring at the ships and ferries in the bay. It wasn't that she'd loved her job that much - she actually despised the tawdriness of the place, the stink of cigarette smoke and constantly getting felt up by drunken boy sailors. She'd always seen herself as a "good girl," not a woman of the night, turning tricks in the alley like so many of the *Tin Can* girls did. Her love life, she rued, was a complete zero. Most of the men couldn't hold a conversation with her for two minutes without staring at her chest. Being smart and having interests seemed off-putting to the men she met. In fact, she read everything she could get her hands on and spent her free hours in the library near her rooming house. Rita wrote a letter a week to her siblings, but answers soon dwindled and she lost interest in writing, receiving no news from home. Sadness began to stretch into most of her days, She had to put on a "face" for the boys at the club, but the anchor of loneliness weighed heavily on her feelings.

Well, here I am on my own just like I wanted. What was I expecting? Prince Charming on a white horse? I've gotten by on good looks, but now the war is over and the sailor boys have gone back to their mommas and girlfriends. The Tin Can Club wasn't for officers, so I didn't meet any eligible, educated men. I guess being dumped by the club isn't such a bad thing. This has gotta be a sign for me to get off my cute ass and do something worthwhile.

The club was kind enough to pay her $100 severance, but her decent savings would dwindle quickly if she waited for unemployment insurance. Grinding her cigarette under her heel, she recalled that smoking was a habit she'd picked up at the club because the sailors would often offer her a smoke. Now she had a pack-a-day habit and knew she had to quit. She couldn't afford to feed this worthless habit anymore.

After gazing awhile at the waters of San Diego Bay, she turned and found herself looking at a painting of a chubby-looking woman on a big, glass window: *Momma's Home Cooking* seemed to beckon her toward its friendly doors.

It was 4:30 in the afternoon and the dinner crowd hadn't started arriving. As she walked through the front door, the bell tinkled her presence, and standing there was her "boyfriend" from V-J Day welcoming her with a smile and a menu.

"Hi, Rita! Nice to see you again!" Howard said enthusiastically. "Let me show you to a our best booth."

"Just a coffee, honey. I lost my job today and can't afford a dinner."

"Really? What happened?" Howard asked as he seated her.

"Well, the sailor business dried up and the club couldn't keep us all on the payroll. So, they had to let some of us go. I think who stayed had a lot to do with how the girls treated the boss, if you know what I mean."

"Uh. No, I can't say I know what you mean, but it sounds pretty bad. No worries, Rita. What'll ya have? I get to give a few complimentary meals to friends, so you're my dinner guest tonight. The burritos are especially good. I even helped make them."

Howard's bright, shining smile touched Rita's heart, and she smiled back, her eyes glistening. "Why thank you, Howard. You don't even know me, and here you are buying me dinner. To what do I owe this pleasure?"

"Well, I've never forgotten how nice you treated me that day in the street. I'm older now. I'll be fourteen in March, but you treated me like a man back then, and buying you dinner is the least I can do for you." With that, he spun on his heel, and fetched Rita a cup of coffee and a glass of ice water. "One burrito dinner coming up."

Rita sat back and slowly took in the restaurant. It was spotless and with only a few customers, quiet and peaceful. A radio played softly in the background, and she could see who she presumed was Howard's mother working in the kitchen next to a shorter, stouter, older woman, both preparing for the coming diner surge.

Delivering her burrito dinner, Howard ventured, "Can I get you a beer, or something else to drink?"

"No, thanks, honey. This is fine. You've been very kind."

After a brief pause, Howard offered, "Oh! I talked to my mom and grandma just now. Two evening hour waitresses quit yesterday . We're pretty busy even with the war ending, so it's really hard for just the family to keep this place humming. Have you ever waitressed in a family restaurant? I remember you telling me you had some experience."

"Yes, I have. Before I came to San Diego, I worked at a local cafe in my small, Iowa town. Made good tips, too, at least for the area with the depression hurting every farmer around. Before my last job, I worked at

Rosie's Cafe up Broadway."

"Great. Sit tight," Howard announced, beaming.

He returned with an application and pen. "If you like, fill this out and give it to me before you leave. Sorry I can't sit and chat, but I gotta get ready for the evening crowd." He smiled at Rita and returned to the door to seat some incoming customers.

Maybe this is my lucky day. I wonder what it would be like working for this family?

Rita finished her dinner—*the kid's right. This stuff is great!*— and filled out the application. Howard, noticing her finishing the meal, came by to bus her dishes. He took the completed application too. "I'll be right back."

"I talked to my mom and grandma about you, and showed them your application. Stick around. They want to talk to you when they get a break. More coffee?"

"Thanks, Howard. Sure, I'll have another cup. I have nowhere else I've gotta be."

After the first group of diners had placed their orders, Howard waved Rita back toward the office, where he introduced her to his mother and grandma. After handshakes and smiles, he dashed back out to the restaurant to make sure everything was going smoothly.

"Miss Jurita Collins from Coon Rapids, Iowa. Why you come to San Diego?" asked Anna, clearly the one who would direct the interview.

"I got tired of being around sad farmers. The depression hit our area hard, and a lot of people were starving. I saved up my tip money and the fifty cents per hour the cafe paid me until I had enough for a bus ticket and headed west. The bus stopped here. The buildup was happening, so I got a job at Rosie's Cafe until the owner died. Then I worked the USO on Pacific Highway for a couple months. I ended up dancing at the *Tin*

Can up the street to pay the bills. That's about it. I had just turned twenty-one without any prospects or money for me to go to college. I was lucky to have had the waitressing job in Iowa, but felt the call to travel. Guess I've an independence streak. And, well, here I am."

"*Da*, Jurita," said Anna. "Husband and I come to America from Ukraine. All on our own. And here we are." The three women laughed lightly together.

"Please call me Rita." She said, flashing her best smile at Anna and Lois, who immediately smiled back.

"Can you cook, Rita?" Lois asked.

"Sure. The cafe where I worked needed me to cook whenever the regular cook didn't show up or was drunk. Also, being the eldest kid, when my mom got sick, I had to cook for the family. She died a few years ago. By then, I'd trained my kid sister to cook. I didn't feel too bad about leaving Iowa after that."

Lois followed up. "What's the best dish you make?"

"I'm really good at making stews. We had a few sheep on our farm, so lamb stew was my speciality. We kept our root cellar filled with carrots, onions and potatoes, so we had stew a lot. When we slaughtered a calf, of course, beef stew was on the menu. You gotta get the thickness of the liquid just right so it isn't too watery."

Anna: "How you do in school in Iowa?

"We only had one schoolhouse for first to twelfth grade. My graduation class was fourteen and I ranked fifth, so, I did all right, I guess. We only had three teachers, so it was kinda like a family business. I'm good at math and even helped teach algebra when I was a senior. I liked school and enjoyed giving speeches, too."

Rita noticed the positive, non-verbal feedback from Lois and Anna. They looked her in the eye and not the clock. They smiled when Rita smiled.

"Please wait, Rita," Anna said. "Only couple minutes." Rita returned to her table.

Ten minutes later, Lois waved Rita back into the office. "Howard really likes you, and we think you have exactly the skills and personality we're looking for. Ours is truly a family restaurant run by a very close-knit family, so we want our employees to feel they are part of that family atmosphere. Anna and I would like to offer you a position as waitress. We pay a dollar fifty per hour and you keep all your tips. Tomorrow is our busiest night of the week. Can you start tomorrow?"

"Yes! Thank you! I'll come in for the lunch crowd to learn the ropes of the restaurant, and stay for dinner. Will that work?"

"Oh yes. We'd want you here for both meals anyway. We're about to shorten our hours to eleven-thirty in the morning to eight at night. Can you handle that workload?"

"Oh, yes, ma'am. How many days a week?"

"Well, we're closed on Monday and only do lunch on Sunday. You'll get plenty of hours and tips. Are you with us?"

"I am! Thank you! If it weren't for your terrific son, I wouldn't have had this chance. Can I say 'bye' to Howard on the way out?"

"Sure, and welcome to Momma's."

Rita thanked Howard and waggled her fingers at him as she walked out the door. The five block walk to her tiny, furnished room passed quickly, with her feeling as if walking on clouds of marshmallows. The relief of knowing she could pay the rent and buy food was not a small thing for a young, single woman who had escaped the vagaries of the Great Depression in a small town filled with failure, hunger and sadness.

I'm gonna make it! I'm gonna go back to school! Was it luck or providence that made me sweep up that boy in the street for a dance? He seemed like an all-American boy, and that's sure what I needed after bein' pawed by sailors for the past couple years. No more smokey bars and drunken sailors for this girl! I gotta new job!

"So, mom…You hired Rita? She's really nice. Pretty, too. She'll be good for our business, don't you think?"

"Yes, Howard. Your recommendation was completely accurate. She starts tomorrow. I want you to show her everything you know about running this place. Your grandpa and dad will join us tomorrow, now that the long factory hours have stopped. Be sure to introduce her to them. I want you to check the tallies at the end of lunch and dinner every day. Like we did with the other waitresses, we want to make sure that she's being honest and not skimming the bills. Can you do that?"

"Sure. What time will she be here?"

"Eleven o'clock. Oh, and she says she's good at math. Even taught algebra when she was still in high school. How's that? She might even be able to help you," Lois said, chuckling.

Chapter 25

Inflections

In 1948, the 200 inch George Ellery Hale telescope atop the Palomar Mountains in northern San Diego County became operational, giving astronomers orders of magnitude more information about the universe. California Institute of Technology operated the instrument, and in association with the Mt. Wilson Observatory in Los Angeles, among other places, emerged the idea that the universe began with a "big bang" where all matter abruptly came into being. No theories yet existed explaining how that might have occurred. It's just that the expanding universe suggested that there must have been a starting point. Einstein's 1915 general theory of relativity predicted what astronomers in 1948 were only now discovering.

In the meantime, the now defunct German military rocket industry, desperately coveted by both the West as well as the Soviet Union, resulted in Wernher von Braun, the chief German rocket scientist and his closest colleagues defecting to the United States, thus giving new life to America's cosmic research.

1948 was also Howard Savage's sixteenth year. He was at the top of his high school class in most subjects. His friendship with Rita Collins deepened. Rita had just turned twenty-eight and was still working at *Momma's Home Cooking*. Her vivaciousness and intelligence gained the entire family's trust such that she soon kept the books for the business.

She quickly became a trusted and valuable member of the Savage family and was invited to all their gatherings. Anna Savage made Rita a large, beautiful cake for her surprise birthday party at the restaurant that year, and Howard bought her a charm bracelet with a little gold heart attached.

"Thank you Howard. That's the sweetest gift I've ever received. I hope I find a boyfriend some day just like you." She gave Howard a big hug and kissed him on the cheek, causing everyone to laugh at his blush and the lipstick print left on his face.

The war being over, relief was slowly followed by the return of joy to the Savages, and Rita found herself thanking "her stars" that she had fallen in with this robust, all-American family that seemed to have unbounded love for one another. Rita found herself accepting them into her heart as family.

One morning in April, 1949, Rita burst through the restaurant's door and proudly announced, "Hey, everybody! Come see my new car!"

Howard was the first to respond "What did you get? What color is it?"

"Come and see for yourself."

Parked at the curb was a dark green 1940 Hudson coupe.

"Wow, Rita. How much did it cost?"

"I got a good deal, Howard. The owner said her husband died just after they bought this beauty and she didn't drive. I paid three hundred bucks for it. Do you like it? How about the color? It's practically new."

Before Howard could answer, Lois and Anna joined the two. "Very nice, Rita," Lois said. "Now you can get around town. Visit the mountains and drive up the coast. You'll have to take us for a ride some time."

Howard said, ""Rita, can you take me for a spin…maybe even let me drive it some?"

"Sure, Howard," Rita replied. At Lois' approving nod, she climbed into the driver's seat and added, "Let's go!"

Once away from the restaurant, Rita told Howard how she had learned to drive a tractor when she was just ten. "The moment my feet could reach the pedals, I had to become a farm hand and drive that clunky old tractor. Good thing our land was flat, or I'd have turned it over more than once. Did you know that the industry with the most injuries and accidents is farming?"

"Really?" Howard exclaimed. "I'd have thought it would be soldiering."

Rita laughed. "Not too many battlefields in Iowa, baby."

Once they reached Mission Valley, Rita pulled over, put the column-mounted gear shift in neutral and pulled on the hand brake. "So. How would you like to take us for a drive into the cool air of the mountains?"

Rita arched her back and stepped over Howard's body as he slid under her and into the driver's seat. In the last year, he'd become taller than Rita and his long legs required him to move the driver's seat back a couple of notches.

"The clutch is still a little stiff and engages all-of-a-sudden. You gotta find the point where it engages or it'll stall."

It took a couple of jerking stalls before Howard learned to feather the clutch; all the while, Rita was stifling giggles at his embarrassment. "Don't say I didn't warn you."

"Thanks a lot. Learning the different feel of different cars takes some doing."

After achieving a smooth start, Howard headed the Hudson east toward the Laguna Mountains. "Let's go up to Julian and have lunch," Rita suggested. "Did you know that Julian was almost named the capitol of California?"

"Nope. Why would anyone want a state capital twenty miles from the

Mexican border? I guess some smarter people finally figured that out."

"Sweetheart, you're so smart yourself. I've enjoyed helping you with algebra and the math part of physics. You're gonna be really great at something. The only thing I really wish for right now, is for you to find a nice girlfriend.Any prospects?"

"I sometimes have lunch with Janet Jenkins. She's really pretty…and smart, too. We haven't gone on a real date, mostly because I've been so busy at the restaurant and studying. Some classmates tease me about being a book worm. If it weren't for being a good baseball player, I doubt I'd have any friends at all."

"Sure. Well, a man—as you'll soon be—needs to have balance in his life. You're handsome, strong, smart and the nicest guy I've ever met. I'm glad we're friends. I'm too old to be your girlfriend, but you are giving me lessons I need to pick a boyfriend for myself. And right now, I'd like my man to be very much like you. If that sounds like I'm saying I love you, good, because I do. It's a kind of family-type love, not the romantic kind. Do you understand?"

"I think so. I love you too, Rita. You're my best friend ever, and I always feel happy when you're around. I never had a sister to compare, so I just guess that the love we share—is uncluttered by any of that other stuff that gets people in the kind of trouble I've read about. I hope we stay friends forever…"

An awkward silence ensued until Rita shrugged and said, "I'm thinking about going to night school and taking auto mechanic classes now that I have a car." After they'd both stopped chuckling, Rita continued. "Maybe I'll meet a nice guy there. And, if he tries to patronize me with the "little lady" bullshit, I can crease his skull with a wrench."

They laughed for a while at that remark as they climbed into the mountains.

"Rita, I want you to be happy. But it seems to me that if you just grab the next available guy, you might end up turning into someone you're not just to please him…"

Another awkward silence ensued.

"You're so damned smart. Where'd you learn all that? How does an 'almost eighteen year-old' come up with that? But, to your point, it IS a worry. You also know me to be stubborn. Having had to deal with all those sailors and Marines during the war taught me a lot about men. Since then, I made a list of things I want in a man. I keep adding and subtracting from it, so it's a moving target."

"Well, you met guys who had been away from home for the first time, probably missing their moms and girlfriends. I'll bet you also met lots of Marines and sailors who'd just come home from combat, too. They surely needed somebody like you to remind them they were human, let alone men. One Marine who came to the restaurant told me that the savagery in combat was more horrible than he had ever imagined. Then, he started shaking and tears poured from his eyes. We treated him to the meal. I felt so bad for him. It hurt to see this big, strong guy crying. The war must have been way worse than we could imagine living here.

"Maybe you did more good for the war effort than you ever realized, Rita. Your decency also showed these men that there were such women still around. It's those things that make me love you too. I know I was still a kid when I first met you, but you've helped me grow into a good man more than you'll know. I'm glad you bought this car and took me for a drive. I feel like we've become closer in our friendship."

"I feel the same way, honey. Thanks for saying those things. You said them so much better than I could. Your goodness is what makes me love you, too. Yes. Buying *this* car for *this* drive into the mountains on *this* day is one of the most important things I've ever done in my life."

As Howard turned off the highway and into Julian, Rita located a little cafe. They parked and went inside. The lunch of hamburgers and french fries solved their immediate hunger issues. The drive back to San Diego, with Rita driving, was silent, the two lost in thought. Nearing home, Howard finally spoke: "I want to get a scholarship to UCLA. My grades are good, and the family has saved money for my college, but I want to earn my share. What do you think of that?"

Chapter 26

Transitions

The 1950s featured a dramatic shift from the public horrors of "hot" war to the more secretive but no less damaging elements of the "cold" war. Albert Einstein warned the world that even an accidental nuclear war could destroy all life on Earth.

President Harry Truman ordered, with great reluctance, the sending of U.S. troops to an obscure nation in French Indo-China called Vietnam, at the same time authorizing the construction of thermo-nuclear weapons, also known as H-bombs.

There were now eight million televisions in households around the country. America was galloping into the second half of the twentieth century, its figurative ears laid back, sprinting into the future. Howard Savage was positioned perfectly for his vision that looked to the stars.

On 27 March 1950, the Savages celebrated Howard's eighteenth birthday. The next day, he received an acceptance letter from UCLA, and to cap off his excitement, he received a full tuition scholarship to pursue his burgeoning interest in aeronautical engineering.

The Savage household was ecstatic. His grandfather tightly hugged the now strapping lad for what seemed an eternity to Howard. He hugged him back as well. When Virgil Savage finally let go, Howard saw tears of joy and pride streaming down his grandfather's normally stoic face. That embrace was followed by a similar hug from his grandmother Anna. With a shaking voice, she said, "You making us proud, grandson. Long journey from old country worth it. Were peasant and cook. Now have grandson who will build airplanes. How far we come."

"Rockets, Grandma. I want to build rockets. I want to help get men into space and maybe even go to the moon. You and Grandpa kept telling me to look far. You taught my father those things, and he passed them on to me.

"Just the other day I was thinking about how lucky I am. You also taught Dad the value of education and work." Turning to his father, Frank, he continued, "Dad, you never asked me to do anything that was just busy work. You always explained the reasons for what you asked me to do. I intend to make you proud of all your work with me. I'm gonna build a moon rocket someday. You'll see."

That last remark brought applause from both parents and grandparents. Howard's snapping blue eyes reinforced his stated intent and determination. The first generation of this multi-generational family was going to college! A great sense of accomplishment washed proudly over the entire group.

Then, Andy Billings walked in from work. "What's everybody so emotional about?"

Everyone laughed at Andy's astonishment. It was the perfect offset for the emotional moments just past. "I'm going to UCLA, Grandpa," Howard stated matter-of-factly. "I got a scholarship!"

"That's GREAT news!" Andy replied, beaming. "Let me add my own hug of congratulations."

Wrapped in Andy's arms, Howard could smell the sweat and chemical residue from the electrician of great ships, but all he felt was joy. "Howard, I can see your mother's fairly shakin' with excitement. Makin' her happy makes me even happier. Frank, we need a party for our college man here!"

"Good idea. Let's close the restaurant early tomorrow. Would steak be okay, college man?"

"Sure. Can I invite Rita?"

"Of course. Mom, we're gonna need a cake that says somethin' about Howard's eighteenth birthday, too. Can you do that?"

"*Da*. Of course. Can already see cake in head."

Later that day at the restaurant, Howard led Rita to the rear of the kitchen and told her the news. "Oh, baby, that's just great! Going to college! That's REALLY great. But I'm sure gonna miss you. What will I do for good conversation? Who will I talk to when I'm blue? You have to promise to write. Often. Won't you?"

"Of course. I'll be just a hundred and twenty miles up the road, so you can drive up and see me and the campus, too. I'll take you to a football game. And if I make the freshman baseball team, you can watch me play!"

"You bet. I'm so happy for you. And at least you're staying within striking distance."

"My folks are throwing me a party tomorrow night and I want you to be there with me. I'd really like you to be there…"

"Wouldn't miss it for the world, baby. Maybe now that you're a college man, I won't be able to call you that…" Rita wrapped her arms around Howard's neck, stood on her toes and kissed him deeply, pressing her entire body against him. As he returned the kiss, he became more aware of his feelings for her. He'd never felt this sort of passion from any other woman before.

"Wow, Rita…"

"I know. Sorry, I just had to do that. Did it hurt much?" she asked winking.

"No...not exactly...I hear customers coming," he said breathlessly. "Talk to you later."

The next day, Howard's party was nothing less than grand. Anna's cake was a widely agreed upon masterpiece. Rita smiled a lot, dabbed away a few tears, said little, and this time kissed Howard only briefly afterwards as he walked her to her car. Leaving him with a dazzling smile, she said, "See you tomorrow, my beautiful man, my college man. Now go get some rest."

As spring gave way to summer, Howard enjoyed his final year of high school baseball. He continued playing into the summer with the best players in the city.

His college tuition, being paid for by scholarship, wasn't a problem. Though he'd saved every dollar he could of money from his restaurant salary and tips, the living expenses, lab fees, student activity fees and school supplies quickly added up.

On the early September day Howard was to leave for college, Rita surprised him, insisting on driving him there. The two silently packed her Hudson coupe to the brim. Frank handed him a cashier's check to deposit in a bank account he'd opened near the Westwood campus. "Wow, dad! That's a lot of money! Thank you!"

"Yes, it is, Son. It's what all of us have been savin' up to give you when you left for college. This is only half of it. You know how your mom and grandparents are: 'Always keep somethin' in reserve'. I trust you to be frugal. You know how hard all of us have worked for this day."

Everyone hugged Howard good-bye while he fought back tears. He and Rita climbed into the overloaded coupe and drove north.

Blessed with an early, but mild Santa Ana wind, the sky was a crystal clear, deep blue, and the drive up the coast on U.S. 101 was beautifully scenic. They stopped in San Juan Capistrano to share a picnic lunch Rita had made just for the occasion, then continued up through Laguna Beach and on to Westwood.

Their chatter increased steadily as they approached the UCLA campus. Howard used his campus map to re-discover the dormitory in which he'd be living. Rita helped him unpack and haul his belongings up to his room on the second floor. It was an all-male dormitory, Rita eliciting wolf whistles and comments as she helped Howard move in.

"Well, that does it, baby. Walk me out to my car and save me from these wild animals you're going to be living with."

When Rita got to the car door, she turned and repeated the birthday kiss from March. Some of Howard's new dorm mates stuck their heads out their windows hooting and whistling. Rita and Howard remained unfazed. Rita broke their clinch, and stepped back, stroking his cheek lovingly. "Gotta go, my dearest Howard. I do look forward to seeing you soon. Write me tonight; I miss you already." And she was gone in a cloud of dust made golden by the lowering sun.

The first semester involved taking prerequisite courses needed to satisfy the basic requirements of the undergraduate College of Arts and Sciences. Howard quickly adjusted to the accelerated pace of learning from professors and teaching assistants. His social life became a blizzard of new acquaintances.

Despite the frenetic pace of academia, he religiously wrote his parents and Rita, though they were quite different letters. Rita did visit and attend a football game at the Rose Bowl with him. She seemed distracted throughout the game, though Howard knew she relished his company. There was no passionate kissing this time, and Howard caught her looking at him with sad, sometimes teary-eyes. After the game, sitting together in her car in front of his dorm, she reluctantly offered, "Howard, I really can't keep seeing you. It's not healthy for either of us. I'm not getting younger and you're not aging fast enough. I'm terrified of falling into that kind of love with you that would lead us down a road that neither of us want right now. I'm approaching thirty and my body keeps telling me I need to get going and find a husband if I'm ever going to have a family."

Taking both his hands in hers, she continued. "I'm only waitressing, and doing payroll and bookkeeping part time at the restaurant. I've taken a job as a clerk in a small accounting firm in San Diego, and taking more night classes. Truth be told, I've met someone who likes me a lot and I've gotta give him a fair shake. You understand, don't you? We've known all along this day would come where I had to push myself away from you. Don't get me wrong. You and the family have been wonderful and will always be precious to me. We can still stay in touch, of course, but I've gotta get my life going. I hope you'll understand..."

"I've no choice but to understand. But you know, it's become clear to me during this first semester that I'm heading in a very different direction. It's a direction where you have no permanent place. It breaks my heart to say that. I'll miss you, of course, but I'm getting so busy that it's hard to break away from my studies even to write you good letters. You've always been my best friend. And, yes, I've often thought about us as a real, romantic couple, but then this voice calls me to do something special with my life."

Howard's eyes suddenly sparkled as he continued. "I want to build and fly rockets, Rita! Ever since I read H.G. Wells books, I've felt a pull to see what's out there in space. Then, when I read the English translation of Hermann Oberth's *The Rocket into Interplanetary Space,* I was hooked. I must have inherited the itch to explore from my grandparents. Without it, I wouldn't be here. America's just beginning to investigate rocket and space sciences, and I want to be in the middle of it! After I graduate from UCLA, I want to go to Cal Tech and work in the Jet Propulsion Labs so I can work with the right people. It's no longer just a dream. I can feel it all coming true, and I need to be ready when the time comes.

"You understand, don't you? By the time I finish my schooling and get established in a job, it's going to be six or seven years. Yes, my dear Rita, I wish my selfishness wasn't so great, but truthfully, we are headed in different life directions.

"I hope this new guy turns out to be right for you," continued Howard, "and makes you really happy. He better or he'll have to answer to me. You are a precious jewel in my life and I'm a better man for having you in my life. I hope you'll always be there. I do want to stay in contact. We've been through a lot together and you've helped me become…an adult."

"You're right about all those things, of course, my dear Howard," Rita replied. "You're almost always right. It's one of the reasons I love you. Your loyal friendship had made me feel secure enough to look at my own life. You've given me a great model for finding a husband. With that said, I think we can chalk up our relationship as a success. Wadda ya say to that?""

Tears glistened in both their eyes.

"Absolutely," stated Howard with resolve. "And I hope I find a girl who is as good for me as you've been."

Rita smiled, that special smile, leaned over and hugged Howard awkwardly over the car console. She kissed him long and warmly, then reluctantly let him go. After Howard exited the car, he watched Rita drive away with the morning sun silhouetting her head. What he couldn't see were the two very large tears streaming down Rita's cheeks. He waved to her departing car, but received no response. She was gone.

PART V
DESTINY FULFILLED

Chapter 27

Rocket Man

The 1950's also saw the rapid development of two new technologies. The first was rocketry, the second was bioastronautics. The seeds of both had been firmly implanted as early as 1947 when the US military launched fruit flies aboard a V-2 rocket to determine the biomedical effects of space radiation.

As Howard coursed through his freshman, sophomore and junior years, he redoubled his effort to become a top scholar in aeronautical engineering. He read everything he could about rocketry beginning with the "Great Trilogy" of Russia's Konstantin Tsiolkovsky, Germany's Hermann Oberth and America's Robert Goddard. In doing so, he discovered Wernher von Braun and Theodore von Karman as well as the Russian rocketry pioneers Glushko, Korolev and Tukhachevsky. He learned about "mist curtains" and other techniques to cool rocket nozzles heated by exhaust hot enough to melt them and blow up the rocket. When high-energy kerosene fuels began replacing alcohol, more problems arose, for example, whereas the new "standard" J-4 jet fuel worked excellently in turbojet engines, it contaminated high-precision rocket engines.

Internal gyroscope control of rocket trajectory was still rudimentary though theories were already emerging in the literature. Information from Chuck Yeager's X-1 rocket-plane flights was also just emerging. A Princeton student and engineer named James Wyld developed a "regenerative" rocket nozzle cooling system. It used liquid oxygen or combustible fuel to cool the nozzles, which was then added to the combustion process. This "new" rocket engine was smaller, more lightweight and vastly more powerful. Four of them powered the X-1 to high altitude supersonic speeds.

Howard visited the Jet Propulsion Laboratory (JPL) at California Institute of Technology, (called by the research scientists who worked there, "Cal Tech,") every chance he could to attend lectures and demonstrations. With support from his professors at UCLA he was soon sharing lunch—as a silent listener and observer—with some of the foremost rocket scientists of his day. He couldn't get enough of it.

One day at JPL, he summoned his courage and asked one of the jet engine engineers, Franz Loeffler, to explain jet propulsion to him. To Howard's surprise, the ex-patriot from Germany who had come to the United States with Wernher von Braun. replied jovially, "*Ja*. Of course. *Also*. It is quite simple, really," and ushered Howard into his laboratory.

"Here. I take off outer covering and show how it works." Franz undid several bolts and had Howard help him slide the housing off a full-scale jet engine. Howard saw two separate fan-like structures with several discs each surrounded by blades. "*Also. Ja*. So, air coming in from front makes big fans spin very fast. These spinning discs—at twenty thousand rpm—compresses the air. You see how each fan-wheel gets bigger and bigger while the blades on each fan get smaller and smaller as we get closer to combustion chambers. So, compressed air is pushed very hard into narrowing area—the combustion chamber tubes. The air is now very hot—maybe two hundred degrees Celsius. These little nozzles then spray fuel—a kind of kerosene—into the chamber and the mixture is ignited. *Ja*. Now, very hot burning gasses pass across second spinning disc, the turbine wheel, causing it to spin very fast. As you see, turbine wheel is connected to shaft that connects to compressor section. *Ja*? So. As long as fuel lasts, everything will keep spinning." The exhaust exits and blows against this other fan wheel. You see it?"

"I see, Franz. Pretty simple so far. What happens next?"

"*Ach*. Of course. Gasses flowing out the back expand as they cool creating forward thrust. That's how to measure the power of jet engines: It's thrust…in pounds. *Verstehen Sie*?"

"Yes. It's like a rocket that breathes its own oxidizer, the air, right?" Howard offered.

"*Ja, ja! Sehr gut!* You will be engineer—rocket scientist—before you know it!"

Howard Savage graduated from UCLA *cum laude* with an aeronautical engineering degree and immediately applied to Cal Tech. Since he had formed relationships with many of the scientific staff there, his acceptance was immediate. Doctor Harald Osterholm, a colleague of the famous chemist, Linus Pauling, took an immediate liking to Howard and started him working on rocket fuels right away.

Osterholm was a graduate of Massachusetts Institute of Technology and was recruited by Dr. Pauling himself after having finished his doctoral work on alternative fuels. His first conversation with Howard was to warn him about how the Soviet Union was rapidly building intercontinental rockets that could deliver a nuclear device to the United States. "We are very concerned about that threat, Howard. Everyone in Washington is pushing us to come up with an intercontinental ballistic missile, or ICBM, capable of carrying a thermonuclear warhead to Moscow. Some say we are already in an arms race for the survival of our country.

"But here's the thing: I had the privilege of watching our first thermonuclear test at Eniwetok in 1952. Unlike the *fission* devices used on Japan, this new, so-called hydrogen bomb is a *fusion* device. It crushes heavy water, deuterium, creating an explosion like that in the sun. And like the sun, the products are mostly helium and orders of magnitude more heat than fission devices. It requires, however, a very hot spark. A small fission device was necessary to start the fusion reaction.

"I was over twenty miles away, because no one knew what might happen when the explosion occurred. I stood not twenty feet from Edward Teller, the fusion bomb's inventor. The light of the blast was so blinding even with dark goggles. What followed was a heat wave that lasted for minutes. The shock wave that followed rocked our ship like a toy boat in a bathtub. It struck my chest like somebody punched me." The atomic bombs dropped on Japan exhibited maybe forty to fifty thousand tons—kilotons—of TNT. The Eniwetok device produced fifteen million tons—MEGATONS—of power. That's two orders of magnitude more destructive force than our atomic bombs. If one of these things was dropped on New York City, for example, seven million people would die instantly. The city from Yonkers to the Statue of Liberty would be vaporized.

"It makes me recall a statement by Robert Oppenheimer after he witnessed the test explosion of the plutonium bomb in 1945 at the Trinity site. He quoted a passage by Vishnu in the *Bhagavad Gita*: *"I am become death, the destroyer of worlds."* So you see, we now have at our fingertips the energy of the universe here on Earth, and building our own ICBM is very important."

The look of shock on Howard's face prompted Osterholm to continue. "The Soviets are building huge rockets and exploding nuclear devices, too. What else are we to do?

"That is not a rhetorical question. What you and I will try to do is develop this technology to *explore space*, maybe even someday send humans to the moon. For that, my boy, we need new ideas, new equipment, new plans and new engines that will require new fuels. Are you willing to dedicate yourself to that effort?"

After an awkward pause, Howard took a deep breath and replied, "Nuclear weapons scare me, too, but I've wanted to get involved with rockets since I was a boy. And space exploration sounds like a much better reason to make powerful rockets than bombing cities. So, where do I start?"

Chapter 28

Tragedy and Sadness

The next year saw the first glimmerings of what would later become the Apollo program, appearing in the "egghead" literature. President Eisenhower pushed hard for ICBM technology and the results were improved liquid-fuel rockets like the Atlas, and reliable, two-stage, solid fuel missiles like the Titan. These two types of rocket engines were powerful enough to carry payloads halfway around the world, but could also put an object into orbit.

Howard Savage kept his head down and learned everything he could about rocket engines and fuels. He had his own laboratory now, cluttered with engine parts, fuel lines and turbine pumps that forced fuel into combustion chambers. Slowly the romance and adventure of his childhood gave way to a real effort making all the science fiction and fantasy he'd read about become real.

Dr. Osterholm's major interest remained in alternative fuels, but he insisted that Howard first learn all the details of rocketry. "Only when you see for yourself what's been done, how it worked and the resulting problems solved, can you make fuel innovations happen that are worth a damn rather than a waste of money and time. Remember, we all stand on the shoulders of the people who came before us."

He completed his first year of graduate school in May, 1957, barely five months before another milestone that would touch the lives of every person on Earth.

Then, on a sunny morning in June, Howard's telephone interrupted his concentration with a head-splitting ring. Leaping for the receiver to quiet the noise, he heard his mother's voice: "Howard, I have terrible news. Grandma fell at the restaurant and died before we could get her to the hospital. She hit her head on a corner of the preparation table. Your dad is on the way up there to get you. You should pack for an extended visit."

Howard was speechless.

"He'll probably head for my rooming house. I'm on my way."

In his note to Dr. Osterholm, along with his telephone number in San Diego, he said he didn't know when he'd be back, apologized and signed it.

Oh, Grandma. How could this happen? You've been our rock. Poor Grandpa. He must be heartbroken. She was the light of his life. Oh, God, I wonder how dad is. What a horrible shock. Grandma was like a second mother to me. Then the tears began. At the rooming house, he could barely see to get the key into the lock.

An hour later, Frank Savage pulled into Howard's boarding house driveway. Howard ran to him and hugged him fiercely and they both wept into each others' shoulders.

Howard drove to San Diego in record time, grabbed his suitcase and ran into the arms of his weeping, red-faced mother. "Grandpa is at the hospital making arrangements with the funeral home," Lois said. "He should be back in a little while."

"Have you told Grandpa Andy, Mom?"

"I did. He was in the middle of something crucial and couldn't get away. He'll be home as soon as he can."

Virgil Savage drove up the driveway to find his son, grandson and daughter-in-law waiting stoically. Virgil squared his shoulders and reported that Anderson's Funeral Home was making the arrangements. His shoulders then slumped, the only sign of his grief. When he spoke there was a roughness to his voice. He stepped forward, embraced his son and grandson in each of his still-powerful arms, and they felt him tremble, squeezing him back. Frank finally let loose and began sobbing loudly. After a moment, the patriarch backed away, wiped his eyes and embraced Lois, who gratefully melted into his arms like warm bread dough. Virgil held her while she sobbed and sobbed. Finally, Lois regained her composure and announced, "I've made some lunch. It'll help us feel better."

Everyone sat silently around the table, each lost in his or her thoughts. There was nothing to say.

Howard wrote Rita a letter reporting the tragedy. The Savages had thrown her a huge wedding reception at a union hall, catering everything. They'd sent her and her husband Calvin Smith to the Hotel del Coronado as a wedding gift. The two had moved to El Centro in 1954. Cal's auto repair business flourished alongside the expanding agriculture of the Imperial Valley and the new Naval Air station there. Rita became pregnant shortly thereafter and produced a beautiful son whom she named David. David Howard Smith.

The funeral for Anna Savage was a solemn gathering. Andy, Virgil, Frank, Howard and two other husbands of *Momma's Home Cooking* waitresses served as pall bearers. After the funeral, the Savages gathered around the kitchen table reminiscing and telling Anna stories until the emotional exhaustion caught up with them. It was a sad day, but it would mark the beginning of more grief that would visit this group of good people who had worked so hard for one another. Virgil left for bed first, but not before saying to Howard, 'Grandma so proud of you, Howard.

You have much of my Anna in you. You stronger every year. You will do great things. She said so. Good night."

Three weeks after Anna Savage's funeral, with Howard back in his lab, Dr. Osterholm's secretary located him hunched over some calculations. "Howard, your mother is on the phone. She sounds distressed."

Howard dashed to the phone in the adjacent office. "Hi, Mom. What's the matter?"

"Oh, baby, Daddy was killed at the shipyard today. A steel plate fell on him and three other men while they were working on a ship. Something about a crane cable parting."

Lois barely got the words out before breaking into wrenching sobs. "Your dad is coming to get you again. Oh, God! It's coming down on us all at once. He should be there in about an hour. Be safe. See you soon."

Howard fell into the chair next to the secretary and hid his face in his hands. Tears were streaming down his cheeks. The secretary, Alice Clarke, stared at him then offered, "What happened Howard? More trouble at home?"

Looking up through bleary eyes he replied, "My Grandpa Billings was killed in an accident at the shipyard. My dad's coming to get me… again. My family is dropping like flies. I don't know if I've enough heart left to break. Andy—my Grandpa Billings—was the one who coaxed us into moving to San Diego. First my Grandma. Now this. My mom's barely holding it together. I gotta go, Alice. Please tell Dr. Osterholm the bad news. You have my phone number in San Diego, right?"

"Yes, Oh you poor dear. Do be careful. Take care of your mother. She's going to need all the strength and love, now more than ever."

The Savage family endured the second funeral. This time, however, the gloom surrounding the household was knife-cutting thick.

After Andy Billing's funeral, Howard returned to Cal Tech with a heart leaden with grief. He moved as if in a trance for weeks. Dr. Oster-holm kept him busy researching possible fuels for space vehicles, know-ing that work was the best salve for his student's aching heart.

And then, one day in August, two months before a rocketry milestone that would change the way every person on Earth thought, Charlene Young walked through his laboratory door.

Chapter 29

Charlie

"Anybody home?"

A tousled head of black hair poked out from behind a bookcase. "Yes, and who might you be?"

"I'm Charlie Young. Who are you?"

"Uh, I'm Howard Savage. I work here. May I help you find whomever you're looking for?"

"Hope so. I'm looking for Dr. Osterholm. I'm his new graduate student. Do you work for him? The folks downstairs said this was his lab. Am I in the right place?"

"You are. I'm his second year grad student. He's off to some faculty meeting somewhere trying to find more budget money."

Howard emerged from behind his hidden desk to shake Charlie Young's hand. "You certainly don't look like a 'Charlie' to me."

"Name's Charlene, but I grew up with older brothers, so...Charlie's the name that stuck. Don't mind it, really. It gives me a brief advantage when they see me in person."

Charlie flashed her best smile at Howard, who blushed and escorted her over to an empty desk just across the narrow aisle from his. "I guess this will be yours since there aren't any others open."

Charlie bobbed her head of honey-colored hair and plopped onto the chair. She saw that he was gaping, causing her bright, periwinkle blue eyes to twinkle in amusement. "Haven't you seen a girl's legs before? How tall are you? Where're you from?"

Howard fought off the attack of gob smack that was threatening to turn his voice into a stuttering gurgle. "Um. Of course, I've seen girls' legs before. I'm six-one in stocking feet. I'm originally from Cleveland, Ohio, but we moved to San Diego in forty-one. I graduated from UCLA year before last. It's your turn, now."

"Well, I prefer jeans to these damned long skirts. I stand five-ten in my stocking feet. I'm originally from Lexington, Kentucky. My dad wanted me to go to University of Kentucky, so I did and graduated last June with a degree in mechanical engineering. Daddy was not happy with my choice of majors, but after working on the farm tractors and mowers, it seemed natural for me to want to know how they worked and why. I'm here to get as far away from blue grass and horseshit as possible. My dad owns a farm and raises race horses, so we kids shoveled a lot of their shit, and pitched a lot of hay and alfalfa. Our family had enough money to send me to whatever school I wanted. My two brothers opted to join the Air Force so they wouldn't get drafted into the Army. Said they're gonna go to college on the G.I. Bill when their hitch is up. We kids seem to have a knack for pissing off Daddy. Mom would just wring her hands and tell us how much we're loved and how they trusted us to do good things. She saved us from the tyranny of Dad. He's a good guy, but really stubborn and more than a little backward. He'd have been happy if I'd have married the guy down the road and filled his life with grandchildren. Me, I have other ideas. I wanna help get us to the moon."

"Wow!" Howard replied, totally awed. "I want to get us to the moon, too. Me? I'm a city boy. I've never been near a horse. Do you ride? Are there stables around here where you can 'rent a-horse'?"

"Yep. That's the second thing I looked for after finding a room. You wanna go riding? I'm a good teacher. Horses love me."

"Sure. Sounds like fun. Is it like in the movies? Do you often take men on a riding date?" Howard asked, grinning and regaining some poise.

"To be honest, most men are afraid of me. Smart girls scare the shit out of them. Are you afraid of smart girls, Howard?"

"No. I was raised by two of them. My mom worked in the aircraft factory during the war and ended up being a poster girl for the Rosie the Riveter broadsheets. You may have seen her likeness on the cover of LIFE magazine. Mom has run our family restaurant almost single-handedly since my Grandma died. Grandma was the other strong, smart woman in my family. They taught me to respect women. They showed what women can do. My best friend, who's twelve years older than me, is another really smart woman. Rita started working at our restaurant as a waitress after the war ended, and became our accountant, bookkeeper and office manager. She married and moved to El Centro, so I don't see her much anymore.

"That was your mom?! Wow, Howard. She's a real beauty. I can see where you get your looks."

"Thanks. I don't spend very much time looking in the mirror; only when I shave. I think I look more like my grandfather, though. Grandpa is sixty-five and still has a full shock of black hair like me. He emigrated from the Ukraine in nineteen oh eight or oh nine.

"Your parents must be handsome people, Charlie, because you're certainly pretty."

"Thank you. They are. My dad was a football team captain and married the head cheerleader from high school. They started having kids right away. I was born in thirty-three, so I'm twenty-three. You?"

"My birthday is in March. I was born in nineteen thirty-two at the start of the Great Depression.

After a moment of awkward silence, Howard offered, "One of my earliest memories was when my dad bought me this model of a Lockheed twin engine Vega. It hooked me on aviation. When we moved to San Diego, I liked to ride my bike down to Lindbergh Field and watch all the planes take off and land. The last ones I saw were the huge B-36 *Peacekeeper* bombers. I thought they'd never clear Point Loma on their takeoff runs, but then I noticed that they had two jet engines on the wingtips to boost them. Then, one day I read a book on the history of rockets and rocketry, and Robert Goddard became my hero. Nowadays, the Russians are building huge rockets to launch into space. I want to be in on our rocket development. In fact, North American Aviation is bidding for contracts to build rocket planes. I'm gonna keep my eye on them after I finish my graduate degree next year."

Howard suddenly noticed that Charlie Young was staring directly into his eyes.

"Wow. I didn't mean to bend your ear, Charlie. I mean, you just got here. Dr. 'O' should be back soon. Let me show you what we're working on."

As Howard showed Charlie around the lab and adjacent workshops, he couldn't help noticing her relaxed athleticism. The bridge of her nose was splashed with freckles, accentuating her expressions. One of her front teeth had a small chip that made her broad smile even more intriguing. She smiled and laughed easily and presented a self-assuredness to which Howard was immediately drawn. It took less than a half hour before he felt as relaxed with Charlie as he had with Rita.

"Well, Charlie, it's close to lunchtime. Let's walk down to the little cafe around the corner and I'll buy you lunch as a welcoming gesture to our part of the world."

"Sounds good. Let's go! I'm starving!"

The two scientists wolfed their burgers and fries while continuing their back-and-forth banter throughout the lunch hour.

"You were right. These are great burgers, Howard. So, let's go see if Dr. Osterholm is back. I'm looking forward to getting started learning about rocket engine design."

After leaving the lab that night, Howard rode his bicycle back to his rooming house. He felt as if he'd fallen down a bottomless elevator shaft. *What is happening to me? She's really beautiful. I wonder how she looks in jeans. I can't remember ever reacting to a woman like this before. Rita was more than just a friend, but I never had feelings with her like I'm having now with Charlie!*

Cool off, buddy. We'll be working together. You can't afford to be distracted from your goal: to find a job next year that will help take people to the moon. Then again, Charlie wants to do that, too, so…take it one day at a time. After all, you've had very few dates with girls, never mind a woman like this one.

Chapter 30

Whirlwind

Howard and Charlie's days in the lab always began with friendly greetings and cordiality. After two weeks, Charlie became sufficiently oriented to begin working on her own ideas for engine design. Her research identified that sticking valves caused explosions on the launch pads and in the live-fire test beds of Santa Susana Canyon. Charlie, Howard soon discovered, was a skilled machinist. She immediately started making her own valve parts from various metals. One day, after showing Howard some of her work that looked more like jewelry, she looked him straight in the eye and said, "It's time I took you to the stables and taught you to ride. Wadda you say to that?"

"Well...sure. When?"

"How about tomorrow morning? Neither of us have classes, so we're free."

"How did you know I don't have any classes?"

Charlie tossed her hair, arched an eyebrow, and smiled her warmest smile. "Well, I've been watching you and planning for a time when we could go riding. You're as nice a guy as I've ever met. I've seen you interact with others and everyone seems to like you. That makes me feel safe enough to find out more. Clear enough?"

"Thanks," Howard answered awkwardly, blushing. "I'm just not used to meeting girls...er...women who show much interest in me. I've had my head down with school and work most of the time. I gotta say that having my Grandma and Grandpa Billings die recently sort of took the spirit out of me. I'm very attached to my family—as you might have guessed. You seem really nice, too. And I can't say that I haven't noticed how pretty you are. Sure. When and where will we go riding?"

"I'll pick you up. Your place. Eight o'clock tomorrow morning. Now, let me see how this little needle valve works when it's cold and under pressure."

Howard was left standing there with his mouth agape, his reply hanging on his lips as he watched her walk away. Feeling his eyes on her, she turned and flashed him her most fetching smile.

Next morning, Howard heard her car horn and bounded out the door. He'd worn his oldest, most comfortable blue jeans and his favorite lace-up Chuck Taylor basketball shoes. "I don't have any boots, so this is the best I can do," he said as he piled into the front seat of her Buick Special convertible. The top was down and the morning air was sweet as they drove.

"Wow. Nice car."

"I musta shoveled ten tons of horseshit to earn enough to buy this beauty from my aunt. Despite Daddy's fortune, there's little I haven't earned. It's his way. Nice shirt, by the way."

"Oh, thanks. My parents gave it to me last Christmas." He glanced over at Charlie's plaid shirt, and through parted button gaps, noticed the graceful swell of her breasts and smiled. Sensing his look, she turned and smiled back.

After a fifteen minute drive up San Gabriel Canyon Road, they approached a horse stable and farm: "San Gabriel Stables, Horses for hire," the sign said. Charlie pulled into an empty parking space and shook hands with a swarthy man wearing a straw hat. After exchanging pleasantries, the man, in Spanish-accented English, asked Charlie what he could do for her today.

"Well, Jaime, I want to take my boyfriend here on his first horse ride. How about something Western and gentle, an old hand who isn't spooked by anything. I'll take a horse with some spunk in case I want to have a gallop."

"*Si*. I will feex your boyfriend up with Calico. An old mare. Sweet and gentle," Jaime said grinning, showing a gold front tooth. "And for you, *senorita*, I weel saddle Jasper. You know him. He ees very spirited, but has never thrown a rider, yet. Let me saddle them up while you go pay."

"Boyfriend? I'm now your boyfriend?"

"Well, I had to let him know that I wasn't just picking up some bum off the road, didn't I? Besides, I'd like you to be my boyfriend— at least for today. That alright with you?"

Charlie's boldness left him stammering: "Uh. Sure. I've just never been anybody's boyfriend before…except when I was thirteen and Rita asked me to be hers for V-J day. Is riding some kind of bonding experience?"

Charlie laughed out loud. "Well, Howard, that depends. If your horse breaks a leg, then we'd have to ride double on mine. How would that be for bonding?"

"Okay, what's the difference between Western and whatever the other choice was?"

"The 'other' is English. Let me explain: The English saddle has a rounded pommel, so no saddle horn to hang on to. It's called a flat saddle, so it has a low cantle, or the back of the saddle. It has only a single girth; no belly strap. There are many styles of English saddles. The Western saddle has a deep seat designed to cradle and support the hips on long rides over uneven ground. The horn can be used to wrap a rope around or hang things on. It often has several accessories such as a chest or butt strap to keep the saddle from slipping forward or back. Some Western saddles even have saddlebags for carrying stuff, which reminds me…Please get the rucksack out of the back seat. It's our lunch."

When Howard returned, she continued. "Okay, another big difference between English and Western is in the reining. Western style uses single neck reins, held together in the left hand. To 'steer', the reins are pulled across the horse's neck: left to steer left; right to right. English reins depend on the bit. A snaffle, or double bit uses two reins instead one. They are laced between the ring and pinky fingers of both hands. In both types of riding, leg signals are more useful than reins, but the cues differ. For example, to select a lead for cantering in Western, you nudge the desired leg with your toe on that side. In English, you squeeze the opposite leg against the horse's ribcage, curving it around the body to foster the lead with the other leg.

"So let me pay the man and I'll meet you over there where Jaime is saddling our horses."

Howard walked to where Jaime had two large horses tied to a hitching post. "So, my friend, thees your first time for riding a horse?"

"Yes, and I'm a little nervous. Is this my horse, Calico?"

"Oh *si*. She ees a beauty. You know how to mount and dismount? No? Let me show you."

Jaime went to the left side of Calico and put his left toe into the stirrup. He took the reins in his left hand, and holding them loosely with plenty of slack, grabbed the pommel and hoisted himself up into the saddle where he wiggled into a comfortable position. "Very easy. Just don't tug the reins when mounting. If you do, the horse may back up and dump you. "

The two had a laugh at that prospect.

"Now, for dismount. You jes' reverse, except for one thing: Take your left foot out of the stirrup first, bring your right leg back over the saddle, turn to the right and slide to the ground. Sometimes when a horse feels weight shift, it weel bolt or rear up catching your foot in the stirrup. You don't want to go for a ride on your back weeth your leg in the air. Doesn't impress the girls..." Jamie said with a toothy grin, nodding towards where Charlie was approaching.

"So, my friend, you theenk you are ready to make friends with Calico? Here are some carrots. Go pat her on the nose and cheeks, and feed her two of these. Save the rest for later. You two will end up falling in love weeth each other I am sure." With that, Jaime handed Howard a small bag of carrots and walked towards the stable. Howard fed a couple of carrots to Calico who crunched on them happily. When she nudged Howard's chest, he gave her another. Their love affair was beginning.

Charlie smiled at Howard and walked over to her car, where she pulled out a broad-brimmed hat and positioned it on top of her head. She also extracted a large box. "Here, boyfriend. This one's for you. You gotta look the part," she said, grinning, her eyes twinkling at the deer-in-the-headlights look on Howard's face.

Howard opened the box to find a large, white straw hat.

"Try it on. I had to guess at your head size. It's gotta fit snugly while riding."

Howard put on the hat, tugged it down until it was bending the tops of his ears outward.

"Perfect," Charlie chuckled. "I haven't entirely lost my eye for sizes. Okay, Howard, ready to ride?"

"Jaime explained how to mount and dismount, so I guess I'm ready."

Charlie glided over to Jasper, slipped the backpack over her shoulders, undid the reins, fed him a carrot, then hoisted herself into the saddle in one fluid motion. Howard patted Calico on the neck, loosened the reins from the hitching post, and carefully hoisted himself up into the saddle. Calico didn't move.

"Howard, we're gonna head up that trail. Pull the reins to the left—gently—and gently squeeze her flanks with your feet. If you squeeze too hard, she'll think you mean for her to break into a trot or gallop. Go slow and learn the feel of your horse." Charlie then directed Jasper toward the trailhead.

Howard did as instructed and, to his pleasant surprise, Calico obeyed immediately. He squeezed his knees together and Calico picked up the pace. He soon found himself bouncing in the saddle and needing a tight grip on the pommel to stay steady. "Let your hips become part of the horse," Charlie called from ahead, looking back,. "Let them rotate with the horse's movement. Watch me. You won't mind watching my hips, will you?"

After a couple hundred yards Howard was beginning to relax, getting into the rhythm of Calico's gait. He even got her to trot. Looking back again, Charlie, gauging Howard carefully, said, "I don't think you're ready to gallop, Howard, but if we do, you'll just want to stand in the stirrups and use your legs as shock absorbers…"

They rode up the canyon a few miles, until they came across a small, clear creek. Charlie reined in, dismounted and led Jasper to the creek where he drank thirstily. Howard followed her lead. Calico joined Jasper and began drinking. Charlie pulled their lunch from Jasper's saddlebags. She showed Howard a steel thermos with cold lemonade, sandwiches and four apples.

"Two apples apiece?" asked the novice rider.

"Nope. One each for us and one for our horses. They love apples.

You'll see." Charlie tied her horse with a long lead so he could nibble the grass along the creek bank. Howard followed suit.

Finding a dry, flat grassy spot, Charlie snapped out a blanket.

"You certainly think of everything, don't you?" Howard said.

"Well, mister, if I do something, I do it right. I never met any guy in Kentucky who could put up with me. After I let them play with my tits, they thought they owned me. The college boys at yoo kay were all the same. I'm not own-able. When I commit, it's gonna be all the way. I'm not gonna be somebody's toy or ornament. Know what I mean?"

"I think so. I've never had a 'real' girlfriend, Charlie, so you're the first woman I've ever really gone out with.

"By the way, my dad's a master machinist, and to see your fine work is VERY impressive. You must have been popular at yoo kay."

"Not really. Spent more time in the wallflower garden at school dances than I care to remember. My parents always insisted I go to those damned things, because that's what 'proper girls' did. They even planned a debutante ball for me. That's when I put my foot down. As they say back in ol' Kintuck, 'I aint no gussied up china doll. Now pass me the jug.'"

Howard, mouthful of sandwich, folded over laughing at her sudden 'hillbilly' affectations. "Do they really talk like that back in Kentucky?"

"Well, ya gotta go pretty deep in the 'hollers'—that's Kintuck fer *hollows* - to hear that kinda accent. You can go so deep, especially in coal country, that their speech is unintelligible for the first hour until you get used to it. I had a roommate at yoo kay who came from the 'hollers' and it took me most of a year to understand her and teach her to speak so she could be understood. The speech classes were the hardest for her."

After the couple finished their sandwiches, they shared the cup-lid from the thermos to drink the lemonade. Each ate an apple, smiling, looking at each other for long, wordless moments. Howard felt an aching in his chest and a stirring in his loins. Without thinking, he leaned across the blanket and kissed Charlie, who wrapped her arms around him and kissed him back with a sense of urgency Howard hadn't known since Rita kissed him on his birthday years earlier. They remained entwined until the horses, smelling the apples, started whinnying and stamping their feet.

"Guess we better to take care of our horses," Charlie said breathlessly with hooded eyes.

"Just hold out the apple? Is that it?" Howard asked, trying to catch his breath.

"Yep. They'll know what to do with it,"

After feeding their horses, Charlie packed up. Howard helped her fold the blanket, kissing her sweetly each time they came close. "We'd better get these critters back to the barn before they have stories to tell. You mind being my boyfriend today?" she asked.

"No. You okay with being my girlfriend today?"

"I hoped that this was where we were going. I've never had a boyfriend quite like you, Howard. I hope you're as good a man as you are a sweet one. Know the difference?"

"I think so. I've never felt like this with anyone. Rita and I talked a lot about relationships, so I think I know the basics. I was taken with you the moment you walked into the lab. Is that what some call 'chemistry'? If it is, it's working for me."

"Good. Now let's get back. We have a lot more to discuss."

With Charlie's cryptic comment ringing in his ears, they rode back to the stables. The horses, of course, knew they were returning and Howard had to reign Calico back. Back at the stable, the two "friends" dismounted, fed the horses the remaining carrots, and thanked Jaime. They jumped into Charlie's car and sped down the canyon onto the highway. Charlie roared into her driveway, and said, "Help me unload the stuff, will you?"

Howard grabbed the blanket and their hats and followed Charlie into her tidy studio apartment decorated with pictures of horses and what he guessed were her parents and brothers. There was a large painting of a beautiful, darkly colored horse with a white blaze on its forehead. "That's my boy, Adam," she said. "He's been my pal since I was two."

The living area was large, but the kitchen was small with only a two-chair, drop-leaf table at one end. Charlie put everything away and told Howard to take a seat on the sofa bed. Without asking, she brought him a cold beer and joined him on the couch with one of her own. "There's nothin' like a cold beer after a long, hot day in the saddle, is there?" she said grinning.

"Well, my butt is a little sore from the abuse, but the beer sure takes the dust out of my mouth. How's your butt feeling?"

"Why Howard Savage! How dare you ask?" Charlie stood up and wiggled her backside in Howard's face. "How does it look?"

Following their spontaneous script, Howard replied, "Why ma'am, that's the finest ass I've ever seen."

"Correct answer." With that, Charlie downed the rest of her beer, curled up in Howard's lap and directed his hands to her softest places and the buttons that needed undoing. "I know we're both dusty, but we can shower later," she said between kisses and with a husky voice he'd never heard from her before.

They quickly discovered they were both technically virgins. After some awkward moments, the instincts from millions of years of perfecting the lovemaking process, they engaged in tender, deep, physical love that ended in multiple breathless climaxes for both of them.

Lying naked in each others' arms, Charlie, ever the quipster, offered, "Well, that wasn't too bad for a couple of rookies. I'm still tingling in all those places where tingle is supposed to occur. How are you doing, boyfriend?"

"Well, I don't seem to have lost my desire or ability to visit more of your tingle places."

They then wordlessly rejoined their bodies, making love slowly, delighting in the newly-found pleasures of each other's bodies.

Some time later, Charlie propped on an elbow and looked into Howard's eyes while stroking his chest. "Howard. This is everything I'd ever hoped it would be. I'm so glad I met you, and that you are you. Am I crazy to feel so safe and secure with you?"

"No, you are not crazy. I was about to ask the same thing. And yes, I've had fantasies of what it would be like, but I never expected to feel so much primitive pleasure with anyone. I'm here for you, Charlie, as long as you want me. I guess that's a commitment and one I'm not afraid to make."

"Oh, shit! I just realized, we've managed to use up the whole day! Well, if you're up to it, we might as well enjoy the rest of it. No saddle jokes, please," Charlie said, mugging a wry smile. Charlie and Howard once again explored the newness of intimate sex and the new-found magnetism that seemed to keep drawing them closer in every way. This time, Charlie took the lead, guiding them both to shuddering climaxes.

"Time to hit the showers, big boy," Charlie stated as the rays of sunlight became horizontal. Here's my plan: You take your underwear into the shower with you and I'll hang it to dry later. I'd like you to spend the night, so it should be dry by morning. And I've always wanted someone to scrub my back in the shower. You won't mind, will you?"

"Yes to all of the above, and, no, I don't mind. Shall we go out for dinner, or make something here? I used to work in a restaurant, so I'm pretty good at short-orders."

"Let's see how good you really are in the kitchen before I decide to keep you. Shower time first..."

The showering acted as much a symbolic ritual as did the lovemaking for the bonding of two people who found love on this day.

"Did you know you have a small mole where your back meets your butt?" Howard casually mentioned as they toweled each other off.

"Yes, I DID know that. And I'm glad you were looking closely enough to notice. Now, wring out your skivvies and let's make something to eat. I'm starved."

The refrigerator contained eggs, cheese and bulk sausage. Howard discovered tomato sauce, canned mushrooms and Tabasco in the cupboard. "Charlie, do you have any ketchup?"

"Of course. I'm civilized, you know," she replied with false indignity.

"How about a couple of omelets? Any beer left? I didn't see any more in the 'fridge'."

"Good point. I'll run down to the store and get some. Or would you prefer wine with dinner?"

"You know, it already feels as if we've been playing house for months instead of just a couple hours. Feels like a real whirlwind romance. Hurry back!"

Chapter 31
Whirlwind—Part II

On 4 October 1957 the world awoke to the beep, beep, beep of the world's first space satellite, a mysterious, shiny, Soviet, basketball-sized globe called Sputnik—meaning "fellow traveler"—and the "Space Race" began.

The two young lovers, aware of it's significance in terms of their work, however, were busy sharing a romantic dinner together. Howard and Charlie wolfed down their food, saying little, and struggling to take their eyes off one another. After the dishes were washed—both knew the routine from childhood—they settled once again into each other's arms onto the folded out studio couch.

"What the hell is happening, Howard? Everything's happening so fast! But it feels so right."

"I know. These last few weeks at the lab have been really hard for me to concentrate on my work. I found myself peeking at you out of the corner of my eye, noticing a curl was in a different place from the day before. I watched the look of intensity on your face as you worked on your next experiment. All the while, I ached to hold you—like this. Today was the relief valve springing. I let go of my emotional safety handholds when you entered the lab that first day. The pressure from my recent grief and drive to succeed at my work needed some offsetting balance. You have provided that balance. Lucky me. I just want to enjoy our time together. For the first time—maybe in my life—I feel whole."

Charlie kissed him, rolled him onto his back and stared into his impossibly blue eyes. "Well, I don't know if I had that kind of revelation on that day. There was a lot of other stuff on my mind. But, as we talked more and became familiar, it felt like you were somebody I wanted to be around more and more."

Howard smiled back up as her hair dangled and brushed his cheek.

"Most of the men in my life have been nothing but tension and competition. You have no idea how hard it is to be a woman in a man's world, especially a smart woman. Yes, I know I'm smart. My grades, awards and scholarships proved it. My father wanted me to be a combination of strong farm girl and a pink-laced little doll at the same time. When he caught me chewing tobacco while feeding the horses, he came unglued."

Howard laughed at the thought of that sight.

"My two brothers were always bullying and teasing me. No one saw me as more than an object to control or play with. I don't get any of that from you. I had some boyfriends in high school and college, but being tall was another handicap. Being taller or as tall as most boys limited my field of dating possibilities. I never got used to having boys or men stare at my chest before they looked into my eyes. But I also don't get that from you. Don't you think I have pretty eyes?"

"Especially when they're looking at me like this."

"Well, cool off, my dear. I'm a bit sore from all our earlier activities."

"Okay. Just know that I don't like you just for your beautiful, lovely, sensual body," Howard said through a smirk.

"You know, lover, it was a big challenge for me to figure out how to get us to this place. Right from the beginning, I wanted to see if we were really compatible, but wanted my first lovemaking experience to be with someone with whom I would feel comfortable and secure. And, baby, you are all about comfort and security! I have NEVER met anyone with your kindness and attentiveness" she said, smiling wickedly.

"I probably have less experience with women than you do with men," Howard countered. "All I've done is work, study and play baseball. I never stopped to think about what women looked for in a guy, but until you, I apparently wasn't it. My big question now is, 'Where do we go from here?'"

"Good question. Right now, I have to go pee. Think about an answer. I'll be right back."

When Charlie returned she sat cross-legged on the bed and offered, "So, where *are* we going from here?"

"Well, I know I want more of this with you. Every day, I look forward to our time together. Right now I feel like I don't want to ever be away from you. Does that answer the question?"

"Correct answer. I feel exactly the same."

Charlie chuckled deep in her throat and added, "By the way, you should know that my period ended yesterday, so no worries about knocking me up from today's lovemaking. That said, we should start taking precautions. I couldn't bear having an unwanted pregnancy when there is so much left to do. I don't want to put either of us in an awkward position, just because I'm falling in love with you. Serendipity is one thing, but really loving another is both wonderful and scary as hell."

With that, Charlie's lips quivered and tears began coursing down her cheeks. Howard reached for her and she fell into his arms, hugging him and quietly weeping.

"Charlie, I think I have long-passed the 'Am I really in love with this woman?' threshold. Today merely put an exclamation point on it all. I'm sure I've been in love with you, at least at some level, from the moment I first saw you."

"Oh good." She sat up abruptly , wiped her cheeks with the back of a hand and smiled a winsome, crooked smile. "So, does this mean we're 'going steady'?"

They both laughed, and looked adoringly at each other. "Yeah. I think that's what it means - and more. So what do we tell our parents?"

"Do your folks know about me, yet?" Charlie asked with a pout.

"I've mentioned you a couple of times as my new lab partner and that we share lunches together, but I haven't told them about my feelings toward you. Have you told your parents about me?"

"Only my mom. I swore her to secrecy, so my dad wouldn't get all frothy. I just told her that I'd met a 'very special guy'."

"Should we tell them that we're an item?"

"I have an idea," Charlie said, brightening. "Let's drive to San Diego for the weekend and I can meet your whole family. Never been there, and I'm told that it's a beautiful city."

"Excellent! It's still early, so they won't be in bed, yet. Hand me the phone. I'll call my folks and set it up."

Chapter 32
Whirlwind—Part III

Their drive down the Pacific coast highway was leisurely and bucolic. The morning clouds of this late August Saturday had burned off, letting the sun bejewel wave tops as Charlie's Buick cruised along the bluffs of Southern California. With the top down, the loving couple basked in the warmth of the late summer morning. Conversation was minimal as they became lost in their own thoughts. They pulled into the Front St. drive-way just after ten o'clock.

"I'm suddenly a little nervous," Charlie said.

"No worries. Just watch what happens next."

What happened next was Lois Savage came running out of the back door with outstretched arms to gather the tall, beautiful woman into her embrace. "Welcome, Charlie Young. We're *so* glad to meet you!"

Next out the door was Virgil's son, Frank, who hugged Charlie while flashing a broad smile, reminding her of Howard. "Well, well, well. It looks like my boy has found himself a beautiful woman at last. It is our pleasure to meet you, Charlie. Welcome to the Savage home."

Next came Virgil Savage, the patriarch. A bit more formal, he none-theless offered an even broader smile, taking Charlie's hand in both of his. "Very pleased meet you, Miss Young. I go to restaurant for lunch rush. You two come with me. I show you…"

"Grandpa, let me show Charlie to her room and give her the cook's tour of the house first."

As they walked through the spacious first floor, Charlie whispered, "I can see where you got your good manners and warmth. Are your folks always like this when meeting strangers?"

"Well, you automatically became family the moment I told them I wanted them to meet you. So, no, they can be somewhat standoffish with strangers, but still polite."

Howard showed her into the guest room, plopping her overnight bag on the bed. "Here's your room. Here, let me open the window and air it out."

Charlie followed him closely and, after opening the window Howard turned around and she wrapped him in her arms and kissed him. "My god, Howard. I'm overwhelmed! I can't believe how I've fallen in with a family that loves me simply for who I am and not what they think I should be. Am I right?"

"Oh yes. That's how I was raised. Otherwise, I'd be just another damned fool staring at your tits…lovely though they are."

That remark got him a gut punch. "Okay, wise guy. Let's go see the eatery."

A short time later, Virgil Savage was proudly ushering the two into *Momma's Home Cooking*. The restaurant was already bustling with lunch customers. Virgil introduced Charlie to the entire crew, who greeted her with smiles and hugs. Then they greeted Howard and quizzed him about school and his 'girlfriend'…all without a break in food preparation or service.

"Mr. Savage," Charlie asked. This is really a nice place. Everything is so well-organized. The menu is most varied. How do you do so much every day?"

"My late wife, Anna was boss. She organize 'special dishes'. San

Diego tough town for restaurants, so we have to stay good. Make enough to pay bills and put money in bank. You will have dinner with us here tonight."

"I can't wait."

Virgil drove everyone back to the house and found Lois preparing lunch. Frank asked Charlie if she'd like a beer. "Thank you," she said. "I'd love one. It's gotta be five o'clock somewhere," causing everyone to chuckle. Howard opened the beers, then kept quiet while Frank and Lois quizzed Charlie in attempts to get to know her. Feeling accepted, Charlie opened up to them as she had with Howard, recounting for his parents her life growing up in Kentucky and her schooling as a mechanical engineer.

"Constantly having to repair tractors and other farm equipment, it was natural for me to become an engineer. I had to fight my father about that, but I eventually won. I can be very persuasive when I want to be."

That comment elicited an eye roll from Howard. Frank put the coals on the grill and began getting them ready for the burgers. Virgil returned to the patio and helped his son stoke the fire. Howard soon joined them, bringing his father and grandfather a fresh beer.

"There you see three generations of Savages, Charlie," Lois said as she opened beers for Charlie and herself. "Has Howard told you about the trip his grandpa and grandma made fifty years ago to get here? When I met Frank, and then his parents, I knew that I was in great company and among some of the best people I'd ever know. Frank Savage just swept me off my feet. We got married just six months after we met. I can count on one hand the times we've gotten crossways with each other. I thank my stars every day for my life with him."

"Funny you should say it that way, Mrs. Savage…"

"Lois. Please call me Lois."

"Okay...Lois. I've been feeling exactly that way with Howard. And meeting you all today, made exactly those kinds of bells ring in my head. I've only known you for a couple of hours, but I feel loved and accepted." Tears welling, she continued.

"You know I'm completely in love with your son, Lois, and if he asked me to marry him today, I'd say 'Yes' without a moment's hesitation. Am I being too forward? Is there something I'm missing?" she asked, as she wiped away lingering tears.

"No, my dear. What you see with Howard and our family is exactly what there is and what you get if you throw in with us. I can't tell you how thrilled I am that Howard met you. We always worried that he would become an 'all-work' guy and never find someone to bring joy to his heart. And from what I can see, you're already a special person in his life."

"I hope so. Listening to your story with Frank sounds a lot like the trajectory we're on."

"Howard is a good man. He's never even angered a teacher. Even the school bullies left him alone knowing he would stand up to them. It has always seemed that if anyone gave themselves a chance to like Howard, they did. I'm sure you know that by now."

"I do. Thank you for taking a few minutes with me to help me know more about Howard and your family. Oh. The grill is hot. What did you put in those hamburgers that smells so good?"

"I just marinate the meat in teriyaki sauce, salt, pepper and something called *Liquid Smoke®*.

Usually, I like to let the meat marinate for an hour or two, but they do smell good already. Come help me cut up some onions and slice some cheese. Then, we won't have to explain the tears in our eyes," Lois said, smiling knowingly at Charlie. The two women walked out and stood beside the grill, beers in hand.

On the way back into the kitchen, Lois commented, "Frank makes his own barbecue sauce. I think you'll love it."

"At the risk of sounding corny, Lois, I don't think there's anything around here that I wouldn't love."

Everyone sat around the patio table and enjoyed the burgers, Charlie being constantly drawn into conversation as the Savages continued their inquiries into her past, her present and her intended future.

"I want to be involved with space science. Our nation has been forced to consider what we're going to do about space, given the Sputnik satellite 'shot across our bow'. I think that event started a race to be the first to put humans on the moon. We're going to do it. I feel it, and I want to be a part of it."

Frank and Lois looked at each other knowingly. "Howard's dreamed about that since he was a boy. It sounds like you are well-matched, career-wise," Frank offered.

Charlie and Howard exchanged knowing looks and smiles. "Yeah, Dad. We've talked about that since Charlie arrived in our lab, and almost constantly now that the Soviets have thrown down the gauntlet. Companies like Rocketdyne, Grumman and North American Aviation are already working on methods, fuels and rockets needed to do just that.

"Of course, the scare of the Soviets having the bomb, the biggest rockets and now a satellite has created a fear in our government that if we don't so something equally outstanding in rocketry and space science, we'll be left entirely behind - 'in the dust' so to speak. I hope our two nations will eventually join up to explore space for the benefit of all mankind. There are a lot of scientists at JPL and Cal Tech who are working day and night to catch up. It's getting really exciting there, and Charlie and I are totally involved in it all."

The Charlie and Howard whirlwind continued when Charlie—with barely any effort—persuaded her lover and would-be fiance to fly to Lexington for Thanksgiving, see the farm and meet the Youngs.

Abner Young took an immediate liking to Howard, calling him "my boy" almost immediately. Margaret Young also took Howard into her heart and fussed over him constantly during their visit. Over Thanksgiving dinner, to everyone's joy, the two announced an official wedding date for the second week in January 1958.

Later that night, Charlie confided to her parents that, "With the 'space race' suddenly underway following the Soviets' launch of Sputnik 1 last month, and our nation's accelerated efforts to chase them and their technology, it looks like there's going to be plenty of work for the two of us after graduation. I'm getting my master's degree the same time as Howard, so we'll be jumping into the job market together. As for our wedding, we'd like to have it here. There are only three in Howard's family, but so many more on our side. We can help them with the travel expenses, can't we?"

"Of course, my dear," Margaret chimed in, giving Abner that special look of spousal certainty. "Do give me their contact information, Howard, so we can get to know them a little and discuss plans."

Howard, smiling, handed them the index card he'd already prepared.

"Well, my boy," Abner commented, "I'm always impressed by someone who is organized and prepared, but are you fully prepared to be married to this headstrong, stubborn daughter of ours?"

"Thanks, Mr. Young, and, yes, I am. We get along great and, as would-be engineers, work out our problems step-by-step. We seem to be able to switch gears and points-of-view when we have to."

Charlie spent the winter holidays with the Savages, pitching in at the restaurant as needed. She and Howard purchased wedding rings, filled out invitations and bought presents for everyone. Sadly, Rita Smith sent her and her husband's regrets, but her life was suddenly busy with David, her son. She sent a picture of her and David, but didn't mention a word about Cal or the garage business. Howard wrote her back, wished her well and included a picture of himself and Charlie.

"Do you think your mother will like this necklace, Howard?"

Charlie held up a thin, gold chain from which a stylized golden sun dangled.

"Oh, I think she'll love it. She doesn't wear much jewelry—the restaurant, you know—but she'll wear that because it's from you."

"What should we get your father?"

"Oh, he has everything. But he's now taking up golf, so maybe a nice set of woods. Can we afford that?"

"Pfft. Of course," Charlie replied. "'My daddy's rich and my momma's good lookin','" she sang in parody to the song from *Porgy and Bess*. "My biggest problem is what I should get you. I think you need a new pair of boots for when we go riding. Those Chuck Taylors just don't work in the saddle."

"Wow. But aren't you supposed to surprise me?"

"Don't worry. The design will be the surprise. So, what are you getting me?"

"Oh, no! Can't tell you! But I am going shopping by myself tomorrow. I'll get you something from whatever mood strikes me. For today, let's go get dad's golf clubs and buy a couple of nice shirts for Grandpa."

The next day, while wrapping the gifts, Charlie, suddenly blurted out, "Can't wait!" and presented Howard with the boots. They were hand-tooled with patterns reflecting familiar scenes of the Cabrillo Monument, Mt. Soledad and Coronado beaches.

"Oh my God, Charlie! These must have cost a fortune!" Howard exclaimed as he gingerly tried them on. He walked around the room, showing them off to his family. "They fit perfectly and are way more fancy than any riding boots I've ever seen."

"Don't worry about the cost, Buddy. You'll earn it," she said saucily, causing everyone watching to laugh.

A big box with her name on it lying next to the box of boots intrigued everyone. "Go on! Open it, Charlie," Lois chimed. "We can't stand the suspense."

Charlie excitedly opened the box and extracted a white, Stetson western hat with a large, feathered hatband. Inside the headband was an inscription pressed into the leather that said, "For the love of my life, a hat for all occasions. Love forever, Howard."

"Oh, Howard, it's beautiful! Does this mean I should throw that old, ugly straw thing away?"

"Nope, it has too much sentimental value. Just enjoy the new one."

After New Year celebrations, the four Savages and Charlene Young flew to Kentucky and began preparations for the wedding. Charlie and Howard were not the least surprised that the two families got along swimmingly. Abner invited Frank to his stables and allowed him to ride one of his best horses around the training ring awhile. Some laughter and a couple of cold beers afterwards cemented their friendship. Virgil, while visiting the barn with Abner, began recounting his earlier days of sleeping in a barn not all that dissimilar. The smell of the horses brought tears to his eyes as he recalled working with his horses back in the "old country." Abner quietly listened and then shared similar adventures in the care and training of his horses, cementing their friendship too.

The wedding occurred in the local church just outside Lexington that the Youngs had attended for generations. The reception was held at the Moose lodge, complete with a band and a catered sit-down dinner for

just over a hundred guests. Charlie was resplendent in a modified itera-
tion of her mother's wedding dress re-designed to compensate for her
height. By the time the photographers finished, Charlie's and Howard's
faces were cramping from smiling so much, and dotted with lipstick
from well-wishers. Howard felt that he couldn't possibly shake another
hand or endure another pat on the back. Kentucky bourbon flowed
alongside French champagne to delight the different palates. As the party grew in energy, everyone began dancing with the bride and groom.
Charlie, in her infinite wisdom, had worn a pair of comfortable, low-
heeled shoes. Being taller than most of the men there anyway, she felt it
made good sense not to have to be looking down on bad haircuts and
bald heads.

Before the cake cutting, the garter snap and the bouquet toss, Virgil
steered Howard and Charlie to a quiet corner. With a shaking voice, he
said, "So happy my precious grandson find such wonderful wife. You,
Charlie, much like my Anna. Very smart. Very strong. Very much love.
You must hold each other close. I very lucky to meet my Anna back in
Trieste. Our son, Frank, married very smart, strong and loving woman,
too. Lois never tired. You make Anna and me proud. When I see her
again, will tell her what a fine woman our grandson married. I love you
both with full heart."

Virgil Savage wrapped his still powerful arms around his grandson
and Charlie, holding them tightly. When he released them, he slipped an
envelope into Howard's hands and quietly walked away, wiping the tears
from his aging eyes. Howard and Charlie wiped tears too.

The cake cutting, a solo dance by the now married couple and they
were off on their honeymoon. Frank, Lois and the Youngs conspired to
send the couple to Hawaii's big island for a week of joy and relaxation
before returning to their work in California. They'd booked a small hotel

on the Kohala Coast , The Royal Inn, that proved perfect.

The two scientists hired a car and drove to the top of Mauna Loa, the island's large volcano less than four hundred feet shy of it's sister volcano Mauna Kea. The breathtaking view stunned them. The Hawaiian archipelago stretched out before them. From there they traveled to Volcanoes National Park and stood at the rim of Kilauea, the world's most active volcano, watching the lava lake burble and smoke. Traveling south, they walked on some of the newest real estate on Earth. Some of it was still warm from the latest flows that showed that the Earth was still under construction.

The whirlwind portion of Howard and Charlene Savage's life together was followed by a period of bliss and love neither could have imagined just a few months ago. They were now as certain of each other as they were that they were going to be immersed in an exciting future, another whirlwind that awaited their return to CalTech and the burgeoning world of space exploration.

Chapter 33

Breaking New Ground

The Soviet Union had been developing rocket technology decades before The Great Patriotic War - as they called it. But after World War II ended, they were repurposed to build missiles that could carry thermonuclear weapons to all parts of the world, specifically the United States.

In the late 1950s, two up-and-coming American companies were vying for dominance in rocket-powered flight. North American Aviation purchased an abandoned factory in Downey, California, once used by Consolidated-Vultee. Rocketdyne built a factory in Canoga Park, California, near the Simi Hills, and a rocket engine test facility in the nearby Santa Susana Canyon. Rocketdyne eventually became a subsidiary of North American Aviation before Rockwell International acquired and renamed the company North American Rockwell.

Charlene Savage, née Young, and her new husband, Howard, graduated together in June, 1959 with masters degrees in aeronautics and astronautics. Together with their field experience in rocket fuel chemistry and engineering at CalTech, they immediately became highly attractive to the companies trying to combine these sciences with the physics required to do what it took to achieve the ultimate: put a humans on the moon.

Both were actively recruited by the new North American/Rocketdyne consortium, and seemed a perfect fit for the massive effort of sending Americans to the moon. Charlie Savage interviewed with North American Aviation for a design engineering position in the space flight department that was developing the X-15 rocket plane. Rocketdyne liked Howard's work and were especially impressed with his publications on the flight characteristics of rocket-powered vehicles. One especially intriguing component of Howard's work was his work with rocket fuels. He was immediately offered an engineering position making design decisions on upcoming NASA projects like Gemini and Apollo, the moon project.

Howard and Charlie called their parents to announce that they would be removing themselves from the umbilicus of parental support and promised to make the investments they made in their children worthy of those parental efforts.

On the phone, Virgil Savage said to his grandson, "So. Going to moon. Great voyages is family history. I walk across mountains, then drive to California. Proud to see you continue journey."

"I'm not *really* going to the moon, Grandpa, but I'm certainly going to help us get there. You and my parents were my support system all along, and now I will be working on projects that are most important. I promise to make you proud of what I do. Charlie had just finished telling her parents the same thing. Her dad clearly groused about her making grandchildren for him and Margaret."

Virgil continued: "No matter. I live long enough to see what I need to see. You the most I could hope for in grandson. Keep doing good work *you* want do. Will always be very proud."

Virgil's comments would stay in Howard's ears for as long as he lived.

Howard and Charlie moved into an apartment on Dickens St., off Ventura Boulevard near its junction with Sepulveda in Sherman Oaks .

The necessities of job-related commuting quickly dictated that they become a two-car family. Charlie's drive south to Downey was twice as long as Howard's north to Canoga Park. Howard had had to take a taxi to his interview, and would continue to do so until he received his employment papers to show the Ford dealer on Ventura Blvd. He came home after his first day of work in a new 1959 Ford Fairlane. Charlie still had her beloved Buick convertible and would not give it up even though it burned gas like lions eat meat.

Their two salaries were a necessity for them as the fifties bled into the sixties. "Budgeting" soon became a major topic for the newlyweds.

"Howard, your salary should cover rent and your car payment with a hundred bucks a month left over. Mine can cover utilities and groceries plus some play money for movies and maybe a baseball game in the Dodgers' new stadium in Chavez Ravine. Take a look at my budget items and tell me what you think."

"Looks great, Sweetheart. We both get life insurance and medical benefits. The only other things we have to worry about are dentists. I like the idea of going to a Dodger game now and then. We're gonna be working our asses off, so we'll need some entertainment."

Charlie quickly became immersed in helping to design the X-15 rocket plane. Previous rocket planes experienced uncontrollable spins at very high altitudes and speeds. Once the engines were turned off on the fringes of space, the aircraft lost vector stability and began tumbling in the extremely thin air where control surfaces were useless. The innovation Charlie was working on solved this problem for the X-15, by using hydrogen peroxide-powered stabilization thrusters to keep the vehicle pointed in the right direction until it re-entered the heavier atmosphere where the control surfaces were once again effective. Her math, physics and lab skills helped the chief engineers perfect that design, and the test flights were uniformly successful.

Howard was assigned to rocket engine design for ICBMs. The brain-child of William Bollay was, the giant F-1 primary booster engine. It was designed to lift the lunar vehicles' mass off the Earth's surface and get it into orbit. Howard's assignment was to develop an engine and fuel for a spacecraft that could fire, cut off and re-fire several times during spaceflight. After doing some heat reaction exercises on paper, Howard suggested, in a staff meeting, that nitrogen tetroxide oxidizer be mixed with un-symmetric dimethyl hydrazine. His reasoning being that these two chemicals were hypergolic; when mixed together, they would spon-taneously ignite. All the engine would need would be valves that opened and closed. Eliminating liquid oxygen significantly reduced vehicle weight. In addition, the energy released would produce five times ten to the third power KiloJoules; a major increase in power per weight-vol-ume of fuel. The hydrazine tank would require heating, though, since that chemical froze at two degrees C.

After engineering staff discussions, Howard's idea was approved for experimentation, and tests proved that the reaction was more than 90% efficient. Design of the engine proceeded. It would eventually be used in the Apollo Command Module and the Lunar Module. For their accom-plishments, Howard and Charlie celebrated with a dinner of "Savage burgers" and champagne.

Chapter 34

"This is How We're Going to Get There."

President John F. Kennedy took office on 20 January 1961, and in his famous inaugural address, challenged Americans to think about what they could do for their country instead of what their country could do for them. The speech announced the arrival of the next generation of Americans dedicated to moving to the next level of civilized governance.

On 12 April 1961, the Soviet Union launched Yuri Gagarin into a one orbit spectacle that stunned the world.

The first American into space was Alan Shepard on 5 May 1961. It was a sub-orbital lob that lasted only twenty minutes. But it was a start. NASA, formed in 1958, was already working on the concepts and details of what it would take to send an American from Earth to the moon before the Soviets. Living under a "red moon" struck patriotic and panicky chords in the hearts of Americans. On 25 May 1961, President Kennedy spoke to a joint session of Congress and initiated the United States' greatest undertaking in its history: *"If we are to win the battle that is going on around the world between freedom and tyranny. If we are to win the battle for men's minds, the dramatic achievements in space which occurred in recent weeks should have made clear to us all, as did the Sputnik in 1957, the impact of this adventure on the minds of men everywhere who are attempting to make a determination of which road they should take.*

"Now it is time to take longer strides—time for a great new American enterprise—time for this nation to take a clearly leading role in space achievement, which in many ways may hold the key to our future on earth.

"I believe that this nation should commit itself to achieving the goal, before this decade is out, of landing a man on the moon and returning him safely to earth. No single space project in this period will be more exciting, or more impressive to mankind, or more important for the long range exploration of space: and none will be so difficult or expensive to accomplish."

Work was already well underway within industry to make this happen. NASA conducted information tours for all employees at major contractors to explain how it would be accomplished and the problems needing solutions.

Rocketdyne was well along in testing and developing its huge F-1 liquid fuel rocket as well as the J-2 that would be used in third stages of the launch vehicles, even though, in 1961, the overall concept of how to actually get to the moon and back had yet to be completely defined.

In Downey, Charlie Savage had become one of Harrison Storm's *Storm Troopers,* developing designs for the Apollo vehicles.

At Rocketdyne, Bill Winters visited Howard's office cubicle one day with Bill Ezell. "Howard, meet Bill Ezell. He's been involved with the S-II stage propulsion aspects of what we're now calling the *Saturn* moon rocket. We'd like you to join us for some coffee."

"How do you do, Mr. Ezell. What can I do to help?" Howard replied politely, feeling growing excitement.

"Call me Bill. You've been recommended as liaison engineer between us, North American and Grumman. Why Grumman, you ask? They are lead contractor for developing the moon lander. Interested?"

"Sure. But what is a liaison engineer?"

"Good question. We aren't sure, other than we're going to need somebody who has a grip on the propulsion systems that must be integrated into the entire project. Your wife works for North American, right?"

"Yes."

"Good. What's she working on, if I may ask?"

"She's working on the S-II design, so she'd be 'on board' with what you're proposing. She's also just beginning work on the command module for Apollo. She's one of the *Storm Troopers*."

"Perfect," replied Ezell. "If you accept, you, she and the rest of Stormy's people will be coordinating designs, testing procedures and actual manufacturing methods for the project. You'll be at the cutting edge of the Apollo project because we've never done anything like this between companies before. Are you *still* interested?"

"You bet! In fact, this is what I've dreamed of since I was a kid. I read Oberth's book, and that was it for me."

"Great," replied Winters and Ezell.

"I'll get you sorted out and moved immediately closer to me and Dave Aldrich. Oh, I almost forgot. NASA will be visiting for a combined employee seminar starting tomorrow. They want everybody in the company to know how we're gonna pull this thing off. The seminar will be at one of the hangers at Van Nuys airport. You'll be there, of course," Bill Winters said, winking.

Howard and Charlie shared a ride to the Van Nuys airport next morning as her department was scheduled for the seminar too. At North American the seminar was being touted as the biggest dog and pony show in the history of aviation. And it was. Fliers were passed out to everyone at the door as they entered. The flyers were entitled, *This is How We're Going to Get There.*

Several NASA administrators were already on-stage waiting for the several hundred engineers, scientists and managers to get settled. Factory workers and maintenance staff would attend an afternoon session. Even the cafeteria staff would attend after lunch hour. George Low, the NASA director, introduced the on-stage members present. Christopher Kraft began by summarizing the basics.

"Thank you. My first slide will list the basic successes we must achieve in order to get astronauts to the moon. Be advised, NASA is already vetting and training the next astronaut class to add to those, staying with us after Mercury and Gemini are completed."

"Okay. The first step was getting a manned spacecraft into space and returning it to a water landing. We did that with Mercury. Next, we had to put a manned spacecraft into orbit. We did that beginning with John Glenn's flight in February. With project Mercury, we feel we've wrung out all the necessary issues surrounding weightlessness and both manual and automatic re-entry.

"Next, we need to perfect extra-vehicular activities. The astronauts will have to be outside a spacecraft while they're on the moon, so we intend to do that with project Gemini, now currently in planning. Sorry, Rockedyne, but Martin's Titan II is going to do the heavy lifting for Gemini. Gemini will also have to accomplish a third goal: rendezvousing with the command module—docking with it in orbit, and then use an Agena booster to push the whole assembly to higher orbit. This will simulate the burns we need to get to the moon.

"We're just learning about orbital maneuvering, but one of our second batch of astronauts, Edwin Aldrin, wrote his doctoral thesis about orbits and trajectories. He's been invaluable in developing our plans, plans that are still being written in crayon."

This remark brought a laugh from the audience.

"Someone in our first collection of engineers remarked that rendezvous and docking was like a person standing in the front yard of a house and throwing a ball over the roof while a person in the back yard would try to hit it with another ball. A little far-fetched, but you get the idea. Oh, and this will all take place at sixteen thousand miles per hour, a hundred miles above the Earth's surface.

A collective sigh rose from the audience.

"Gemini must stay in orbit for as long as a round-trip to the moon and back. New guidance, controls and life support systems will be fine-tuned during those missions. We're learning how to do this as we go, so there is plenty of room for innovation.

"Now, how do we get to the moon, land, walk around, collect some rocks and fly home? The most plausible concept involves discarding parts as we go so that only the command module returns with the three astronauts. We begin with the huge Saturn five booster and second stage S-two pushing the entire load into orbit around the Earth. Those first two stages, using the F-one engines, will lift the entire assembly into orbit before being jettisoned. While in orbit, all systems will be checked for go/no-go status.

"If all systems are go, the S-four-B will fire in what we call TLI, or trans-lunar injection. Once escape velocity from Earth's gravity is achieved— somewhere around thirty thousand miles per hour— the crew will discard the S-four-B and be on their way. About half-way to the moon, the CSM, or Command/Service Module, will separate from the trailing service module and extract the lunar module that's been riding along behind. They will dock with and pull the LM, or Lunar Module, out of the service module's shroud.

"At this point, we now have the parts that are going to the moon. If necessary, the SM, or Service Module, engine will burn for course corrections. Once we get there, the SM engine will burn again and bring the entire assembly into lunar orbit. At each step, systems will be checked and go/no-go decisions made by Flight and the Mission Control Center in Houston...when it gets built."

That brought more chuckles.

"So now, we're ready to go to the surface of the moon. Before I get too far, I've been told that one of your young engineers here has developed a new fuel concept for the SCM and LM that is lightweight and highly reliable. His name is Howard Savage of Rocketdyne. Stand up, Howard. Well done. You've allowed a lot of people up here to sleep better."

There was applause and muted cheers from the Rocketdyne contingent. Those sitting around him pounded Howard on the back and head. Charlie just elbowed him in the ribs and gave him a broad smile.

"In the wake of all the space junk we've left behind, the SCM and the LM will orbit the moon while the two LM astronauts get into the LM, suit up, undock and descend to the surface. Since there is no air on the moon, the physics of orbital dynamics will come into play. The LM will have many control thrusters as well as the descent engine allowing the pilot/astronaut to land on a dime.

"After the LM detaches from the SCM, the control module pilot will remain in orbit during the lunar exploration. Okay.

The LM is made of a descent stage and an ascent stage. Obviously, the descent stage will land the entire assembly and the astronauts will exit the LM, climb down a ladder and do whatever we tell them to do on the moon. I say that last bit advisedly, because we just don't know how tired they'll be, or how well their life-support will work under stress. That, and other such items will be tested in Gemini. Virtually every step they take will have been thought out, written down and rehearsed before the crew leaves Earth.

"When the astronauts have completed their lunar activity, they will climb back into the LM and launch the ascent stage, return to lunar orbit and dock with the SCM that has been patiently waiting for their return. Once docked, the SCM engine will burn to initiate TEI, or trans-earth injection. Somewhere along the way, the LM ascent stage will be jettisoned.

"Finally, as the SCM approaches earth, there will be correctional burns using the SCM engine. Once the correct trajectory is established, the SCM too will be jettisoned leaving only the command module to re-enter Earth's atmosphere and splash down somewhere where we can find them. Any questions?"

The spellbound audience was silent. Finally, a hand went up.

"When are you planning to land the first men on the moon?"

After the groans and catcalls stopped, George Low stood up to the microphone and said, "Some time before 1 January, 1970."

That brought more groans and laughs. After the audience re-settled, Low stopped smiling and said, "We are planning to have a moon landing mission somewhere between Apollo eight and Apollo twelve. A lot of it hinges on when the lunar module will be finished, tested and made available for test flights. As you know, North American is building the S-two and command modules for these missions, so a lot of our schedule depends on how well you each perform your jobs. NASA is deeply grateful for all your efforts so far, and will work as closely as possible with everyone here to fulfill these expectations and goals laid before us. There's going to be plenty of work for everybody, so without any further questions, I bid you farewell and good work. Thanks for attending."

As one, the audience rose and gave the speakers a standing ovation. While clapping with the crowd, Charlie and Howard looked at each other with wide grins. "It's going to be a hell of a ride, my beloved," Charlie offered.

"And we're gonna get to work together to make it happen," Howard responded.

Chapter 35

Following the Vision

The date *22 November 1963 will live in infamy alongside the attack on Pearl Harbor as a day when the earth moved underneath the American psyche. The assassination of President John F. Kennedy literally ripped the soul out of an idealistic nation.*

On the one hand, some experienced a re-doubling of patriotism, a sense of duty and dedication to the late President's vision to place a man on the moon before 1970, while others thought the space program was a waste of money and resources. President Lyndon Johnson, long a proponent of space exploration, fanned the embers and kept the Apollo program at the front of national priorities even as the nation's military involvement in Asia escalated.

Relations with the Union of Soviet Socialist Republics moved away from imminent nuclear war to something more like two angry neighbors yelling across the fence. The race to the moon was seen by both countries as a national duty not unlike the world-wide efforts to defeat tyranny during World War II.

Evening conversations across the land included discussions about recent missile tests, satellite launches or the growing war in Vietnam. But the conversations between Charlie and Howard Savage went deeper.

"Howard, you've got to see the elegant design for the interior walls of the command module! It's an aluminum honeycomb core laminated between two aluminum sheets. It's incredibly strong, though it's very hard to make. Adhesion has to be perfect across the entire assembly. It's like the heat shield's honeycomb that has to be precisely filled with bubble-less epoxy. The whole process is more of an art form than just making an assembly."

"Sounds interesting, sweetheart. How exactly are you involved?"

"I'm writing up the instructions for the module's assembly. One of my major problems is keeping the thousands of bundled wires inside the module from chafing or fraying. Some of the wires are quite small and fragile. With all those panel doors opening and closing, I worry that some of them might get damaged and cause a short.

"And what have you been doing since you got back from Long Island, dear husband?"

"Well, Grumman is working hard at finalizing the lunar module de-sign. I sat in a meeting where the chief engineers were busy trying to find ways to dump weight. For example, they have the astronauts sitting in large, reclining couches in the LM. That meant large windows. Win-dow glass, of course, is much heavier than the metal skin. Anyway, I asked why the pilots had to be sitting. Why couldn't they just stand? They would be flying for less than an hour before landing. Removing the seats would save hundreds of pounds. You should have seen the looks I got,"

"That sparked discussion over whether the controls could be located closer to the windows allowing the windows and the whole module to be smaller. Someone there calculated that these two changes alone would reduce LM weight over ten percent. You cold have heard a pin drop.

"With the weight reduction, the engines would need less fuel and thus save even more weight. I gotta say it was one of the most exciting meet-ings I've ever been to."

"Wow!" replied Charlie as she threw her arms around Howard's neck. "That's great! Which brings up a concern I have." Howard's body suddenly tensed. "It has to do with the module's inner atmosphere during ground tests. With Mercury and Gemini, pure oxygen was pumped into the spacecraft. Everybody was so afraid of failed life support in the space suits, so they wanted plenty of oxygen inside the capsule, just in case."

"So, what's worrying you?" asked Howard.

"Well, it's about the ground testing. In space, five-point-five pounds per square inch internal pressure is necessary to maintain the shape-integrity of the module. But on the ground, the tests have to be done at the fourteen psi of Earth's atmosphere PLUS the extra psi to simulate the internal environment in space. Sixteen or seventeen psi of pure oxygen sounded really dangerous to me, especially if any one of those wires I was talking about happened to short."

"Ummm," Howard mumbled.

"Well, I told my boss, Moe Goodman, about my concern, and he asked me to run an experiment, which I did. I placed some materials from inside the spacecraft into a lucite pressure chamber, then pumped it full of oxygen and hit a sparker. The interior materials exploded in flames. It happened so fast and so powerfully...it scared the crap out of me. I called Moe in to watch a replay. I was astounded when he said he wasn't surprised. He said that this was the way NASA did all its ground tests of spacecraft and he doubted they'd be able to change their minds at this late date. I wrote up the report and gave it to Moe. The incident left me even more conscious of the workmanship quality necessary to secure the electrical connections against any sparking."

"That *is* concerning," Howard said. "How's assembly of the service module going? The fuel cells and cryogenic tanks weigh a lot when filled. I'm always looking for ways to save weight so the Service Power Supply engine still has enough fuel for all the maneuvers needed, and then some. I hear you guys are doing a great job with the service module. You're gonna have to give me a tour some day soon."

"Anytime, sweetheart. Apollo One is due for testing in January, sixty-seven. Maybe we can wrangle a trip to Florida to see it."

"Maybe we could babysit the SCM as it's being flown to Florida?" Charlie offered with a big smile. "Have you seen the *Super Guppy,* yet? I couldn't believe that a modified cargo airplane could look that ugly. It looks more like a cartoon whale with wings than a guppy. Can't wait to see it fly…if it can. Well, people above our pay grade are making those decisions. We're just worker bees trying to get the pieces finished in time. I just hope we're not rushing so much that we end up sacrificing safety for the details."

"No kidding," Charlie affirmed. "Management is already planning the second production lot of command and service modules. And we're already starting to construct the fuel cell tanks for the coming production lots. Did you know the fuel cell oxygen has to be heated before mixing with the liquid hydrogen to make electricity?"

"No, Miss Smarty, I didn't. You're becoming quite the expert on all things Apollo."

"I should be,"Charlie finished. "I just hope we can track all the modifications from one lot to the next so no unforeseen events occur…"

The two fell into mutually concerned silence.

Howard was the first to break the silence and took Charlie's hand in his. "My dad once told me how design changes came daily when he was building the B-twenty-four bombers. The critical changes often had to be implemented in downstream units before they were test flown. The biggest changes were reflected in 'model' letters after the designation.

You know, like 'B-twenty-four-D' is significantly different than a 'B' model. The 'D' model incorporated enough overall design changes to receive a new letter. I wonder if they'll do that with Apollo?"

Chapter 36

"Go Flight!"

The evening of 27 January 1967 was chilly in Florida, but on top of the Saturn V rocket assembly sat the Apollo I command module and its three astronauts strapped into their couches. Gus Grissom, a former Mercury astronaut, Ed White and Roger Chafee, both Gemini veterans, were performing a plugs-out test meaning the unit was detached from all ground support. Communications quality between the Apollo module and ground control were very bad. Grissom became impatient and let NASA know in the strongest possible terms what he thought of the situation.

Below his feet, millions of electrons were moving quickly through the bundled wires. Two adjacent wires were frayed and some of those electrons moved rapidly from one exposed wire to the other creating a burst of plasma called a spark. That spark created enough heat to explosively combust nearby materials inside the spacecraft. The high-pressure, pure oxygen environment facilitated the event. The fire spread so rapidly, that it created enough smoke and internal pressure to blow off the outer shroud and injure men in the white room adjacent to the module's hatch. None of the astronauts survived. The fire breached their suits and they died of asphyxiation in a matter of seconds.

Months earlier, engineers at North American Aviation, the company that built the Apollo command module, petitioned NASA to reconsider using pure oxygen under pressure during ground tests. The petition was ignored. Charlie Savage's worst fears were tragically confirmed this terrible day.

Everyone in NASA and the companies building the Apollo vehicles were deeply concerned that the Apollo tragedy might end Kennedy's vision of going to the moon in the decade of the 60s. As it happened, a Senate hearing initiated a complete re-design of the command module to eliminate any possible repeat of the Apollo I disaster. Frank Bormann, an Apollo astronaut in training, testified before the committee and, in a moving statement, reiterated the agency and its astronauts' resolve to move ahead and fulfill Kennedy's directives. It was a near thing for Apollo, but the redesign produced a much superior module.

Howard Savage's work as liaison engineer began dwindling as all the Service Module projects finished testing to everyone's satisfaction. His ideas for using hypergolic fuels worked beautifully, the engine started and re-started perfectly every time. The new catchwords at NASA were, without question, safety and reliability. Howard's initiatives satisfied both requirements.

In late 1967, Howard received a call from Bob Gilruth's office asking him to visit Houston and consider working in mission control. Gilruth, the project director, Chris Kraft, the head flight controller, and others were training back-up teams for the upcoming Apollo flights and beyond. Howard's interview with Gilruth and Kraft was the most in-depth technical interview he'd ever experienced. On 4 December, Kraft offered him the job as back-up EECOM, the acronym standing for *Emergency, Environmental and Consumables* controller for Apollo. He was told he would have to move to Houston to train, then shadow the dean of EECOM controllers, Seymour Liebergot, who, had manned that console for most of the Gemini flights.

"When can you start?" was the magic question from Kraft, leaving Howard to reply that he had to talk with his wife. Kraft handed him a phone. Non-plussed, Howard called Charlie at work and told her what had just transpired.

"Holy shit, Howard! Houston! Take the damned job! We'll figure out how to get to Houston later."

"My command module engineer says, 'Take the damned job', so I guess I'll take it."

"Great. Let me finish showing you around and introduce you to the Mission Control administrative assistant who will get your paperwork going and find you a temporary billet. Expect twelve to fifteen hour days to get up to speed. Welcome aboard, Howard. Gotta go. Mazie will finish the tour." With those few words, Kraft returned to the bowels of Mission Control, leaving Howard staring open-mouthed at Mazie McCreary.

"Well, don't just stand there, young-un. Start fillin' out these forms! When yer done, I'll show you tah your quarters. Temporary, of course. Oh, and when you pack for here, be sure tah include a sleep mask an' a loud alarm clock. Just in case yah missed it, y'all gonna be workin' rotatin' shifts at all hours. Yer gonna be learnin' everbody's job. So yer gonna need all the rest yah kin git. EECOM is the toughest of the lot, so git ready to work harder than you ever have afore. One more thing. When you git here, stay away from the honky-tonks. Too many rednecks who don't cotton to what they call 'Yankee eggheads'. Oh, an' Nice tah meetcha," Mazie drawled. She smiled, shook his hand, then handed him a pen.

Charlie, having largely completed her work with North American Aviation, announced her resignation to everyone's disappointment and, with a nice chunk of money in hand from her "I-don't-have-time-for-a-vacation" time, her employee savings portfolio and two-week withholding check, she was ready to start her next adventure with her husband. She called Howard, instructing him to find them an apartment and to send her the list of job openings at NASA-Johnson Space Center. "I refuse to become a kept woman, Big Boy. Besides, I don't think you can keep me in the manner that I desire."

Howard flew to Los Angeles, where in-between episodes of passionate "I'm going to miss you" lovemaking, he packed his clothing and drove the three days back to Houston.

Virtually, from the moment he arrived, he began observing controllers. He shadowed Sy watching and noting his actions when he switched jobs. He saw how the controllers rehearsed and simulated events along with the astronauts in the CM simulators, every day. Howard worked his way into those rotations as he became more familiar with the Mission Control and Texas-based lexicon. One day he asked his mentor Sy when to say "Go, Flight!"

"Yeah. Good question. Look, there's this thing called *go fever*. Controllers have a tendency to say 'go' even though their parameters are not optimum or they're dancing on the 'no-go' line. Don't do that. 'Flight' refers to, of course, the Flight Controller. He is god and we all answer to him. Chris and Gene Kranz insist we give them the straight scoop. No guesses. Guessing creates problems and problems create, well, bigger ones. So, when you hear one of us say 'Go, Flight', that means our numbers are straight down the centerline. If they aren't, we are obliged to say 'No go' just as emphatically. You understand?"

"Yessir. Thanks Mr…"

"It's Sy, Howard. And I'm just 'EECOM' around here. You're gonna be working my console at some god-awful times of the night, but your 'Flight' will be asking you for status reports on a regular basis no matter what your shift."

"I'm a GO on this, Sy. Thanks."

"No problem. Do your best every day. Those guys floating around a quarter of a million miles away depend on it."

Chapter 37

The Pride of Generations

The Apollo project continued moving through the necessary stages of development, methodically testing and perfecting each system in turn until it began seeming routine. Except that there would be no "real" routine until Mission Control finally integrated the functions of various systems in preparation for a "real" launch. In the words of Chris Kraft: "We will bring the astronauts home safely every time". That meant no mistakes, despite the constant string of "glitches" that constantly popped up with every attempt at systems integration. Human errors continued to appear at every stage too often for NASA's management to accept. What made Apollo succeed was the total commitment by everyone involved to identifying and correcting each problem. The daunting statistics associated with total quality control showed that with even 99% correctness in a system with, say, 100,000 parts and assemblies, 100 things could go wrong, any one of which could be fatal to the astronauts.

While NASA engineer-managers were committed to perfect control over every aspect of the proposed lunar missions during 1968 , the rest of the world continue to struggle with crises after crisis. The war in Vietnam raged and grew. Civic unrest and anti-war protests in the U.S. were constantly in the news. The police rioting against demonstrators at the Democratic National Convention in Chicago that year illustrated the agony the country was experiencing.

Howard Savage quickly mastered the EECOM console and came to serve on that duty station on second shift after Sy Liebergot finished his turn. Charlie found employment as a maintenance supervisor with a small aircraft company servicing private airplanes at Hobby International Airport in Houston. She liked the work as it was much less pressure than with Apollo-related projects. The Savages found a roomy apartment in the rapidly developing seaside community of Seabrook. The stress of moving to Texas seemed like child's play compared to the difficulties they'd had to confront over the last several years.

Howard ended up working as Sy's EECOM backup for Apollo VII, VIII, IX and X. Each textbook flight was accompanied by much fanfare.

Apollo VIII was especially visible to the world as it was America's first circumlunar trip. But Grumman still didn't have a viable LM ready, so EIGHT went to the moon without one. The crew orbited the moon and returned to Earth having tested every maneuver except the moon landing itself. Apollo VIII relayed spectacular photographs of an Earth rise over the surface of the moon while it was in orbit. This flight over the Christmas holiday included messages sent by the crew of Bormann, Lovell and Anders that connected what was happening to the entire world. As one telegram to NASA said, "Thank you for saving 1968."

Apollo IX did have an LM, which they tested in orbit around the Earth.

TEN, however, was the final "dress rehearsal" for the first Moon landing, testing all the components and procedures just short of actually landing. The LM flew with two astronauts inside to within 50 miles of the moon's surface before firing the ascent stage and returning to the CM for the return trip to Earth.

In June, 1969, Frank Savage called his son and, with a concern Howard had never heard before, asked him to return to San Diego. "My dad isn't doin' so well, Howard. He's losin' weight and seems to've lost his spark. I'm really worried that he may be comin' up on his time. I want you to see him at least one more time while he's still alert and able to care for himself. Bring Charlie."

"Sure thing, dad," a shocked Howard answered. "I'll let you know in a couple days when we can be there. Say hello to everyone. Let me speak to mom."

Howard's mother confirmed that Grandpa Virgil was slipping. "He talks about you almost constantly, Howard. Please bring Charlie. He talks about her as the daughter he never had."

It took a week for Mission Control to adjust EECOM schedules and release Howard.

Virgil's appearance shocked Howard and Charlie. He had lost a lot of weight and his hair had turned all white. He did, however, pump them about every detail of their jobs. "Like to watch landing on moon with you. You do that?"

"Yes, Grandpa. My bosses have trained us all so well at Mission Control that we can do each other's job in our sleep. I told them all about you and they wish you well." Virgil nodded his appreciation.

Charlie added, "My job is not nearly as important as Howard's, but my boss is a pretty cool guy and told me to tend to my family. If he didn't give me the time off, I'd have quit. I think he knew that. That's the kind of job security I have."

Virgil smiled and nodded his agreement.

"Do you still work at the restaurant, Grandpa?" Howard asked.

"No. Go there with your mother. Watch everyone work. Remember Anna working in back," he replied, his eyes tearing. "Read books to make time go. News on TV awful. How in hell did we get into awful war over there? You not getting drafted?"

"Nope. I just had my thirty-seventh birthday, Grandpa, and have a pretty good deferment situation right now." Everyone laughed at that.

Later that day, Charlie and Howard drove Virgil to the restaurant and, under his watchful eyes, helped bus tables and even do some food preparation. Everyone pumped Howard and Charlie about their work on the space program. "They build some parts for that big Saturn rocket down here at Solar Industries, Howard," Lilly, a cook said proudly.

"Yeah. There's more than enough work for everyone. For now..."

On 16 July, the Savages gathered around their new, color television and tuned to Walter Cronkite's narration of the launch of Apollo XI. During the countdown, Howard and Charlie added their own narrative about what was going on in Mission Control and inside the Command Module. When the final countdown ended and the five mighty Saturn V F-1 booster rockets ignited, seven and a half million pounds of thrust created so much noise they couldn't understand the television announcer. When the rocket cleared the launch tower, the exhaust plume extended a hundred feet below the nozzles

After launch, Howard narrated the finer details of what was going on inside the spacecraft and what he would have been doing if he were at his console. The camera suddenly flashed inside Mission Control, and Howard said , "That's my boss, Sy Liebergot! He'll be glued to that console for another twelve hours. His relief will likely have to drag him away.

"I hope I'm not boring you...It's just that with so much training and the other flights I worked that I know this like the back of my hand."

Lois replied for them all: "Oh no, Howard. It's all really interesting. I had no idea you needed to know so much."

"And I love it that my son knows all this stuff," added Frank, smiling broadly. "Your college education was clearly worth every dime. And you brought home a fine woman in the bargain. Charlie, tell us more about your work."

Virgil kept proud eyes on Howard, smiling as if saying , "My work is done. Mission accomplished."

Charlie jumped in and provided her own description of the SCM and what they would soon see happening. "I worked on the parts that will go to the moon and back."

"After TLI, we should eat dinner and go to bed. Don't worry," Howard a added. "They'll be sleeping up there, too. They've had a long, busy day. Tomorrow we'll tell you more about what's going on while they're traveling to the moon. Right now, they're speeding along at thirty thousand miles an hour, but have already begun slowing down. The Earth's gravity will still tug at them until they're two-thirds of the way there. Then, the moon's gravity will catch them and they'll start speeding up again. Let's eat. I'm starved."

The next morning, Virgil gathered his son and grandson around the patio table. Lois and Charlie had already left for the restaurant. Virgil began with a soliloquy about his travels and adventures, summing them by saying, "Howard. Seeing you remind me of my travels. My journey from barn to beautiful home here. Savages all travelers. Your moon mission make me grow big with pride. My grandson…helping men go to moon…that even bigger journey than sailing across ocean, *da*? You build ship to go to moon…like you made—what is word?—made destiny come true. Yes. Destiny.

"My son bring me here from Ohio. Got into cars to come here. Went through Great Depression and world war all together. My son is every hope I had for him. And now, is wonderful to see what HIS son has done. Savages are men of adventure. 'We ask what is over next hill?" And we find women to make adventures good. See, reading books give me more words.

"Getting old now. Hard to walk up stairs. Frank, you and Howard help move me to guest house, *da*? Maybe this last time all three Savage men be together. No man is more proud of son and grandson. Never knew my father, but he would be proud of us, too."

Frank and Howard started to speak at the same time, but they were waved into silence by Virgil.

"Let me finish little speech. We are nation of immigrants, immigrants' children and grandchildren. Everyone have immigrant story to tell. Only people NOT immigrants are Indians. They here before white men come to take land. Coloreds brought here to be slaves. Had no choice. I old man, watching country behave badly. Frank, Howard. Please do something to fix wrongs during years have left. Make difference. Start with small step.

"I look with pleasure at my grandson. The immigrant's grandson. Proud to be your grandfather."

Howard, with tears streaming down his cheeks , embraced his grandfather and thanked him for his love and support through all the years. "And I'm also proud to be your grandson. My father's been my rock and you've been his. We have the goodness that began in your heart to guide us, Grandpa. I've so missed our talks while I've been away."

That night, Howard and Charlie together reflected on their accomplishments. The point that Virgil Savage had made was that theirs was a true American story. Apart from the mindless prejudice of weaker souls, people like Frank and Lois, Howard and Charlie were building a nation populated by people from all around the world. Everyone, is an immigrant's grand daughter or grandson. Howard's and Charlie's contribution to perhaps the greatest human adventure underscored what good can come from good people no matter their ancestry.

Epilogue

The Savage family, along with a billion other people around the world, gathered around their TVs again on the afternoon of 20 July 1969. They watched in breathless awe as Neil Armstrong stepped off the lunar module footpad and half-jumped onto...the surface of the moon. The TV image was grainy and blurry, but the event was unmistakeable. What the people like Howard and Charlie accomplished in sum was best voiced by Armstrong's words from the moon's surface: "...a giant leap for mankind."

The family followed the module's ascent from the moon's surface, the docking to the SCM the next day, and the return to Earth. The Savages, along with millions of others who participated in this culminating event, toasted their "personal" accomplishments with champagne. When the helicopter deposited the three astronauts on the deck of the aircraft carrier, President Richard Nixon was there to greet them. After a brief quarantine, parades and accolades began and kept coming for the Apollo XI "heroes".

A few days later, Howard and Charlie quietly returned to Houston to resume their equally quiet but very important jobs. Before he left, Howard helped his father move Grandpa Virgil into the guest house.

Two weeks after they returned to Houston, they were suddenly called back to San Diego. Virgil, the family patriarch had died in his sleep. When Lois came down to make morning coffee one morning, Virgil wasn't there waiting at the breakfast table as he usually was. After an hour, she went out to the guest house and knocked on the door. No answer. She looked through the front window. Nothing. When she looked through the back bedroom window, she saw Virgil's body lying with slack jaw. Her fears were confirmed when she let herself in and found him cold and unresponsive. Frank, awake by now and preparing for work, saw the stricken look on his wife's face as she ran through the house to him. He realized that the day of his father's passing had arrived.

The funeral was small with only a few friends attending. But one of those friends was Rita Smith. To Howard, she seemed haggard. She'd brought her son, David ,who looked like a frightened rabbit standing next to her. Her husband, Cal, wasn't there.

"What's wrong, Rita?" Howard asked taking her by the elbow to a private corner of the funeral home.

"Oh, well, I couldn't miss Virgil's funeral, now could I?"

"No, but that's not what I mean. What's *happened* to you? Where's Cal?"

"We broke up," She replied stoically, then started to cry. "I could only tell you, Howard, but at one point he beat me to the point where I couldn't walk without pain. It began when he started drinking. A lot. He began accusing me of all sorts of things including secretly having an affair with you. It didn't matter that you were hundreds of miles away. I finally had enough when he pointed a gun at David and me. I packed a few things and ran, taking David with me. We ended up in El Cajon last night, where we're staying in a cheap motel. I accidentally saw Virgil's obituary in the paper and here we are." She paused to hug the boy clinging desperately to her leg. "The truth is,I'm frazzled, my dear Howard, and don't know what to do. I have this beautiful son who keeps asking me why I cry all the time. Please tell me: What should I do?"

Without listening to another word, Howard waved his mother over. "Mom! Good News: Rita is moving back to San Diego with her son. She and her husband broke up. Is there still a place at the restaurant for her?"

Lois put her hand over her mouth as she listened to the details of Rita's story. "Oh, my God, Rita. Of course you can have your job back. If you like, you and David can stay in the upstairs apartment for free until you get your feet back under you. We'll talk more about that later. When the funeral is over, you'll come with us to the wake at the restaurant and we'll get some food into you both."

Rita broke into sobs of gratitude and relief, and fell into Howard's arms, crying openly for minutes. When Charlie came over and learned what had happened, she immediately offered,. "C'mere, Rita. Let's get you cleaned up."

All the fears and worries of Howard and Charlie about configuration control flared up again with the Apollo XIII near disaster. An earlier version of the cryogenic tanks for the SCM fuel cells was not updated to accommodate the more powerful currents used to "stir the tanks" so that oxygen would be able to react with the hydrogen and create electricity. The internal temperature gauge pegged out at a much lower temperature than the dry test produced, burning off the insulation from the wire leading to the heater. The tank was then filled with liquid oxygen and loaded aboard the Apollo XIII SCM. The routine mid-flight "stir" created a power surge in the bare wire and the oxygen tank exploded, blowing away the the side of the SCM itself.

Sy Liebergot, the EECOM, was immediately called to action. After a perilous four-day journey with every engineer on the ground assisting to fix problems, the crew ended up using the lunar module as a lifeboat during their return to Earth. The ascent engine of the LM worked perfectly to push the entire assembly into a free trajectory slingshot around the moon and back toward Earth. The hypergolic fuels of Howard's research performed exactly as required. Without the intense training everyone had undergone, Apollo XIII could have been a fatal disaster. It wasn't. Failure, indeed, was not an option.

When the program ended with Apollo XVII, only twelve humans had walked on the moon. Howard decided it was time for him to leave NASA and return to San Diego. He told Charlie what he wanted to do and she responded by saying, "Wither thou goest, my love, so, too, will go I."

Returning to their favorite city, they purchased a lovely, three-bedroom home in Ocean Beach where they could listen to the surf pound all day long. But neither were idlers or beachcombers. They ended up taking the necessary classes and examinations to become public school teachers. Charlie taught all the science and math classes she could find. Howard, even with his heavy science background, heard his grandfather's request to right wrongs and bring enlightenment, and ultimately taught social studies, history, math (schools ALWAYS needed math teachers) and volunteered to coach baseball.

Frank Savage passed away at age seventy-three from heart failure. Lois Savage lived another seven years and, like her mother, worked in the restaurant until she collapsed and died from a massive stroke. That left Howard to assume sole-ownership of *Momma's Home Cooking.*

Rita managed the restaurant and was able to put her son through college at San Diego State University. Throughout the time, she stalwartly maintained that David was more Howard's son than her ex-husband's—who died from gunshots in Mexicali, Mexico shortly after Rita and David had run for their lives. Howard mentored David to help prepare him for future undertakings.

The final chapter in Howard and Charlie Savage's working lives was dedicated to writing their memoirs and working together on behalf of civil rights organizations.

As the curtain descended on this wholly American family, readers of Howard and Charlie's memoirs were reminded that it doesn't matter from where one's ancestors come. What matters is that the family of man must recognize the concept that allows the species to live together in harmony and to accomplish great things. These accomplishments extend from the family level to the entire planet's population.

The United States of America is a great experiment in democratic nation building, and it was built by European and Asian immigrants. Slaves and native Americans also produced subsequent generations that added to the fabric of America in spite of the travails and social upheavals plaguing the nation. This great nation still struggles, vacillating between egalitarianism and the cult of racial dissension and bigotry. New stories like Howard's and Charlie's are written every day. This is a success story that is purely and truly American. The tapestry of the Savage saga has been repeated millions of times across this great land, and each story has suffered its own vagaries, passions, failures and successes. Without mentioning or examining the problems and difficulties, the genre of this story would be a fantasy, not historical fiction.

About the Author

Vern Turner is a world traveler, scientist and industrial engineer specializing in automation, robotics and sophisticated electro-chemical processes. He holds a BS in Zoology and Chemistry and a MS in Biology, having taught anatomy, science and language arts in post-secondary and secondary schools, and serving as a combat medic in the National Guard. Writing op eds for the River Cities Daily Tribune, many of his columns still appear in The Oklahoma Observer. He is the author of six non-fiction works and five published novels. He is also a Savant editor and proofreader as well as an aspiring screenwriter.

Consider these other fine books from Savant Books and Publications and it's imprint Aignos Publishing

Essay, Essay, Essay by Yasuo Kobachi
Aloha from Coffee Island by Walter Miyanari
Footprints, Smiles and Little White Lies by Daniel S. Janik
The Illustrated Middle Earth by Daniel S. Janik
Last and Final Harvest by Daniel S. Janik
A Whale's Tale by Daniel S. Janik
Tropic of California by R. Page Kaufman
Tropic of California (the companion music CD) by R. Page Kaufman
The Village Curtain by Tony Tame
Dare to Love in Oz by William Maltese
The Interzone by Tatsuyuki Kobayashi
Today I Am a Man by Larry Rodness
The Bahrain Conspiracy by Bentley Gates
Called Home by Gloria Schumann
First Breath edited by Z. M. Oliver
The Jumper Chronicles by W. C. Peever
William Maltese's Flicker - #1 Book of Answers by William Maltese
My Unborn Child by Orest Stocco
Last Song of the Whales by Four Arrows
Perilous Panacea by Ronald Klueh
Falling but Fulfilled by Zachary M. Oliver
Mythical Voyage by Robin Ymer
Hello, Norma Jean by Sue Dolleris
Charlie No Face by David B. Seaburn
Number One Bestseller by Brian Morley
My Two Wives and Three Husbands by S. Stanley Gordon
In Dire Straits by Jim Currie
Wretched Land by Mila Komarnisky
Who's Killing All the Lawyers? by A. G. Hayes
Ammon's Horn by G. Amati
Wavelengths edited by Zachary M. Oliver
Communion by Jean Blasiar and Jonathan Marcantoni
The Oil Man by Leon Puissegur
Random Views of Asia from the Mid-Pacific by William E. Sharp
The Isla Vista Crucible by Reilly Ridgell
Blood Money by Scott Mastro

In the Himalayan Nights by Anoop Chandola
On My Behalf by Helen Doan
Chimney Bluffs by David B. Seaburn
The Loons by Sue Dolleris
Light Surfer by David Allan Williams
The Judas List by A. G. Hayes
Path of the Templar—Book 2 of The Jumper Chronicles by W. C. Peever
The Desperate Cycle by Tony Tame
Shutterbug by Buz Sawyer
Blessed are the Peacekeepers by Tom Donnelly and Mike Munger
Bellwether Messages edited by D. S. Janik
The Turtle Dances by Daniel S. Janik
The Lazarus Conspiracies by Richard Rose
Purple Haze by George B. Hudson
Imminent Danger by A. G. Hayes
Lullaby Moon (CD) by Malia Elliott of Leon & Malia
Volutions edited by Suzanne Langford
In the Eyes of the Son by Hans Brinckmann
The Hanging of Dr. Hanson by Bentley Gates
Flight of Destiny by Francis Powell
Elaine of Corbenic by Tima Z. Newman
Ballerina Birdies by Marina Yamamoto
More More Time by David B. Seabird
Crazy Like Me by Erin Lee
Cleopatra Unconquered by Helen R. Davis
Valedictory by Daniel Scott
The Chemical Factor by A. G. Hayes
Quantum Death by A. G. Hayes and Raymond Gaynor
Big Heaven by Charlotte Hebert
Captain Riddle's Treasure by GV Rama Rao
All Things Await by Seth Clabough
Tsunami Libido by Cate Burns
Finding Kate by A. G. Hayes
The Adventures of Purple Head, Buddha Monkey...by Erik/Forest Bracht
In the Shadows of My Mind by Andrew Massie
The Gumshoe by Richard Rose
In Search of Somatic Therapy by Setsuko Tsuchiya
Cereus by Z. Roux
The Solar Triangle by A. G. Hayes
Shadow and Light edited by Helen R. Davis
A Real Daughter by Lynne McKelvey
StoryTeller by Nicholas Bylotas
Bo Henry at Three Forks by Daniel Bradford

Kindred edited by Gary "Doc" Krinberg
Cleopatra Victorious by Helen R. Davis
The Dark Side of Sunshine by Paul Guzzo
Cazadores de Libros Perdidos by German William Cabasssa Barber [Spanish]
The Desert and the City by Derek Bickerton
The Overnight Family Man by Paul Guzzo
There is No Cholera in Zimbabwe by Zachary M. Oliver
John Doe by Buz Sawyers
The Piano Tuner's Wife by Jean Yamasaki Toyama
An Aura of Greatness by Brendan P. Burns
Polonio Pass by Doc Krinberg
Iwana by Alvaro Leiva
University and King by Jeffrey Ryan Long
The Surreal Adventures of Dr. Mingus by Jesus Richard Felix Rodriguez
Letters by Buz Sawyers
In the Heart of the Country by Derek Bickerton
El Camino De Regreso by Maricruz Acuna [Spanish]
Prepositions by Jean Yamasaki Toyama
Deep Slumber of Dogs by Doc Krinberg
Navel of the Sea by Elizabeth McKague
Entwined edited by Gary "Doc" Krinberg
Critical Writing: Stories as Phenomena by Jamie Dela Cruz
Truth and Tell Travel the Solar System by Helen R. Davis
Saddam's Parrot by Jim Currie
Beneath Them by Natalie Roers
Chang the Magic Cat by A. G. Hayes
Illegal by E. M. Duesel
Island Wildlife: Exiles, Expats and Exotic Others by Robert Friedman
The Winter Spider by Doc Krinberg
The Princess in My Head by J. G. Matheny
Comic Crusaders by Richard Rose
I'll Remember by Clif McCrady
The City and the Desert by Derek Bickerton
The Edge of Madness by Raymond Gaynor
'Til Then Our Written Love Will Have to Do by Cheri Woods
Aloha La'a Kea edited by Robert "Uhene" Maikai
Hawaii Kids Music Vol 1 by Leon and Malia
William Maltese's Flicker - #2 Book of Ascendency by William Maltese
Retribution by Richard Rose
Shep's Adventures by George Hudson

Poutine and Gin by Steve Rhinelander

Coming Soon
I Love Liking You A Lot by Greg Hatala
Lion's Way by Rita Ariyoshi
The Power of Dance by Setsuko Tsuchiya
Hot Night in Budapest by Keith Rees

http://www.savantbooksandpublications.com
Enduring literary works for the twenty-first century

www.ingramcontent.com/pod-product-compliance
Lightning Source LLC
Chambersburg PA
CBHW051246260626
47162CB00002B/630